THE END GAME

GERRIE FERRIS FINGER

THE END GAME

MINOTAUR BOOKS
A THOMAS DUNNE BOOK
NEW YORK

This is a work of fiction. All of the characters, organizations, and events portrayed in this novel are either products of the author's imagination or are used fictitiously.

A THOMAS DUNNE BOOK FOR MINOTAUR BOOKS.
An imprint of St. Martin's Publishing Group.

THE END GAME. Copyright © 2010 by Gerrie Ferris Finger. All rights reserved. Printed in the United States of America. For information, address St. Martin's Press, 175 Fifth Avenue, New York, N.Y. 10010.

www.thomasdunnebooks.com
www.minotaurbooks.com

Library of Congress Cataloging-in-Publication Data

Finger, Gerrie Ferris.
    The end game / Gerrie Ferris Finger. — 1st ed.
        p. cm.
    ISBN 978-0-312-61155-2
    1. Ex-police officers—Georgia—Atlanta—Fiction.   2. Children—Crimes against—Fiction.   3. Kidnapping—Fiction.   4. Child molesters—Fiction. I. Title.
    PS3606.I534E53 2010
    813'.6—dc22

                                                    2009047495

First Edition: May 2010

10 9 8 7 6 5 4 3 2 1

For my husband, Col. Alan J. Finger, USMC (Ret.)

ACKNOWLEDGMENTS

Thanks to my family and friends for their support and patience when I immersed myself in a world where they could not go. They were happy to assist me in the real world, though. My daughter Paula's knowledge of computers is simply astonishing. Dale, my son, who knows guns, dogs, and automobiles, didn't hesitate to tell me when something didn't add up.

I want to thank Ruth Cavin and Toni Plummer at St. Martin's Press. Especially to Ruth: Thank you for selecting *The End Game* as the Best First Traditional Mystery Novel in the 2009 Malice Domestic/St. Martin's competition. I'll never forget that phone call.

To the experts at Crimescenewriters.com, I'm indebted to you. There isn't a question I've asked that you didn't answer, or guide me to someone who could.

To those who work tirelessly to protect children, you are the best.

A note: Certain streets, places, and towns in this novel have been fictionalized.

THE END GAME

ONE

Satisfied, Lake and I lay apart on the king bed. The breeze through the window flitted across my skin, fine-tuning the pleasure of cooling down. In a little while, we'd get up, throw on sweats, and run the 10-K to Piedmont Park. We'd drop onto a bleacher to watch a pickup softball game—maybe join in if idle gloves lay nearby. Right now, though, an après snooze was the plan.

Not to be. A train horn moaned into my nap. The bedside clock said the seven A.M. from Birmingham was smack on time, the chug-rumble growing louder by the wheel turn. It's a miracle how the bricks and mortar of this old cotton warehouse—now lofts—withstand the shakes and have for more than a century. Lake lives on the third floor, and whenever our schedules give us a weekend together, we alternate between the burbs, where I live, and this place, which I adore.

I also adore train squalling. This behemoth's air horn warbled loud and long like an off-key contralto. I lifted a finger and tapped

Lake's broad back. "Engineer Number Two." My brain's chock-full of useless knowledge, like knowing the signature sounds of seven air horn maestros.

Lake rolled his shoulder toward me. "Your cell."

"Huh?"

"It's playing your song."

I got up, impressed again at his ability to hear my cell phone tinkling out Mozart with the train screaming by. My cell lay on the windowsill. I hoped it was a wrong number, but the display said otherwise. " 'Lo, Porsh."

Portia Devon yelled in my ear, "You in a tornado?"

Cranking the industrial window, I yelled back, "Train. Hang on." The chill in the room was no match for the cold lump of apprehension beating along with my heart. Last night, Portia and I closed a runaway girl case. It had taken me three days to trace the sixteen-year-old to San Francisco. Within an hour, I got the call she was a DOA. Portia and I salved our failure with a drink in her chamber. We said our good nights, and she told me to rest up, we'd talk Monday. "What's got you up so early?" I asked.

"You and Lake need to put your clothes on. Guess you haven't been watching the television."

"No," I said, looking at Lake, who'd raised himself on his elbows. "We haven't been watching television."

Lake grinned about the same time his landline rang. He listened for a few seconds, then his face lost its soft edge. He grabbed the TV clicker.

Portia said, "The fire's in Cabbagetown." Her voice crackled like the flames leaping on the screen, a replay of the fire that occurred earlier. "Two people dead. Man and wife. Foster parents. Two girls gone. Sisters."

2

"Gone?"

"They weren't in the house, dead or alive."

"How old?"

I watched Lake slam his phone receiver and head for the bathroom.

Portia said, "One's nine, one's seven. The seven-year-old is deaf. You're hired."

Portia is a juvenile judge, and I own Child Trace, Inc. I search for missing kids, and my main client is the Search and Rescue Division of the Juvenile Court System. "On my way. Which street?"

"Cotton—by the old converted mill. I'll catch you there with details and bring photographs."

"Lake's on the case, too?"

"I talked to the Major Crimes commander. Thought you'd like that."

"Yeah, thanks."

Pressing END, I went for my backpack, slid the cell in, and thought about my poor overworked lover. A big-city detective lieutenant couldn't count on two whole days to himself unless he escaped to a desert island and changed his name. Neither, it seemed this morning, could an ex-policewoman turned child finder.

I pulled clothes from a wardrobe while I watched the tragedy on the tube. A helicopter hovered above the scene. Video caught firemen tromping through a gutted house and horrified people clinging to each other. The chopper ranged the neighborhood where searchers darted like fire ants. Closer to the ground, the lens tightened on a Search and Rescue dog pulling its handler along an overflowing ditch. Another SAR dog zigzagged across a playground with swings and seesaws.

Lake came from the bathroom toweling his chest. We exchanged glances. I said, "It was really nice while it lasted."

"Really nice?" he mocked, flinging boxers and socks from a drawer onto the bed. "You say better things about my wardrobe."

He's a tall, broad-shouldered man, but it's his face that captivates—all angles and irregularities merging to make him beautiful. Then my brain's devil-voice said, *you're not the only woman in Atlanta who thinks so*. I didn't have the time to dwell on my jealous side and whirled for the shower. I said over my shoulder, "It appears you're on loan to me."

"Isn't owning me enough?"

If only I did. "Portia made sure you got the gig."

"Lovely Portia."

As I washed hair and scrubbed body, I said goodbye to an amorous weekend and set my mind on the reality of what lay ahead. Kids going missing after their house burns down. Foster kids. Troubled kids. My kind of kids.

Out of the bathroom, dark hair dripping, I snatched up pants, shoved into them, and reached for my shirt. While I zipped and buttoned, Lake strapped on his cop gear, cell, radio, guns—his police issue in a shoulder holster and his personal Glock in a paddle holster at the back of his waist. He stuck his arms into his blue jacket, strung badges around his neck, and clamped on his trademark panama—a navy straw now it was spring. All the while, his eyes were riveted on the TV screen. "Those wooden houses are tinderboxes," he said, shaking his head. "A spark is all it needed." He flicked off the remote, and I slipped on my backpack—a compact leather thing with enough room to carry my mini-laptop, PDA, cell phone, and wallet. I'm licensed to carry, but my gun's at my house, not that I thought I'd need it.

Our footsteps on the wooden planks resounded like thunder through the hall and down the narrow steps. Apologies to the neighbors later. We bolted across the street to a security fence. Lake flashed his palm across the scanner, the gate opened, and we dashed to the unmarked police car.

As Lake raced through downtown, my heart beat to the pulsating blue teardrop lights mounted on the dashboard. This wasn't the weekend we'd planned, but I was ecstatic to be working with him again.

As if he'd read my mind, he reached to squeeze my hand. "Me, too, Dru."

My name is Moriah Dru, and except for old friends I'm called Dru, thanks to my cop days and M DRU etched on my metal name tag. I met Richard Lake when we were assigned to patrol the Atlanta Police Department's Zone Two. Within three weeks, we'd become lovers. When he got promoted to the Homicide Unit, I couldn't adjust to another partner, mainly because each man assumed he was taking Lake's place in my bed. After two lothario-type sidekicks, against whom I could have brought harassment charges, I quit and started Child Trace, something Portia had been pestering me to do since my maternal instincts (ha!) led me to my first lost child.

TWO

Lake's loft is in the Castleberry Hill community, and if you're driving at street speed about ten minutes from Cabbagetown. As we flew along Memorial Drive startling the early birds on foot and on the road, I watched black smoke ballooning over the city. At a railroad crossing, Lake had the squad car jumping the hump, and at Oakland Cemetery the tires squealed when he yanked a left. Whiplash added to the thrill, and thank God for seatbelts.

I hadn't been in Cabbagetown for a couple of years, but I wasn't surprised to see urbanization muscling in on the blue-collar neighborhood. The narrow, hilly, one-way streets were cramped with tricked-out cottages close to the curbs. Lake pulled onto Cotton Street and came to a dead halt. Heedless of the flashing light, tense-faced people darted in front of the un-marked. Some sobbed. Others bounced off the fenders. "Chaos like this could give a claustrophobe the screaming meemies," I said.

Lake flipped the siren for a second and stuck his head out the window. "Please, move aside. Police."

Near the scene, yellow tape stretched across the street, but the crowd still packed in close to the emergency vehicles. A cop hollered through a bullhorn, warning the multitude to stay back. Lake turned up a side street and made a left onto a street running parallel to the fire scene. At an intersecting alley, two uniformed policemen were surrounded by another group of hysterics.

Frantic voices called from every direction. Jessie! Dottie!

Lake wheeled away from the crowd, into the alley, and came to a vacant lot in back of the smoldering house. He parked and darted back to the cops trying to keep the search organized.

Deciding the mob didn't need another body in the hubbub, I made my way through soggy rubbish to the side of the house. Did I smell charred flesh, or did I dredge up the horrific odor from other fatal fires? I know I didn't imagine the smell of gasoline residue. Lake can hear a spider crawl across the floor; I can flat smell.

A low stone fence surrounded what was left of the cottage. I skirted the fence and fat fire hoses to the front sidewalk. Facing the ruin, I noticed the roof and a door at the back left corner hadn't been destroyed. Two blackened porch columns stood—reminders of two cindered bodies inside. I imagined what it would be like to be consumed by flames. In another life, high-minded citizens probably burned me at the stake.

Shaking the spooks, I looked away to see a yellow plastic windmill whirling under a scorched dogwood tree. Further away, a hundred-year-old oak showed off its unspoiled spring leaves. The trunk supported two youth bicycles—one pink, one purple. My mind drifted into pity-land, but a sudden commotion behind the house snapped me out of it. Leaping hoses and dodging firemen, I ran to the vacant lot.

A handsome German shepherd with its nose in the air loped down the alley. Lake and a uniformed officer trailed the dog. The officer carried a pink bicycle helmet. The shepherd whisked past me and stopped at the back steps of the cottage. He looked at his handler and gave a high-pitch whine—his way of alerting.

Another dog came into the alley, a black Lab, his nose to the ground. The air-scent and the ground-tracker had begun at opposite sides of the neighborhood's boundaries, but ended at the same place.

"The girls are gone," I said to Lake. He clutched my shoulder in a buck-up gesture. Lake, the handlers, and I gathered in a circle. Watching the dutiful dogs at the hips of their masters, seeing the pink headgear in the men's hands, it was enough to soften a callous heart, and mine—well, thirteen-plus years in law enforcement, and I still wasn't hardened enough to suit myself.

Lake asked the air-scent's handler, "How easy, or difficult, is it for dogs to sniff out people when they live in the area?"

"It's tricky," he answered. "These dogs are trained for urban searches where you have a lot of overlying scents. People have opened their houses, crawl spaces, sheds—about any likely place the girls might find shelter. But right here is their strongest scent." As gloom settled on his features, he reached down and patted his dog's head. Then he kicked an old Coke can. "The K-9s are telling us this is where the kids were before . . . whatever happened. Buddy and Jed here hate not making a find and getting their reward."

I looked down at Buddy. His nose wriggled into the wind.

His ears were sharp, his eyes vibrant, his tail wagged loosely. Jed, the Lab, had the same flashing energy. "What's their reward?"

"Buddy likes Frisbee and Jed likes tug-of-war with one of my smelly socks."

Lake asked, "How far away can they pick up a scent?"

"Depends," the handler answered. "Sometimes quarter of a mile. Air-scents are good when the weather's bad. This morning's air is heavy after last night's storms."

At one time I'd thought about transferring to the APD's K-9 Division, so I learned how dogs detect a scent mere mortals can't. First off, dogs can pick out individual odors against a myriad of other smells because they have more olfactory DNA than humans. Then, the scent we throw off is made up of gases we emit and dead skin cells we shed. Such scent is as individual as fingerprints.

The handler went on. "Later, if the sun comes out, Jed will get the scent because the heat breaks it up and pushes it to the ground. But ol' Buddy here, he's a good ground-tracker, too."

The discussion exhausted, we lapsed into thoughtful silence.

A helicopter came clattering above the tree canopy. Lake glanced up; so did I. Apparently getting a copy of the video being shot from the chopper occurred to him at the same time as me, because we looked at each other and nodded in our mind-meld way.

Lake said to the handlers, "Get the pups water and a snack, then go to the cemetery."

The cemetery. A flock of blackbirds chose that moment to flap across the sky. Atlanta's famous Oakland Cemetery is a few blocks west of here. As a kid, I used to beg Daddy to take us to a picnic by the Lion of the Confederacy. But these days, too many kids were turning up dead between the soaring headstones of too many cemeteries.

"It's across a busy street," I said. "And the cemetery's fenced."

"Got to try," Lake said. "Who knows where kids will get to?"

"*If* it's just the two of them."

"Let's hope that's the case."

I shook my head. It wasn't.

Dogs and handlers trotted away, and I followed Lake to the front of the house where the head fireman broke away from his crew and hurried toward us. CAPTAIN was stenciled in the medallion of his large metal helmet. An acrylic face shield topped the helmet. The breast tag on his long slicker read: C. Turquin.

Lake knew him. "Mornin' C.T. What have we got?"

Soot blotched Captain Turquin's face, covering strong facial muscles that had tightened into a mask of command. He wore fireproof gloves and waved one toward the house. "The neighbors say four people were in there—two adults, two children. We located two adult bodies in a bed in that corner." A finger roamed to a section where the roof had collapsed to the cellar. "No other bodies were in the bunk-type beds, or anywhere else."

The young small bodies wouldn't have burned completely. I could see a hint of wood here and there, and plastic, and red fabric.

"Any cause yet?" Lake asked.

"None official. Couple of points of origin, hot spots."

"Arson," Lake said.

"I'm not the expert on fire forensics," Turquin said, "but I'd say a delayed starter. A candle and rigged match, or could be a more sophisticated device."

While they spoke, I examined faces in the crowd. Arsonists like to linger and gloat over their evil work. Sometimes they can't conceal their glee. Although I didn't see any shining eyes, my bones told me the arsonist was here. My certainty was curious because the gathering was mostly older women and small children. The more able-bodied were elsewhere, crashing through streets and yards, searching.

My gaze settled on a spaghetti-thin woman who stood on a porch across the narrow street. She dabbed at her eyes with a hankie and then tucked it in a skirt pocket. I studied her while she steadied herself on her cane. She had gray hair arranged at the back of her head, although wisps straggled down her neck and the sides of her face. Her eyes were focused on Lake, but then they shifted to me. A strange strumming started in my chest because I felt she was telling me something.

I bobbed my head at her and turned to the fire captain. "You know the dead people's names?"

"Neighbors said Barnes. The girls' last name was Rose."

Lake asked, "When was the nine-one-one?"

Turquin reached inside the slicker and took out a computer printout. "Six-twenty A.M. Woman across the street told APD she heard a whoosh," the captain said, gesturing his head in my lady's direction. "In no time the whole place was engulfed."

Lake gestured at the house next door to the Barnes. "That house wasn't touched, C.T. It can't be more than a couple of yards from the fire."

I studied the dollhouse cottage. The pansies in their beds hadn't even witted. "Fireproof siding," Turquin said. "He's lucky we got here before the flames melted it. The fire started on the alley side of the house, where the bedrooms are, and in the front."

"Can you spot the lucky guy who owns the house?"

The captain looked over the crowd. "Don't see him. Probably out with the searchers."

"You see him, let me know," Lake said.

I glanced away, taking in the panorama of despair. At the top of a hill stood the redbrick cotton mill that was no longer a mill. It had been turned into a gated loft community. Unlike Lake's loft, it was fancy and expensive. Ironically, the mill that had supported the residents of Cabbagetown—from the aftermath of the War Between the States until the mid-1970s—now stood behind concrete and iron fencing as if it had turned its back on the angst of the past.

My God. I recognized the man coming down the sidewalk. He walked stiffly and looked above the heads of the crowd as if the missing Rose girls were ascending into the sky. Sudden anger always makes my face hot. My blood pressure shot up twenty points as I recalled that Conrad Hugle lived in the mill lofts. Except for monsters I've put in jail, I could count on one finger the people I loathed. Conrad Hugle, the bureaucrat's bureaucrat, was that one.

Captain Turquin cleared his throat and tipped his head in Hugle's direction. "Dr. Hugle was here earlier, asking questions. The media came and got a little too close to him. Now he's keeping his distance."

Lake's brown eyes fixed on me, his mind obviously wondering what vulgarity I'd come out with.

I kneaded the side of my neck in a futile effort to ease my tension. "Dr. Hugle's here to be seen by the cameras. He won't be speaking until he gets his scriptwriters scrawling his plea for money."

Conrad Hugle's state agency, Child Protective Services, was taking a drubbing in the press for losing children in the system and placing kids back with violent parents. Teflon Con was good at going on television to beg for more money as if upping the ante made up for incompetence. But with today's catastrophe, which involved CPS as well as the Juvenile Court, things needed to cool down before he made his call for more cash. If I were under his cloud of distrust, I wouldn't be anywhere near here, but who understands the motives of slicksters like him.

When Hugle's eyes met mine, he halted and threw his hands in the air as if he remembered he left something behind. He whirled to hurry back the way he'd come. I was used to his snubs, but the fool wasn't going to avoid me for long.

"Has the Amber Alert gone out?" I asked the fire captain.

He looked at Lake. "It's the lieutenant's call."

Guarded lines dug into Lake's face. "Problem is . . . I can't confirm abduction, although I believe what the dogs are telling us. Give me a little time to talk to some folks first. There's still a chance the kids took refuge and haven't been found."

"Good point," Turquin agreed.

I said, "Portia Devon, the judge in their case, is on her way here with pictures."

Shouts by an avid group of men and women loaded down with notebooks and cameras and microphones intruded into our conversation. Turquin shook his head. "I don't talk to the media, Lieutenant. I'll brief you, though."

Lake's lips twitched. "Thanks for the favor."

Across the street, a television reporter spoke into a video

camera. Several panned the crowd and lingered on Lake. Since he wasn't ready to speak, he hopped-skipped toward two of his detectives who had been interviewing witnesses.

When he disappeared, I felt the cameras' focus on me. I was well known by Atlanta's press corps. When I started Child Trace as a specialized detective agency, news editors and producers got interested. I've become a regular on talk radio, and the newspaper did a spread after my first trace. The photographs with the story showed me to be a tall, blue-eyed, dark-haired woman with a wide smile. Some of my quotes were sappy, but I'd said the words and generally tried to live up to them. I wish, however, the article hadn't included long-ago personal stuff like my daddy's fall from grace and his suicide because of alcoholism, and my mother's subsequent dementia. The writer of the piece concluded that these poignant details turned me into a champion of the innocent. All crap. I leave the high-mindedness to the courts— particularly with Portia Devon—and work like the devil to recover what children I can.

All of a sudden, the restless crowd hushed and parted. I had a vision of Moses passing his rod over it. Portia Devon marched up the divide. A bulging soft briefcase hung from one arm, and in the clutch of another was a large manila envelope. She wouldn't come up to Charlton Heston's biceps, but her Roman nose alone conveyed as much force. Those who crossed her in court flinched under her piercing black eyes. "Officer!" she bellowed.

A uniformed policeman rushed to her. "Yes, ma'am."

Jamming the envelope into his hands, she said, "Pass these flyers to the press and the searchers." She turned to me. "I faxed photographs to the news organizations and police HQ."

The cop opened the envelope. I reached for a picture of the

girls. Both had blond hair in tight curls. They could have been twins, except one was taller than the other. Their eyes were blue, and their fair faces were shaped like hearts, wide at the cheeks and pointed at the chin. I touched each face and prayed they were safe.

When I looked at Portia, anxiety appeared to seep from her pores. She made the sign of the cross, stirring up a stew of memories. We'd met in second grade at Christ the King Catholic school, became lapsed in college, and now made the sign of the cross mainly at funerals. She asked, "You learn anything yet?"

I shook my head. "The dogs came up empty so far."

She studied the crowd, and her eyes settled on Lake. He climbed onto the runner of a fire truck, holding a bull horn.

"Please!" his amplified voice called out.

People quieted.

"Anyone with any information about this fire and those missing children, please come forward. Speak to me, or any officer. Nothing is too insignificant to bring to our attention. Again, nothing is too insignificant. These children are somewhere. Time is critical."

The tension in him flowed into me, turning my muscles into steel strips. He was divorced and had a five-year-old girl, Susanna, which reminded me we were supposed to take Susanna to Sunday brunch at Ray's on the River tomorrow. Come hell or high water, we were going to keep the date—having found two blond, blue-eyed tykes unscathed.

Suddenly I heard Portia mutter, "That asshole."

I gaped at her. She couldn't mean Lake. She was crazy about him, and then I saw her eyes drill someone or something behind me. I glanced around. Here came Conrad Hugle, creeping toward us. He reminded me of a speckled snake that hangs out in my garden. I'd caught it slithering, tongue flickering, toward a ladybug. I'd saved that ladybug, but what about the millions I hadn't been there for?

Hugle's reluctance to greet us was obvious. Large, dark freckles on his large face stood out. Rimless glasses magnified bulbous eyes, staring over our heads.

Portia said in whisper, "We're about to make public a report that shows twenty-five kids in the state have died in the past five years after coming to the attention of his staff."

"Plus, I rescued six," I said.

"Seven," Portia corrected.

Hugle sidled to within three feet and stopped.

"Conrad," I said.

He nodded with a dutiful drawing back of his thick lips.

"Dr. Hugle," Portia said in her crisp way. "How long have you been here?"

"Since I heard the sirens at dawn and looked out my window. I live in the lofts."

"And, precisely what have you learned so far?"

He tilted his head back, and I could see the hairs up his nostrils. "Precisely as much as you have, Your Honor. Everything is in turmoil and has yet to be sorted out."

"Don't throw so much information at me at one time," Portia snapped. "My mind can't take it all in. I'm surprised to see you still here, Conrad. You have able spokespeople at CPS."

Portia's sarcasm was flagrant, and Hugle was speechless for a second. Then he said, "I've joined the search." My eyes slid to his shoes, which hadn't lost their shine despite the wet grass and mud. He went on, "My position aside, I'm also part of this community."

Portia turned away—I would guess to keep from saying something she'd really regret. "Come, let's go through the file."

Hugle and I followed her as she kicked aside wet trash and bottles all the way to Lake's squad car in the vacant lot. She laid the briefcase on the hood, opened it, brought out a folder, and put it in my hands.

Captain Turquin came up. "Not too long now," he said, "the medical examiner and the fire forensic team will be here."

I said, "Captain, I'd appreciate it if I can talk with you later."

"Of course," he said. "Be happy to give you all the information I can."

I pulled a card case from my backpack and handed him a card.

After Turquin was out of earshot, Portia asked Hugle, "You know the Barnes couple, don't you, Conrad?"

Hugle rubbed his forehead as if unsure how to answer—as if Portia would ask for biographical details. But she knew, like me, Hugle wasn't the type to get to know the hoi-polloi.

Portia said, "It's all in the folder, but briefly, Ed and Wanda Barnes have lived in this neighborhood all their lives. Ed retired from the railroad at forty-eight after thirty years. Wanda was a retired nurse. He was a deacon of the neighborhood church, and she, the organist. The girls captured their hearts from the start. They wanted to adopt them."

"They should have been allowed to," Conrad said.

Portia's neck muscles flared as she stared up at him. "The father wouldn't agree."

"I would think it would be out of his hands, Judge."

I wanted to rip into him before Portia did. But she gave me a warning glance and, oddly, let silence be her rebuke. "Now to the children," she said, throwing aside one folder and picking out another. "Jessica and Dorthea Rose. Their mother is dead, killed in a trailer fire with a baby son. Their father's name is Timothy Rose. They moved to Atlanta from Apple Creek, a trailer park hollow up in the mountains. He is serving life in prison. His crack operation blew up and started the fire, killing his wife and son. Dorthea was born deaf."

Hugle made a noise like a fart. When I glanced at him, he gave a quick moan. "Suffer the little children."

"We must *find* the little children," Portia said.

I heard footsteps crunching their way toward us. I turned as Captain Turquin beckoned. "Lieutenant Lake asked me to let y'all know he's going to interview the next-door neighbor."

"I'm coming," I said.

"So am I," Portia said.

Hugle opened his mouth like a puppy eager to follow, but we charged away, leaving him standing—if not feeling like a fifth wheel, at least looking like one.

THREE

The route to the Barneses' neighbor's house took us past en-croaching radio and television microphones. A long-armed mike brushed the top of Portia's head as its holder tried to stick it in her face. Hitting the mike with the back of her hand, she said, "Get back, you idiot!"

Reporters called, "Judge, what can you tell us!" "Give us something!"

They also challenged me. "Miss Dru, here!" "How is Child Trace involved?" "Do you have a clue where the kids are?" "Where did the dogs go?"

Past the media swarm, we came to a picket fence. There was a sign on a post inside it. The calligraphy read: STEPHEN ALVIN DOONAN (M.ARCH/M.I.P.). DOONAN ASSOCIATES, P.C. My neighbor is an architect, so I know the alphabet tags mean Master of Architecture and Master of Infrastructure Planning, Professional Corporation.

Lake waited at the stone steps with a young man who was a few inches shorter than Lake, but as fit. I'd guess he was a three-day-a-week, 10-K runner, like Lake and me. A diamond stud took up nearly half of his left earlobe. When Lake introduced him to us, Doonan removed his baseball cap to reveal close-cut blond hair.

Doonan said his throat was parched and invited us to come inside his cottage. He slipped off his mud-caked shoes beside the doormat. His pants legs were crusty, poignant evidence he'd beat the bushes for the two children who lived next door.

His home was a typical craftsman's cottage. We entered into a hall foyer. Five paces ahead, a narrow staircase rose to a room above. Beyond the staircase would be a kitchen, bath, and a small bedroom. To my left was a front room where a draftsman's table stood, surrounded by computers. To my right was another front room, sparse of furnishings. I think straight-line creations are called Mission style.

I turned to Doonan. "Nice place."

Obviously house-proud, he beamed. "I had to tear down the superstructure, but I built onto the old foundation."

"You're lucky it didn't catch fire," Portia said.

He shuddered at the idea. "Yes, ma'am. I am."

In the parlor, Lake got the Morris chair, which didn't look any more comfortable than the hard oaks Portia and I sat on.

When Doonan rushed away to get drinks, Portia looked at Lake. "Sorry I interrupted your weekend, but I wanted you for this investigation."

Lake looked at me and winked. "I wouldn't miss working with my favorite partner again for anything in the world."

It was a struggle to keep my composure when my heart was beating like a rock group's drummer, but I managed an inadequate, "We do good work, don't we?"

Doonan came back carrying four bottles of water and coasters. I hadn't realized I was thirsty until the first swallow. He went across the hall and rolled in a padded desk chair. He sat and sucked water until it flowed from the sides of his mouth. Wiping his chin with his fingers, he cupped the bottle in his hands, hung them between his knees and drooped his head. "Terrible," he said. "Just terrible."

Lake took out a notebook. "We appreciate your help, Mr. Doonan."

"Glad to."

Lake said, "Begin with the fire. Did you hear an explosion?"

"No, nothing like that." Doonan paused, apparently to stare back in time. "It was past six when I woke. It was lighter than it should be. I sleep upstairs, in what is usually the children's room in these places." He pressed his lips together.

I asked, "Was the Barnes cottage like this one? Did the children sleep upstairs?"

"The houses are identical," Doonan answered. "And yes, the kids slept upstairs. I can't see the Barnes house from my upstairs because there's a single window at the front. When . . . it happened . . . I heard a commotion. I looked outside and saw people from up the street running all-out. The woman across the street was waving her cane so hard I thought she'd fall. I thought at first something was wrong with my house. I opened the window, smelled the smoke, and ran down and out. The Barnes house was in flames. I looked for them, for the little girls. People were banging on the windows . . . yelling and screaming. It was truly terrible."

Lake looked up from his scribbling. "Did you or anyone try to go in?"

"A couple of guys tried to break down the front door. I ran to the back. There's a door off the kitchen. Me and a neighbor got the door open, but man, the blast of air threw us back. We couldn't . . ." He finished off his water and wiped his mouth. "Jeez, it burned so hot."

Lake asked, "Was the door locked?"

"Uh, no, it wasn't."

"Go on."

"We couldn't do anything for the people inside."

"Did you hear noises from inside? See movement?"

"None." He squeezed the bottle, cracking the plastic. "You didn't know which way to turn."

"When did you learn there were only two bodies in the fire?"

"After the flames . . . died. The firemen went in. God help them, it was hot as hell. Word went around . . . everybody got upset. Naturally, we thought the girls died, too, but then the firefighters said they weren't in there. We lit out to find them. The dogs came." He took a deep breath. "The one little girl, Dottie, is hearing-impaired. But she was always with her sister. We scoured the neighborhood." He leaned back hard, and his chair rolled back until it hit the edge of a straight-legged table. He walked his chair forward as he massaged his temples.

"Where would they run if they escaped the fire?" Lake asked.

He blinked as if to clear film from his eyes. "Here, or across the street to Miss Goddard's."

"Who lives on the other side of you? Looks locked up."

"A renter. He's in New York now."

"Who does he rent from?"

"I own the house."

"You look inside it yet?"

"Why no. It's locked tight. They couldn't get in."

Lake stopped short of scowling, a look I could read. Already he didn't like Doonan. Lake said, "We'll want to go in. Who owns the vacant lot behind the Barnes house?"

"Me. I don't mind you parking there."

Portia's eyebrows almost shot to her hair line.

Lake's eyes became slits to match his lips. "Obliged. And who owns the house on the other corner of the alley?"

"I . . . own it, too. New tenants move in next month."

It appeared Mr. Doonan had staked a claim in Cabbagetown. I wondered if he'd offered to buy the Barnes house since his property surrounded it.

"You got keys for the rental houses?" Lake asked.

Fret wrinkles appeared on Doonan's forehead. "Of course."

"We need to take a look," Lake said.

"It'll be all right, I guess."

Wrong thing to say, Mr. Doonan.

Lake asked, "How long have you lived in the neighborhood?"

"Aren't we going astray here?" Doonan asked.

"I'd like an answer to my question," Lake said, his voice implying consequences if Doonan got mouthier.

"Let's see, I bought this place ten years ago as an investment, for a rental, but then fell in love with the community. I moved in when this house was renovated three years ago."

Lake looked thoughtful. "I see. Now, let's assume the worst and the kids were taken by someone."

It wasn't typically something a cop would suggest, but his reason for laying it out was clear when Doonan's mouth dropped open as if it hadn't occurred to him. And maybe it hadn't, you never know. Doonan's voice cracked. "You mean . . . ?"

"I mean abducted. It's imperative we determine that as soon as possible. So, think back to last night. Did you see or hear anything unusual?"

Doonan's blond eyebrows came together making one fuzzy line. He shook his head. "It was a typical Friday night. People go out, and come home. Some pretty late, but it's quiet in this neighborhood. No through traffic, so you see the same people and their friends. I went to sleep about midnight, I think. I know it stormed, but I slept through it."

"Are you here during the day?"

"Yes. My office is across the hall. I'm an infrastructure architect. I write for digests and I do renovation projects in historic neighborhoods."

"Did you see anything out of the ordinary yesterday?"

Doonan leaned back and braced both feet on the chair's roller housing, his hands draping the arms. "I never thought about the possibility of abduction. But something did happen yesterday afternoon."

My spine stiffened. Portia's eyes were shining stones. Lake's head cocked attentively, but his lips were pressed with irritation. He said, "Go on."

"It rained almost all day. I was out most of the morning. In the afternoon I saw Jessie and Dottie. It was after school. They were riding their bikes. They always rode their bikes. Everywhere." He put his feet on the floor and leaned forward, his eyes glistening. "You know, they were terribly disadvantaged children."

Portia interjected, "I'm a juvenile judge. I handle their case."

Doonan acknowledged this with a nod. "Then you know the Barneses were lovely people. They bought the girls bikes for Christmas."

Portia said, "Are you saying the Rose girls were out on their bikes yesterday in the rain?"

He shook his head. "The rain had stopped. A car came along and slowed next to the girls. I'd been paying particular attention while they rode in the slick streets, because I didn't want the little one skidding in a puddle and going down. I guess I'm kind of partial to her." He swallowed, bobbing his prominent Adam's apple.

"Describe the car," Lake said.

"Dark blue. Late model. American-made. Like a Buick or Ford. I'm not good with cars. I got a BMW. Oh, yeah, it had a chrome strip missing."

"Ever see it before?"

"No."

"Go on," Lake said, standing and removing the portable radio from his belt holster.

"The person in the car . . . I couldn't tell if it was a man or woman. From my vantage, I didn't get a look when the window came down, but Jessie spoke to the person inside. Then she stepped back and waved. Little Dottie seemed lost in thought, but I guessed it was because she couldn't talk."

Lake asked, "How long did the conversation last?"

"Not very. But I had a strange feeling and went outside. The car drove away at the same time Wanda Barnes came outside, too."

"Did you get a tag number?"

I held my breath and prayed—please, say you did. Redeem yourself.

"I saw the first three numbers clearly: 248. They're easy to remember. Sorry, I didn't catch the last three."

"Then what happened?" Lake asked.

"Wanda asked Jessie if she knew the person. Jessie nodded her head yes. Dottie signed as they went into their own yard."

"Signed?" Lake asked.

Portia explained, "Dottie's going to speech school to learn American Sign Language." She turned to Doonan, "What did she sign?"

"I'm sure it was the sign for Santa." His hand ran down from his chin to his chest, indicating Santa's beard.

"Santa?" Lake asked, and I could almost hear his mind whirling. Santa. Bicycles for Christmas. A predator who knew how special this Christmas was for the Rose girls.

Doonan said, "I wish I'd asked little Dottie what she meant."

"Did you see the car again?"

"No."

"Did you talk to the girls after the occurrence?"

"No, I saw them later in the yard, actually, in my vacant lot. I thought I'd ask about the Santa man, but then I thought I'd wait for another time when I could warn them not to talk to strangers, even ones they know." He rubbed his eyes with his left hand.

"Stick around," Lake said, heading for the door. "I'll be back to go through those houses with you."

Outside, Lake said, "I'll authorize the Amber." He spoke into the radio as he walked away to join his men.

FOUR

Portia said, "Interesting."

"What?"

"You believed Stephen Doonan. Lake didn't."

It was obvious Lake didn't, but I felt ambivalent about Doonan. Something bothered me, but I couldn't sort through his reactions yet. "Withholding judgment for now," I said.

"Doonan's small-minded," she said. "I don't like small-minded people."

You always knew what Portia liked and didn't.

The woman I'd noticed earlier, the skinny one with the cane, still stood on her porch across the street.

"Want to come with me?" I asked Portia. She nodded, looking as eager as Buddy, the air-scent shepherd. I kidded her, "Glad to see you're giving new meaning to the term activist judge. More should get out of their ivory towers and take to the streets."

"If I could, I'd get rid of the damned bench altogether." For a jumping bean like Portia, sitting in a chair more than fifteen minutes was torture, which explained why she was known as the fastest judicial gun in Atlanta.

I waved at the woman with the cane, and she raised it. She knew I would come. She introduced herself as Miss Goddard—no first name—which made me certain she was a spinster, an old-fashioned word for an old-fashioned lady.

Her cottage was an architectural duplicate of Doonan's but there the resemblance ended. The crocheted and embroidered antimacassars on the occasional tables were an extension of Miss Goddard's character. Little figurines, cup-and-saucer sets, photographs of unsmiling people littered the small parlor. The lady also liked to read and knit. Her bag was sitting beside her platform rocker. The weave on the side read, "Millicent's Handiwork." She laid her cane against the footstool. The stress in her face hadn't abated, but she sat arrow straight.

Taking out my notebook, I said, "I can see you were very fond of the family."

"Yes. Very fond," she said, biting her thin lower lip. "I've known Ed and Wanda Barnes as long as they've been on this earth. They were a little younger than me. We all went to the old Grant School. Wanda was a dear, dear friend." Her eyelids flickered to hold back tears.

I would let her ramble for a while. People like Miss Goddard ease into the horror of the moment rather than jump into it.

She went on in a shaky voice, "Wanda and Ed adored those two girls. Jessie was quick-witted and funny. The little one . . . she had a hearing problem. Ed wanted to adopt so he could get her on his railroad insurance and get those special tests and get her to hear. But their daddy . . ." She paused, and, before she could go on, Portia intervened.

"Tell us about the fire, what did you see and hear?" No ease in Portia.

Miss Goddard's voice firmed. "I didn't see what I prayed I'd see. Once the fire got going, I prayed the four of them would rush from the place. They didn't. The neighbors couldn't get to the front door for the smoke and flames. They went to the back. They tried." Her head shook. "They tried."

I said, "Mr. Doonan believes you witnessed the start of the fire. Was there an explosion?"

There was something in her faint frown, and I wondered if she was going to give an impartial witness account or exaggerate. She said, "The sound was like a match being struck to the gas right before the flames. Neighbors came flying from everywhere. It was quite devastating to see." She lifted a leg to the stool. She wore thick stockings—like my mother's varicose vein stockings. "I called nine-one-one. At first I thought maybe Wanda left the stove on in the kitchen. Then I saw it was in their bedroom where the flames first went up. Then, the front room went."

"Go on."

"When help came, the firemen were no match for the flames." She drew a handkerchief from her pocket. "When they got it out, I heard Jessie and Dottie weren't in the house. Now nobody can find them." She breathed in, holding her breath for a second or two before she exhaled. "They were pretty little things. It breaks my heart." She rubbed her breastbone with stiffened fingers. "I pray those girls are safe somewhere, but I fear . . ."

"What do you fear, Miss Goddard?" I asked, hearing the fear in my own voice.

"Harm has come to them. I know I'm supposed to keep up hope, but, you see, at my age, and all my ears have taken in and all my eyes have seen, it isn't easy."

Portia leaned forward. "I understand what you're saying, Miss Goddard. Miss Dru and I work with children. We are aware of the unspeakable things that happen."

Miss Goddard pressed her handkerchief to her lips. "I think somebody set the fire and stole the little girls."

Portia bestowed a critical glance as only Portia can.

Miss Goddard laid the handkerchief carefully in her lap. She leaned back, and her eyes skimmed the bookcases built floor to ceiling on each side of a tiny fireplace. I recognized several Agatha Christies on the shelves. She closed her eyes and rolled her head side to side. When she opened them, her glance made me uneasy. Portia and I exchanged quick looks.

Miss Goddard said in a monotone suggesting evil, "There have been children missing from this community before now."

Portia about shot out of her chair. "Who, when?"

Miss Goddard wasn't prepared for a rapid exchange. Her breathing labored before she said, "A ten-year-old girl . . . about eight years ago . . . up and vanished. Bonnie Yates lived with a foster couple on Ruby Street. Name was Bolton—Andrew and Stella. They were from Valdosta. They did their best for the wild little thing. When the police and the CPS got through with them, they went back home to Valdosta full of anger, and who can blame them. They were good people."

"Eight years ago, huh?" Portia said, obviously trying to remember the case. She shook her head. I'd been a cop then. I searched my mind for the case but couldn't remember it.

Miss Goddard spoke again. "Then, there was another case

three and a half years ago. Sherri Patterson was eleven years old. I guess today's youngsters mature earlier than they did when I was coming up. She was a pretty girl but she had a smart mouth like her mama. Mrs. Patterson was divorced and not always at home when she should be." Her expression of disapproval said more than words, and even though I felt the press of time, I let Miss Goddard go on at her measured pace. "Sherri ran with an older crowd, and when she went missing the police decided she was a runaway. I don't credit it at all, but we in the neighborhood had to tell what we knew about the family."

"Which was what?" Portia asked.

"They were tenants of Stephen's." Miss Goddard let a beat of time pass as if to hint at something we should grasp. "After Sherri disappeared, Mrs. Patterson moved to Florida with . . . a friend."

"Anyone you knew?"

"She had so many."

Portia's expression became impish. "What do you think happened, Miss Marple?"

Her reference to the famous fictional sleuth lightened the air, and Miss Goddard's eyes glittered and she fussed a little. "I guess I have to plead guilty to being a busybody. You talk to others, they'll tell you."

"This community is like a small village," Portia said. "Everybody knows what goes on in small villages, real or fictional."

"I'm a seamstress by trade," Miss Goddard said. "I've sewn up christening dresses, wedding dresses, and regular clothes for forty-five years, ever since Mama taught me how. Mama was the seamstress here before me. We go into homes." Her eyes conveyed you learn things when you go into other people's homes. "My old hands are creaky now, so I don't do much anymore."

"What was the gossip when those girls disappeared?" Portia asked.

"Half believed the police; half didn't."

"What about you?"

"They were stolen. They were troubled youngsters, targets for evil, not runaways."

"Targets for whom?"

Her eyes went from Portia to me. "Why . . . I wouldn't know."

I didn't believe her, nor did Portia by the look on her face. She said, "Stephen Doonan's name keeps coming up. He rented to the Pattersons and he lives next door to the Barneses . . ."

Portia's unasked question hung for a moment or two, and Miss Goddard's slim hands wrenched together while she spoke. "Stephen owns most of the rental property around here, so it was natural Mrs. Patterson would rent from him." She looked past my shoulder, toward the window. "Maybe it's not for me to bring up, and I'm not saying he had anything to do with their being gone, but Stephen was awful fond of the Rose girls, especially the little one, Dottie."

"And?" Portia asked from the edge of her chair.

When she looked at Portia, Miss Goddard shook her head. "A child molester's dream, they were."

"What you're implying is . . ."

"Wicked, yes. I don't say he did anything. Stephen looked out for them all the while he played and joked with them."

"Yet, you found it troubling."

"So did Wanda. We liked Stephen, but he's . . . I know he had trouble with his firm downtown, and they fired him. But he's done well on his own. He's determined to get this neighborhood back to the charm it never had. He's helped me with the three-by-sixes on my porch. He's ambitious, but Wanda wanted him to keep his distance from the little ones. She was going to say something, but I told her I'd bring up with him that he needed to stop being in their playtime so much."

I said, "Stephen Doonan strikes me as a lonely man."

"Lonely?" Miss Goddard said, angling her head right. "I don't know about that, but you got to keep appearances up. Men with little children these days . . .'tis a shame what happens sometimes."

"Mr. Doonan said he saw the Rose girls talking to a man in a car yesterday afternoon," I said. "Did you see that occur?"

"No. Let's see, it was raining yesterday. I went to the store in a cab. Then I had a bite to eat, took a nap, and got up about five in the afternoon. I'm an insomniac, and so I sleep in fits and starts."

"I, too, am an insomniac," Portia said—a new one on me. "Did you sleep through the night?"

"Never do. I was more restless than usual. Stephen's light went off at midnight. The Barnes house went dark about eleven. I can't see the master room from my house. It faces the alley street, but I saw the girls' silhouettes upstairs against the curtains before the lights went off."

"Then?"

"I slept until the wind woke me. I'm afraid someday a pine is going to blow on my place. I watched outside."

"Was anybody out? See any cars?"

Miss Goddard looked genuinely thunderstruck. "A car did go by. His lights were dim."

"His?"

"The driver's lights. I'm old-fashioned using the masculine."

Portia asked, "Were they fog lights?"

"The yellow ones."

"Was it foggy?"

"It was, before later, when the wind picked up and the lightning started."

"Where did the driver go . . . straight or did *he* turn?"

Although Miss Goddard's frown was faint, I read annoyance in it. She said, "The *car* turned into the alley street by Wanda's."

"What was the car? The make?"

"A dark car. I don't drive, but I know what folks around here drive. It wasn't from here."

Jotting quickly, I asked, "So this would have been about two-thirty?"

"Thereabouts. Many hours before the fire, which is why I didn't make a connection."

"And there may not be one," I said. "Anything else you can add?"

"No," she said, trouble gathering on her brow. "I slept again on and off until the storm blew over. I raised the windows, and then I heard . . . the house go." She clutched her breast. "My heart . . . it's not good anymore." She leaned forward; her face looked bloodless. She reached into her knitting bag and brought out a pillbox. I guessed it was nitro for angina. When she spoke she sounded like she had marbles in her throat. "This tragedy . . . I'm afraid when I lie down to sleep, I won't wake up."

"If you need a heart monitor, I'll see you get to the hospital," Portia said.

"No, no. I have oxygen. And my little pills."

"Are you sure?"

"Yes, dear."

Odd to hear someone call Portia dear, although, beneath the brusqueness, she is a dear.

A strident noise intruded—the jarring sound of a vehicle backing up. Portia and I rose to look out the window. The medical examiner had arrived. I watched as Lake and he talked briefly. I flipped my notebook closed. "We'll leave you now. Rest, and if you think of anything . . . anything at all . . ."

She looked up, and I saw a cunning glint in her eyes. "I reckon you'll be back." The marbly throat had cleared.

I reckoned she was right.

FIVE

We walked down Miss Goddard's steps. "Porsh, good going with the Miss Marple thing."

Portia's nose wriggled like a disapproving rabbit's. "That's how she sees herself, and how she wants us to see her."

"Damned woman has an idea whose car it was. She said *his*, even though she tried to cover for saying it," I said.

Across the street, I watched the medical examiner pick his way through the rubble, toward the bodies. What a profession. I knew Lake wouldn't be trailing him through the ashes. Lake trusted what the ME reported, and later would study the photographs.

Lake spotted us coming down Miss Goddard's steps and hurried toward us. The media people stretched their perimeter and shouted. Lake shook Portia's hand for the cameras. Usually he gives her a hug. She turned her back on the men and women of the press and said to Lake, "You need to talk to them before they come at you—grab you by the throat."

"Not until the ME tells me something. It will be hours before they can move the bodies."

Keeping our mouths away from the lip-readers among the reporters, we briefed Lake on our talk with Miss Goddard. Even though Lake wasn't in Homicide eight years ago, he recalled the first missing girl case. "Probably some Cold Case guy will get to it," he said. "They do good work, but they need fifty more detectives, like we do."

"You know what I think?" I said.

His eyelids quivered over his dark eyes. "I never have."

It was hard to ignore the warm prickle in my chest, but this was business, no batting eyelashes and come-on grins. "We'll clear these two cases before Cold Case does."

"Or you'll die trying." His tone was amused, but I could feel the admiration in it. He went on. "I talked to Jessie's teacher. She joined the searchers as soon as she heard about her missing student."

"Anything helpful?"

"No Santas in schools these days. She mourned his loss, along with the Confederate flag."

Portia, showing signs of agitation, said, "I'll get the ball rolling on the missing girls. I have no recollection of a child in CPS care going missing in this neighborhood, but then eight years ago I'd just gotten on the bench."

"You might ask Dr. Hugle," Lake suggested.

I said, "Dr. Hugle's mine. I'll also tackle the background on our architect. And Miss Goddard."

Lake's eyebrows shot up. "Miss Goddard?"

Suspecting an old woman, especially a spinster seamstress, was callous, but at every opportunity I tried to raise my callous quotient. I chided Lake, "Always, always, check out the people closest to the vics. No matter how improbable. Isn't that what they taught you in detective school?"

Lake looked up at the Goddard house. "The curtain fell. She's watching us."

"See?"

"Arson and old lace?" he asked. "Who's her accomplice?"

"Santa Claus," Portia said.

Lake gave his characteristic grin and glanced across the street. "Mr. Doonan's impatiently waiting for us at the door of his tenant's house. Wonder how much property the community is going to let him gobble up?"

Portia snorted. "Vulture. All he has to do is sit tight and wait for their economic worm to turn, then swoop in with the bucks."

"Or wait for their house to burn down," I said.

Without a word, Doonan unlocked the door to the renter's house. Judging from the look on his face and the tremble in his hands, he'd come to the conclusion we didn't believe the missing girls were hiding inside. Lake had deliberately given him time to figure out if the Rose girls were abducted, from our perspective, the stranger-in-the-car story was suspicious, and the Santa Claus story very strange, given it was April.

Doonan led us through a bungalow identical to his own; however, the tenant's taste went to airier wicker and rattan. As Lake went from room to room, a fidgety Doonan stood next to me in the small foyer. He said, "I see you talked to Gossiping Goddard."

"I did."

"You get anything useful?"

"Maybe."

"She and Wanda Barnes ran the neighborhood."

Craftiness gleamed in his eyes, and I wondered if it was to camouflage his nervousness. "I thought Conrad Hugle did."

"He's a joke. Let him be president of the neighborhood association. It's a thankless job. I did it for a year. A whole year of headaches."

"How did Conrad get along with the children in the neighborhood?"

"There were children in the neighborhood? Conrad didn't know it."

I headed for the kitchen. Doonan followed. Lake was there, wearing latex gloves. He shut the pantry door and turned hard, dark eyes on Doonan. "Other girls have disappeared from this neighborhood. Tell me about them."

Doonan washed his hands on each other. "Goddard knows a hell of a lot more than me."

"You weren't concerned about the foster girl and the child of your tenant?"

"Sure. But . . . look, I was working at the firm then. I was out of town a lot. I was concerned, but I was also busy. Very busy."

"This house have a basement?" Lake asked.

"Yeah, the entry's outside."

Lake, still wearing gloves, followed Doonan down the back steps, me on his heels. As we tramped single file to the side of the house, Lake asked, "How did you and Miss Goddard get along?"

"She has favorites," Doonan said, halting, selecting a padlock key from a ring. "You got to be a neighborhood old-timer for her to respect you. I like the old girl. I don't dislike anyone. But she gets her knife into the newcomers when she can."

We came to slanting double doors marking the entrance to the cellar. A padlock shackle hung on a hinged ring attached to the doors, but the U-shaped loop was twisted and not clicked into the lock's body. Lake and I stared at each other; dread seemed to seep from the pores in his face. I couldn't so much as blink before Doonan went into a rant. "Would you look at that, for Christ's sake? Kids in this neighborhood have no respect."

Lake reached to the back of his waist band where he kept the Glock, a gun he'd rather draw than the Smith and Wesson in his shoulder holster. He ordered, "Step back, Mr. Doonan."

His face red from anger, Doonan snarled, "What?"

Lake reached down, and, with the barrel of the gun, nudged the bent shackle from the door ring and reached to pull back one of the double doors. He held the Glock pointing down, into the opening.

Death stench roiled from the cellar. I reeled back.

Gagging, Doonan clutched his throat.

It wasn't the Rose girls we smelled. They may have been dead—I swallowed the liquid filling the back of my throat—but the odor coming from under the house was too ripe.

Ripping open the other double door, Lake asked, "Doonan, you got lights down there?"

"Yeah."

"Follow me. Get 'em on."

The two of them moved down the four steps and ducked into the cramped darkness. The cellar couldn't be more than five feet from dirt floor to ceiling. I squatted and looked down at their retreating backs, breathing through the collar on my shirt when I had to. A yellow light sprang on.

Doonan yelled, "God! It's the dog!"

"What dog?" Lake demanded.

"The Barneses' bull terrier." There was a cry-hitch in Doonan's voice.

The Barneses had a dog? Why were we just hearing about it?

I backed away, and the men climbed up the cellar steps. Lake's stormy dark eyes watched Doonan close the door and kick the padlock lying on the grass. "My tenant is not going to be happy when he gets home to this."

"Don't touch that lock," Lake said, his voice staccato through compressed lips. "Now tell me about the dog."

Doonan looked pasty enough to faint. "It went missing is all I know."

"How long ago?"

"Wednesday."

We moved away from the cellar into Doonan's backyard. The pinks and whites of his early azaleas were waning, but the later variety, the smaller salmons and reds, had to be a source of pride for him. Pride—the man was loaded with it.

Lake crossed his arms. "Why didn't you tell us the Barneses' dog went missing?"

"I didn't think . . . what does it have to do with . . . ?" He threw up his hands. "God . . . I don't know . . . I . . ."

"How and when did you learn it was gone?"

"Wanda came to the house. Asked if I'd seen Buster. The girls were upset. We looked everywhere. In the streets particularly. I hoped the girls didn't have to see their dog squashed by a car. But we couldn't find the dog. That's all."

Lake's hands went to each side of his waist. "That's all? Everybody forgot about it? The girls? The Barneses, too?"

"I think they got in touch with the Humane Society. Look, you can't blame me for everything."

"Who's blaming you for what?"

"You know . . ." His worried eyes roved his shrubs, and then he looked at me. "You talked to Goddard. Did she tell you about her pet, Dwight Judd?"

"No," I said, picturing a big tabby cat. "Should she have?"

"I'm not surprised she didn't talk about him, but he's your suspect."

"Not a tabby then?"

"Huh?"

Lake grinned, like he'd been thinking animal, too.

Doonan wasn't amused. "He's a convicted child molester. He lives on Miller Street, wears an ankle monitor. Nut case, but you wouldn't know it by the old maids and PRO-fessionals living up at the mill. Makes me sick."

"His existence is another thing you should have told us about when we first talked," Lake said.

Doonan snapped a flower head. "I didn't want to accuse anybody."

"So now you did. What'd he do?"

"Molested Susie Ryan."

"Who's she?"

"Neighbor kid."

"How old?"

"Ten."

"How old's Judd?"

"Twenty or so."

"When'd it happen?"

"Two years, I don't know exactly."

"When did he get out of prison?"

"Since Christmas. Got out early for good behavior."

"Does he work?"

"Yeah, with Cyrus Bassett, at Bassett's Grocery."

"Where is Bassett's Grocery?"

"On Windom."

"You keep an eye on Judd?"

"I avoid people I don't like."

"Like Miss Goddard?"

"I like her. I don't excuse her faults."

I couldn't resist asking, "Like Conrad Hugle's?"

The corner of his upper lip rose. "There's a creep for you."

Lake asked, "Is he the PRO-fessional you're talking about?"

"One of them."

"You throw suspicion on a likely named Dwight Judd, what about Hugle?"

Doonan's smile was sly. "Is he the one with the jail record?"

"Not that I know of."

"But you don't know for sure?"

"He's a public figure, Mr. Doonan. Head of Child Protective Services. I think we'd all know if he had a jail record."

"Doesn't keep him from being a creep."

Lake grinned as if to agree, and then looked thoughtful. "It's not hard to know a creep when you see one, right?"

"Right."

"Makes you wonder how he got in the position he's in, don't it?"

"Sure as hell does," Doonan said, flexing his shoulders as if to ease tension.

"So tell me . . ." Lake said, ". . . why were you fired from your downtown firm?" A surprise, almost friendly change of subject is an old cop ploy.

Doonan clenched his upper arms. "I might have known Gossiping Goddard would get that out. I resigned."

"Why?"

The way he looked at Lake, Doonan appeared on the verge of telling him to go to hell. Wisely, he took several deep breaths instead. "We were a small, but very elite firm. Put it down to personal differences. Besides, when I bought here, I knew what my life's work was to be."

"What's the name of the downtown firm?"

"I don't see the necessity of going into it."

"People are dead. Someone set the fire."

"You think I did?"

"I said someone did."

"You're treating me like a suspect."

"Your interpretation."

"I didn't do anything to those girls. Nor the dog. I swear."

"Then answer the question. What's the name of the firm you left?"

"Design Representation Associates. P.C. On Peachtree Street. I've complied, all right?"

"Miss Goddard thought maybe you liked the little girls next door too much," I said.

Doonan slanted his eyes at me. "She knows better."

"Did you ask the Barneses to sell you their house?" I asked.

He grunted. "I knew better."

"Did you ever intimate you would buy their house if they wanted to sell?"

"No."

"Is it your plan to own this neighborhood?"

"Only those houses I'm interested in—if the owners want to sell. I don't twist arms."

"There must be foreclosures, poor saps who can't make their payments."

"A lot of houses came onto the market several years ago. The market has changed."

Lake said, "The Barnes property could soon be on the market."

Doonan balled his fists. "That's warped. If you've finished your inquisition, I need to see to some things."

Lake's face was a rictus of disbelief. "Don't leave town."

Doonan threw his hands in the air, turned on his heel, and trotted to the front of the house.

I turned to Lake. "The neighborhood undercurrents are interesting."

"Someone kills a dog on Wednesday and hides the body in the cellar of a man who is away for a while," he said.

"Local knowledge."

"Local perp."

"Is Doonan smart enough to plot a point-the-finger-at-yourself scheme?"

"Or point a finger at Hugle, or Miss Goddard. Or the child molester?"

"Just what I like, an eeny-meeny-miney-moe of suspects."

SIX

When we left Doonan's backyard, Lake said exactly what I expected him to say. "It's time I had a chat with Gossiping Goddard."

"She told me she reckoned I'd be back."

"She didn't tell you about Dwight Judd, and she knew you'd wonder why."

It took a while for Miss Goddard to answer the doorbell, which rang out a tinny "Georgia on My Mind." Eventually I heard footsteps, and she snatched open the door. Her expression said, "Back this soon?"

She held out her hand, palm up. It took a tick or two before Lake realized she meant for him to give her his hat, which she hung on an old-fashioned hat rack. She offered drinks, a mini-tour of her cottage, and a few comments about Portia—she liked her—obviously intended to delay the inevitable conversation. But, at last, we got to it.

Lake took out his notebook and laid it on his knee. Miss

Goddard's eyelids were jittery whenever she looked at Lake, and I concluded she wasn't easy near virile men.

"Let's talk about Dwight Judd," Lake said.

"I knew you'd find out about Dwight," she said, looking at me. "Does it count against me I didn't tell you myself?"

"Of course not," I said. "You told Portia and me many useful facts." I looked at Lake and hoped he saw my eyes plead for patience. "The lieutenant needs to put the neighborhood in perspective, gather facts for his investigation—and quickly."

Miss Goddard's shoulders lifted, somewhat mollified. She faced Lake. "It's a fact Dwight was convicted, but he got out early for good behavior. It's a fact his name is on a molester list, and a shame."

One of Lake's eyebrows rose. "Why?"

"Because what he did was hijinxing."

I thought Lake's eyes might roll, but they didn't. "Hijinxing?"

If Miss Goddard had feathers, they would have ruffled. "Mr. Lake, I've known Dwight his entire life. I know what he's incapable of doing."

"Miss Goddard . . ." Lake said, mustering tolerance, "I could go to the police and court files and find out the facts of Dwight Judd's crime, but I'd appreciate it if you would tell me your understanding of it, and why it's hijinxing."

I could feel her anguish as she spoke. "Dwight's not got good sense. He was always awkward, saying the wrong things. And then Susie Ryan told her mama he wanted her to touch him wrong. He pleaded guilty because his lawyer told him to. I went to visit him in prison." She stopped for a moment, and then said thoughtfully, "I believe he liked prison."

"Touching a ten-year-old wrong is not hijinxing," Lake said.

"I didn't say he touched her wrong, Mr. Lake. I said Susie Ryan said he asked her to touch him wrong. There's a difference."

Lake looked at me as if to say, the ball's in your court.

She turned slightly in her chair, so it looked like she had given him the cold shoulder. I asked her, "After he pled guilty to molesting Susie Ryan, did anyone think he might have been responsible for the Yates and Patterson girls' disappearance?"

"It came up, but it didn't go anywhere. Dwight was fifteen when Bonnie Yates vanished. He couldn't drive."

"Did he have friends who drove?"

"Dwight didn't have friends, period."

"Mr. Judd could drive when Sherri Patterson went missing, couldn't he?"

"He didn't have a car. His grandaddy was still living and wouldn't let Dwight drive. Dwight never left the neighborhood that anyone remembered, except to wander in the cemetery. They searched the place high and low. They never found either Bonnie or Sherri."

"Tell me about Cyrus Bassett, the man who hired Judd."

"Cyrus was a friend of Dwight's granddaddy. Dwight's daddy and granddaddy are dead now." Her eyes squinted, as if to focus on the past. "The Judd men worked at the mill. Dwight's daddy drank, and never stepped foot in church. Dwight's mama left when Dwight was a little thing. Then his daddy died in a car wreck on Ponce de Leon. His granddaddy died of liver cancer last year."

"What do people in the neighborhood think of Dwight Judd's returning from prison?"

"Half wasn't happy—the newcomers who didn't grow up here. The other half knows Dwight didn't do anything to Susie."

"Does he own a car now?"

"Just the old junk car his grandaddy left. Doesn't work half the time. Cyrus picks him up at six-thirty of a morning and brings him home at three."

"How far away is Judd's house from the Barneses'?"

"Everything in Cabbagetown is in walking distance. Stephen runs the streets every day. Says it's a mile and a half around, not counting the cemetery."

"Then Stephen Doonan would be very familiar with the territory."

"Like the back of his hand."

"One more thing before we go. Who here is called Santa, or calls himself Santa?"

I couldn't say Miss Goddard looked startled. It wasn't quite apparent. But she'd been so forthright her hesitancy was noticeable. She breathed in before she spoke. "At Christmastime we have Santa at church, and in the stores." She paused. "Cyrus Bassett does Santa for the little kids. He's overweight and lets his beard grow out for the holiday. Of course the children know he's really Mr. Bassett."

"What about someone known as Santa at times other than Christmas?"

"I know of no one. Why do you ask?"

"Mr. Doonan believes someone, who maybe plays Santa, was in the car he saw yesterday—the one that stopped for the little girls."

Miss Goddard folded her hands. "Be that as it may . . ."

Lake asked, "You think Doonan's blaming Bassett?"

Miss Goddard looked at him like he'd turned into a piece of fecal matter. "Stephen has his own agenda. Isn't that the new way to say selfish?"

"Any reason to suspect he's lying to us?"

Her voice was firm. "No."

"What can you tell me about Conrad Hugle?"

"More than I want to," she said. Her telephone rang, and she sat forward, preparing to rise.

"We'll be leaving then," Lake said. "We'll be back if we need more information."

"Of course," she said, rising stiffly. "I'll do my civic duty."

The gathering of media had grown. The horde had stretched the yellow tape closer to Miss Goddard's house. When we came down the steps, they assaulted our ears.

"Lieutenant!" a cable news reporter called out. "Speak to us! We need information." The cable news headquarters was ten minutes away. Our tragedy had gone out to the world—another in a parade of appalling, never-ending news stories that fed a public enmeshed in the warped side of humanity.

"It's now or never," Lake said, walking to the bank of microphones. The reporters cheered. His sex appeal and the panama hat made him a media darling—to one media woman in particular. She was my anonymous caller. Twice she called in the middle of the night to brag Lake had left her moments ago, and that he calls her all the time. I asked him about it, and he reassured me I was his lover—there was no one else. But he refused to tell me who Deep Voice was, or might be. I hate these little jealous twinges of mine, so to rid my mind of her voice, I parked my butt on Miss Goddard's steps, unzipped my backpack, and fished out my cell phone.

Dennis "Webdog" Caldwell is a college student and my part-time computer sleuth. If a byte of information finds its way onto a piece of silicon, Webdog will hunt it down. I was certain I'd get him at our office on Decatur Street despite its being Saturday. He kept his own super computer there and spent his free time inventing platforms and sharpening his hacking skills. Webdog is quick to remind people he is a hacker, not a cracker. He defines hacker as a person who likes the intellectual challenge of overcoming artificial limitations put on computers for the sake of making a buck instead of sharing information, which, he says, was why the Web was invented in the first place. A cracker, he says, is a thief.

Webdog answered the phone. "I heard on the radio what happened."

"Portia's called on us once again."

"I hear you. I'm yours for the duration."

I have two employees. One was on a well-earned vacation in the Bahamas; the other—Webdog—needs one. Last year I ordered him to visit his brother in England. He'd no sooner left when I got a parental kidnapping case that screeched for his tracing techniques. I refused to cut his trip short, but he learned about it from cable news. He e-mailed he was on the case and tracked down the man and child from London. Computers have no boundaries, nor do webdogs.

I heard the keyboard tapping as I gave Web instructions to check out Stephen Doonan and Millicent Goddard and Cyrus Bassett.

Putting the cell away, I turned my attention to Lake as he

answered the same questions repeatedly. The dulcet tenor in his Southern accent was captivating. On waking this morning, I'd heard the sweet sound of sensuality in it. The media cuties looked adoring at "Ricky" as I searched each eager face—like I could discern the face of my anonymous midnight heckler. But Lake was mine. For how long, I couldn't guess. I'd had serious romances before, was engaged once, but with the exception of my fiancé, who died, those romances ended after the passion subsided and the obvious became apparent. We traveled different paths. With Lake, I hoped with my whole heart that wouldn't happen. But when I would bring up the anonymous calls, he'd gently chide me for my imagination and reminded me of what I knew to be true. People in the public eye are targets of cranks and dreamers. Deep Voice wasn't crank. She may have been a dreamer, but I wasn't imagining the gist of her phone calls. Honest with myself, I wasn't imagining her having an affair with Lake, but I would get at the truth if it took me to the brink of insanity. First, I'd find out the identity of the sultry-voiced media whore who threatened to take "Ricky" from me, and then we'd get to the nature of the relationship. That there was one, I was certain.

Speaking of media whores, I shook myself. Time to find Hugle.

Hugle was at the back of the crowd, paying attention to Lake's answers. Apparently, Hugle didn't like the questions or the answers. Unaware I was watching him, he shook his head. Once, his mouth opened as if to curse, then it snapped shut. In disgust, his head turned, and he saw me. As I came up to him, he lifted his chin. "Your detective friend is adequately answering the questions about the fire, but he shouldn't be speculating about what happened to the children."

"There aren't many things that could have happened," I said, "and Lieutenant Lake is stating the obvious. It isn't good if the public's thinking gets too far ahead of what the police are saying. We are no longer an optimistic society, in case you hadn't noticed."

"Yes, well, optimistic or not, I don't like the word kidnap until the facts say it is."

"What else could have happened?"

"The Rose children most likely found shelter, and we haven't located them yet."

"It would be rather nice for you, wouldn't it, Conrad?"

Instead of answering, he looked back at Lake, who was talking about the Amber Alert.

Hugle's nose wrinkled. "The public's lurid preoccupation with the sensational shouldn't be encouraged by asking them to interact with the principals in the crime."

"The Amber is an effective tool."

"It's not going to change people's behavior."

"Meaning?"

"Exactly what it says."

Jerk.

"Can I ask you a few questions?"

His lips peeled back. "Haven't you been?"

"How long have you lived in the mill apartments?"

"Must we get personal?"

"Nothing personal. You're not used to being asked routine police questions, are you?"

"I should say not. But, if you must, I've lived at Cotton Bag and Mill ever since my wife died. We lived in Dunwoody, but the house proved too large for me. I have simple tastes—a couple of rooms, a kitchen, and a bath suit my needs. I believe in and support revitalization of the old neighborhoods, and I was delighted to get an apartment in the historic old mill. Plus, I'm ten minutes from work."

"I hadn't heard you lost your wife."

"Long time." He sighed, his eyes on Lake as he spoke. "She died—probably before you became a policewoman, most assuredly before you began Child Trace." His tone of voice left no doubt what he thought of my agency.

He spun on his heel and strode toward the mill apartments. I matched his steps on the cracked sidewalk.

"Do you go to church in Cabbagetown?" I asked.

"I do not. I've continued to attend my Dunwoody church."

"Do you shop at Bassett's store?"

"I've been in the store, yes."

"Often?"

"Why do you want to know?"

"I'm looking for two little girls who disappeared from this neighborhood. I'm asking you to give me your take on your neighbors."

"I know and like them better than most residents of the mill apartments do. As you know, mill residents are not established Cabbagetown folk. We've come from all over the metropolitan area. We've become attracted to the concept of coming back to the core of the city."

"A lot of people have. Lake lives on Castleberry Hill. He used to live in Buckhead."

"Then you understand."

"Lake does. Tell me about Stephen Doonan."

"He's a fine young man. Ambitious. A good neighbor."

"And Ed and Wanda Barnes?"

"Fine, upstanding people. He was a deacon in the church, she was the organist."

At least he was paying attention to Portia when she told him those facts. "And the Rose girls?"

"Nice children."

"Who is their caseworker?"

"Confidential. I've asked a member of my staff to contact her."

"Did you take special interest in the girls?"

"From afar," he said. "They were integrating nicely."

"I've talked with Miss Goddard."

He stopped and faced me. "Of course."

"She was very forthcoming."

"She always is."

"Is she a friend?"

"Not especially."

"What is your relationship with her?"

His nostrils flared. "I don't know what you mean by relationship. We are an active neighborhood; everyone's interested in the welfare of the community. She never missed an NPU meeting that I can recall."

NPU meant Neighborhood Planning Unit. Fistfights could break out at NPU meetings.

"You an NPU officer?"

"The president." He walked ahead.

I skipped after him. "Miss Goddard said two other children

disappeared from your neighborhood. A couple of years ago a troubled girl from a broken family disappeared. But before her, a foster child disappeared. Tell me about the Yates case."

"It was never solved," he said indifferently. "Neither case was."

"I know, but it's important I know the facts of the Yates case. It might help finding the Rose girls." He looked as if he had no intention of enlightening me. I said, "It was on your watch, Conrad. I would think you would know the facts."

He turned his head and showed me too much of the whites of his eyes. "Are you accusing me of something?"

"All I'm saying is she was in CPS, and she lived practically on your doorstep."

"Her parents were in jail. She was difficult. The foster parents had requested she be placed elsewhere. Then she disappeared."

"Never to be seen again."

"We posted her photograph on the Internet. It's still there. Not a word after all these years."

"What do you think happened to her?"

"I think she's dead. Her bones will turn up in a patch of weeds eventually."

His nonchalance gave me the chills. "Who is Santa?"

"Santa?" There was a hitch in his step.

"For the neighborhood children."

He scratched his nose. "Cyrus Bassett dresses up like Santa Claus."

"Would they call him Santa at times other than Christmas?"

"I've never heard them."

"What is your relationship to the child molester on Miller Street?"

"Dwight?"

"Dwight Judd."

He waved a trivializing hand. "Your typical village idiot."

He stretched his stride again, but I kept up. "What really happened to Susie Ryan?"

"Maybe Dwight acted improperly with her, but it was all much ado about nothing."

"Why didn't you intervene to keep him out of jail before he learned some really good methods of molestation?"

"I am not law enforcement, nor a judge or jury."

"Could someone else have molested the girl and persuaded Judd to take the fall?"

Hugle stopped and glared. "Miss Dru, I am not an investigator. You are an investigator, or I should say, you hold yourself out to be an investigator. Now go investigate, and leave me alone."

"You can evade me, Conrad. But you're not above being questioned by the police."

"I cannot reveal confidences, Miss Dru. To anyone."

"I didn't realize you were under the seal of the confessional."

When he hurried off this time, I saw no need to go after him.

How do bureaucrats like Hugle keep their jobs? It's always been a marvel. I'm like every other Jane who thinks if that were me, I'd be canned in a nanosecond. And then, like every other Jane, I tell myself: he keeps secret files on his superiors, secret photos of them in bed with lambs and Labs.

Which made me wonder. With Mrs. Hugle long gone, who did Conrad Hugle keep in his bed?

Arriving back at the scene, I looked for Lake, who had finished his press briefing. I hoped he'd satisfied the rapacious crowd for a while.

Suddenly he was beside me. "Shall we go to Bassett's store where we can grab some nourishment while we talk—if he's at the store? Or shall we go grill Dwight Judd?"

Mentioning food brought on a bout of the stomach growls. But I couldn't wait to meet the misunderstood molester.

At that moment, Lake's radio crackled. "Go ahead." He listened for a few seconds. "On my way. Out." He touched my arm. "The dogs may have found something in Oakland Cemetery. Want to come."

"As if you have to ask."

SEVEN

Oakland Cemetery. Burial place of Margaret Mitchell, author of *Gone With the Wind*. Not far from her monument is the grave of my father. I visit him once a year in October, the month in which he died. The desolation is profound in the fall, but Oakland in the spring is hauntingly beautiful, like an English garden that happens to have wondrous headstones and forceful sarcophagi. Oakland was founded right before The War—what we Southerners call the War Between the States, as if that war is the one and only war in the history of man that matters.

Parts of the cemetery are walled in stone and concrete, and parts are surrounded by tall iron fences. Lake drove through the iron gates like he was driving a hearse, past the seated, life-size statue of Jasper Newton Smith, Atlanta's first real estate tycoon.

As he drove deeper into the quiet place, he fell into reminiscence. "When I was a little boy my family had Sunday picnics here. I'd almost forgotten those idyllic days. That was before Daddy decided to kill himself."

Lake's daddy had been a cop, like Lake, and a suicide, like my daddy.

We crept through the original six-acre part of the old cemetery, alongside paths winding between magnificent oaks and magnolia, passing blossoming dogwoods wavering above the graves of Atlanta's founders. We reached the Confederate section. I'm not fond of the Confederate Obelisk. It memorializes the South's surrender to William T. Sherman and the end of The War, but then I'm old Atlanta. Some of my male ancestors died in the conflict.

Before I heard men's voices, I guessed where we were headed—to the Lion of the Confederacy, a marble monument to a lost cause. For poignancy—for its portrayal of a noble beast dying with grace on top of a Confederate flag—nothing I've seen comes close. Next to the sculpture, Buddy and Jed stood patiently beside their handlers. Alighting from the squad car, we walked toward them.

A bookish man emerged from behind the monument. He extended his fingers, which were soft in my hand, and introduced himself as the cemetery's sexton. When he crossed his arms, his mouth puckered like he'd eaten a vinegary pickle. He glanced back at people who gawked at us from between headstones. "Frankly," he said, "I can't see what the dogs are excited about. I can assure you we have searched throughout the site and don't believe the children could have gotten into the grounds. We are closed after dusk and don't open until past dawn. We were not open at the time of the fire."

Lake asked, "Can't people get in here after closing? A fence is only good if it is topped with razor wire or electrical elements."

"I can't argue there," the sexton said. "Of course we have marauders. But we have security, too."

"How good?"

"A guard at night."

"Just one? All these acres?"

"Eighty-eight," he said precisely. "We are part of the Parks Department, you know. Frankly, we could use more public money. Our foundation is always running short of funds. Frankly, too, we could use a more guardian approach to our monies, rather than the artistic."

We moved closer to the lion. Its symbolic sarcophagus guarded a field containing the remains of unknown Confederate and Union soldiers who died far away from home in the bloody Battle of Atlanta.

The sexton looked at the two SAR dogs. "Frankly, I don't see what they see."

"They aren't here to see," Buddy's handler said as if he'd already explained this to the sexton. "They are here to smell." With that, he scratched Buddy's head and said, "Show me." Buddy went to the corner of the statue, lowered his head and gave a yelp-whine.

The sexton wriggled his nose. "I suppose I understand he's telling you something."

At the spot where Buddy alerted, I saw a bare place in the grass that had a vague imprint in it. "Could it be a small shoe print?" I ventured. "Maybe a sneaker?"

Lake knelt. "Could be," he said.

Buddy nudged against Lake's arm.

"Good enough for me," Buddy's handler said. "One of the girls—or both—has been here at some time."

"I can explain that," the sexton said. "Those kids trespass repeatedly. We are open to the public. They bring their dogs, which is tolerated if they're harnessed. Frankly, from my point of view, children and dogs are destructive, children more so, since they climb the statues. Tsk. Dogs only lift their legs."

"Acidity can damage stone," the handler said.

The sexton folded his hands across the lower part of his body and looked back at the gawkers.

"Is this the only place Buddy and Jed alerted?" Lake asked.

"There were a few places of interest," the handler said, "but not as much as this one. Now, I can't say they were here this morning. It may have been anytime in the last twenty-four hours."

The sexton again chimed into the conversation. "Frankly, I believe yesterday is more likely than in the middle of last night."

"I'll get the crime scene people in here," Lake said as he studied the lines in the mud. He shook his head doubtfully. "Get a cast."

The sexton sighed, and I surveyed the cemetery. Cabbagetown was due east of where I stood. Memorial Drive was due south. Memorial Drive was a major road running through Atlanta and aptly named because the Battle of Atlanta had taken place on its roadbed. To the north, the cemetery bordered the railroad tracks. It was there that General Hood had his headquarters. He stood on the high ground to watch his Rebels fall to canister rockets that shattered their bones. And to the west, outside the cemetery gates, was Oakland Avenue.

"Where does Oakland Avenue end?" I asked the sexton.

"At the railroad tracks," he said.

"Fenced?"

"Indeed. Fortified and razor-wired. Didn't used to be, of course, but when they constructed the commuter rail system next to the train yard, they built concrete ramparts to divide the cemetery and the neighborhood from the yard. Good thing, too. Keeps the hoboes out. So unnerving to have them sleeping on the headstones."

That was all we learned at Oakland, so the dogs jumped into their squad cars, and we loaded into ours.

Passing through the iron gates, I said, "My dear, we have departed Oakland. How many times do you suppose the sexton has seen *Gone With the Wind*?"

"Frankly, my dear, I don't give a . . . flip."

EIGHT

Back in Cabbagetown, we parked behind the Barneses' ruin and went to Miller Street where Dwight Judd lived.

His house was a sorry replica of its neighbors. Unlike the houses on Cotton Street, these were shotgun houses shaped on the outside like Monopoly pieces. On this particular block revitalization had taken a pass. Perhaps Doonan hadn't convinced anyone to sell yet.

An old car was parked in front of Dwight's cottage with two tires hiked on the cracked, weed-ridden sidewalk. There was no front yard. A single step up from the sidewalk led into the screened porch. The screens were rusty. Lake knocked on the porch door. Inside the house, a dingy curtain moved. A wooden door opened, and a small round-shouldered man padded across the porch.

Judd was an old twenty-something. He was going bald on top, and the rest of his hair was wispy. He was trying to grow a ponytail. His face was marred by pox, and his features were pinched, especially when he drew on his cigarette. His eyes were red-brown like our clay soil. He had on soiled blue jeans and a dirty T-shirt with an Olympics emblem on it.

"Come in, I guess," he said, stepping back, sucking his cigarette. "You're police?"

"We are," Lake said, holding out his identification. I held my ID for him to peruse. He studied them for a long while, and I wondered if he could read.

The house reeked of old plaster, old sweat, and marijuana and cigarette smoke. Newspapers and magazines lined the walls three feet high. Lake sat on a cane-bottom chair, and I squeezed into an armchair beside a fat cat. The cat protested and jumped down. It curled protectively in front of a bowl of SpaghettiO.

Judd slumped onto a frayed couch. His left ankle wore the monitoring device. It was plastic and had wires in it that connected electronically to a box on his telephone. It recorded exactly when Judd came or went, but it didn't record where he would go once he left the house. However, it would automatically call his parole officer if he wasn't home when he was supposed to be, or left outside his time strictures.

Lake said, "Mind if I write down what we talk about?"

Judd scratched his nose. "Is this official-like?"

"The house over the way burned down, people died, and little girls are missing. We're looking for them. You're not under suspicion if it's what you're asking."

"I don't need no Miranda?"

"You know your rights, don't you?"

"Sure do. Memorized them."

"You know the Barnes family, don't you?"

"From the time I was little."

"What do you know about the Rose girls?"

"That's what this is about, isn't it?" He crushed the cigarette and reached for his pack.

"Yeah," Lake said. "They're missing."

"I didn't do nothin'."

"What did you do to the girl you're convicted of molesting?"

"Nothin'," he said, flicking the Bic and lighting up.

"Then why were you convicted?"

"They wanted me to be."

"Who's they?"

"Everybody. They told me I did it. Susie said I did. I don't talk about it no more. I'm almost done with my time."

Lake asked, "How many times have you been questioned by police since you've been out of prison?"

"A bunch."

"That's what happens when you go to jail for molestation. Every time some kid goes missing, you get a call."

"I ain't been out of my house. I wear this thing . . ." He held up his leg. "They've no call to come askin' all the time. I didn't harm those girls that live with the Barneses. I never would. Never. Maybe they burned up and ain't been found yet."

"Their bodies are not in the house. Do you have any idea where they could be, or who they could have gone with?"

"I'd of called my parole officer if I knowed."

"When was the last time you saw them?"

He scratched the hair on his chin. "Maybe yesterday. Yeah, it was after I got home, Mr. Bassett drives me. They walked by with their bikes."

"Was this after it rained?"

He thought a minute. "Did it rain yesterday?"

"In the afternoon."

He looked doubtful. "I forget sometimes."

"Were the girls with anyone?"

"Lanny Long."

"Where does he live?"

"Five houses up."

"Did you talk to the children?"

"Jessie asked me if I had their dog."

"Why did she think you had their dog?"

"Because Buster was lost."

"But you didn't have their dog, did you?"

"I wouldn't keep no dog of theirs."

"What do you suppose happened to the dog?"

"Stephen probably killed it. It was wettin' on his yard."

"You really think that?"

" 'Course."

"I guess it means you don't like Mr. Doonan."

"Don't mean that. He's mean. Don't like cats, either." He looked at his fat cat at the bowl of canned spaghetti and flicked an ash at it. "Heh, boy."

"Did he like the neighborhood children?"

"Some."

"Jessie and Dottie?"

"Yeah, them he liked. Wanda knew to keep them off his yard."

"Did the searchers check out your place to see if the girls took refuge on your property?" I asked.

I stumped him with the word refuge. Finally, he answered, "Someone came with a dog and looked in the shed out back. The cellar, too." He looked at Lake and pointed to his ankle monitor.

"You get my parole officer to give the word, I'll go out and look for Jessie and Dottie, too. Bet I find 'um."

"I can't do that," Lake said. "Did the girls say anything about being at the cemetery?"

"Not yesterday."

"But they did go there?"

"Sure. Lots. Wanda lets them go with Lanny 'cause he watches out good for them." He dragged on his cigarette. "Dottie don't talk, you know. She does her hands like."

"She signs," I said. "Can you sign?"

He snickered. "Nah. Jessie would say what Dottie said with her hands."

"Did they talk about a man named Santa?"

His muddy eyes fixed on my mouth. "You mean like at Christmas?" He stubbed out the cigarette.

"Anytime. After Christmas. Lately."

"Naw. Christmas come and gone."

Lake asked, "Do you have any knowledge about the fire at the Barnes house that could help us?"

"Why you askin' me? Ask Stephen."

"You sure seem down on Mr. Doonan," Lake said.

"He don't like nobody that don't go along with him."

"How did the Barneses not go along with him?" Lake asked.

Judd snickered and fished out another cigarette. The room was like a gas chamber. Judd lit the white stick, and said, "Ol' Stevie, he wanted their house."

"How do you know that?"

"I hear things people don't think I do."

"And see things?" I asked.

"Ol' Dwight, he sees stuff."

Lake asked, "What stuff?"

Dwight shrugged and clamped his mouth on his cigarette.

Lake looked ready to strangle him. "If you know or have any ideas about what happened to those girls, or what caused that fire, you better say so and soon."

I asked, "Have you seen cars you didn't recognize cruise the street?"

Judd sucked on his cigarette. I wanted to yank it from his tight fingers. He blew smoke while he said, "Maybe don't mean nothing, but a car went by slow on this street."

"When?" Lake asked.

"Real early this morning."

"What time?"

"After the storm got through. Six, maybe."

"What kind of car?"

"Don't know."

"What color?"

"Dark."

"My God man, that was about when the Barnes house went up in flames. Didn't you think there might be a connection? You've sat here and watched the whole goddamned neighborhood look for those girls and didn't think to say anything about a strange car!"

Judd looked as if Lake had slapped him. He whined, "It's not my fault. I thought it was the cops sneakin' by, seein' if I'm where I'm supposed to be."

"You're wearing a monitor, Mr. Judd. Cops don't sneak by to check up on you."

Judd flicked ash on the floor. "He rolled down the window to get a good look when he went by. Who else was he lookin' for, tell me?"

To cool things down between them, I asked softly, "What did the man look like?"

Judd looked at me like he'd forgotten I was in the room. It took him a while to answer. "I didn't see him good."

"So you didn't recognize him?"

"Nah."

"Was he black, white, what?"

"White, yeah."

"Old, young?"

"Older like."

"Clothing?"

"Don' know."

"Hat?"

"Yeah, ugly one."

"What'd the car do? Where'd it go?"

"It stopped up the street. A light went on, then went off. And the car drove away."

"Fast or slow?"

"Fast!"

"Toward Memorial?"

"Yeah."

"Do you know Conrad Hugle?"

"Yeah." He looked spitefully at Lake. "He watches out for me."

Conrad Hugle watching out for anybody was suspicious. "Any particular reason?" I asked.

"He's my friend. I got friends. I got friends you don't know nothin' 'bout."

Lake's eyes fixed on Judd's face. "Maybe you should tell us about those friends."

"No," Judd said, suddenly flinging his cigarette on the floor and stomping it. "You can't make me. You think I did something I didn't do 'cause kids get me in trouble."

Lake flipped the notebook shut. "You know anything about where those girls might be, you better say it now, son, because if I find you've held back, I'll be back to stuff those fucking cigarettes down your fucking throat, and arrest you for smoking fucking grass and violating your fucking parole."

"I want my lawyer."

Lake stood. "And you have the right to remain silent, you f—" He flung himself from the room before he finished his curse.

Judd stood up and put his hands in his back pockets as if he'd scored a victory.

I said, "The lieutenant is under considerable stress right now. He must find those children."

His lip curled, showing his crooked yellow teeth. "I hope he does, miss. They was real nice to me."

NINE

I joined Lake on the sidewalk. He muttered, "Goddamn my ass."

Lake hates to lose his cool more than anyone I know. For his daughter's sake, he'd been working on cutting down his use of the real hard-core Anglo-Saxonisms.

"Judd got under my skin, too," I said. "He's two pints short of a fifth, but he's more cunning than one might think."

"He honed the instinct in prison. Let's go see if Santa's in his shop."

"You go, I want to find Lanny Long."

"Good enough. Meet up with you later. And go easy on the witnesses, Dru. You can't ramrod these people."

I laughed at his self-deprecation and watched him walk away mumbling curses at himself.

The breeze met me head-on as I trotted up the street. The houses were so close together two people had to walk single file between them. In the old days, no need for a telephone—simply open a window. The fifth house down from Judd's was not much larger than his, but had recently been painted. The name LONG was stenciled on a black mailbox that hung beside the front door. The door was wide open. I called out and knocked on the frame. No one answered, and I assumed the Long family were searchers.

The neighborhood park, which was called the Green Space, was three blocks away. The noise level led me in its direction. The Green Space had been a playground for the boarded-up Grant School. I fell in step with a woman, introduced myself, and asked her where I might find Lanny Long. She said he was probably at the park with his mother and brothers and sisters. She said to follow her. Trespassing through neighborhood shrubbery, we lamented the death of the Barneses and speculated on where the girls could be.

"There's a predator in the neighborhood," the woman said. "Don't know if you know that."

"Mr. Judd?"

"Not him. Too dumb. But there's someone. Happened before, but the police didn't do nothing about finding him."

"Does anyone have a clue who it could be?"

"Oh, people talk all right, but I don't go along with the talk."

"Who do they talk about?"

"You ask around, you'll find out. I mind my own business."

We came to a hillside that looked down on the Green Space. Not much green in what could have been a lovely sunken garden, but was a softball field. An occasional weed patch showed up where a ball was unlikely to be hit. We started down the slope. Erosion had threaded riverlets into the soft mud. I slipped and slid halfway down the hill. "There's Mrs. Long," the woman pointed out.

Mrs. Long was one rumpled woman, and it wasn't just her wrinkled clothes. Short and stout, she had clumps of reddish hair and a face devoted to her cheeks. She couldn't be more than forty, but her mouth sucked in as if she were missing teeth. When I introduced myself, she smiled. Her teeth were as tiny as a baby's.

After we exchanged compassionate remarks about the fatal fire and the Rose girls' disappearance, I said, "I understand Lanny was a friend to the girls."

"Surely was," she said, bobbing her head. "He liked Jessie a lot. He's twelve. You know boys these days. Take to girls younger and younger."

"Where is Lanny now?"

Her eyes gave a quick scan of the park. "He's somewheres. Lanny's always somewheres. Can't keep that kid in my sight. 'Course I got four others to look after. Lanny's a help when he's around."

"I want to ask you a few things that might help us locate the girls." She looked willing, if unsure. "Did you know the Barnes dog went missing on Wednesday?"

"Lanny went to help find it. Probably got up on Memorial and got hit."

"Has anything unusual happened in the neighborhood in, say, the past few days?"

She shook her head. "Yesterday, I was out planting my impatiens. I didn't see nothin' unusual."

"Have you noticed people you've never seen before hanging out?"

"Tch. Stephen has a lot of riffraff workin' for him, too many on his payroll for the work they do. Neighborhood's crawlin' with them. They come and go, 'course they work other places, too. My sister lives in Grant Park. They're there like here, reno-vatin'."

"Any cars go by you haven't seen before?"

"Sometimes. Can't remember yesterday."

"We're interested in finding a dark car, an American make, Ford or Buick."

Her naturally sunny face turned shrewd. "I don't say nothin' to upset Lanny, but it don't take no genius to see somebody took those kids. Waste of time lookin' in the neighborhood. 'Course you got to, just in case. My lands, people are lookin' for kids a lot these days. Search parties and dogs sniffin' the ground. On the news, all the time."

"Mr. Doonan saw the Rose girls talking to someone in a dark car yesterday afternoon. Dottie called the man Santa."

"Dottie don't talk."

"She used sign language."

"Mr. Bassett don't have a dark car."

"Is anyone besides Mr. Bassett known as Santa?"

"I don't . . . think so, but somewhere's in the back of my head . . ." She shook her head and frowned. "I can't recall."

I urged her to give it a little more thought, but it was useless, and I gave her my card.

We walked toward the boarded-up school building. "Did the fire awaken you this morning?"

"I heard the sirens. Lanny came runnin' down the steps and out the door. That boy! I called after him and got myself dressed."

"Miss Goddard called the nine-one-one."

"She sees everything."

"She told me about Dwight Judd."

"She would."

"Do you believe he was wrongly convicted?"

She shook her head. "He meant no harm, but he had no upbringin'. Didn't know what was right and wrong."

"Do you believe he molested Susie Ryan?"

"If Susie got molested, it weren't Dwight. Somebody put the boy up to sayin' he did."

"Who?"

"I shouldn't say it, but I'm goin' to. Conrad Hugle."

"Dr. Hugle?"

"Conrad's been takin' care of Dwight. That ain't like Conrad. And that's all I got to say about that."

"But if people here were sure Mr. Judd didn't do it, it's unfair they let him go to prison."

"Dwight didn't mind going to jail."

"There are lots of folks who take to institutional life," I said.

She agreed with a nod. "He was alone like, once his grandaddy died. Everybody felt sorry for him, but nobody could do nothin' for him. Oh, we cooked and took him stuff to eat, but well, that's not really livin' now is it?"

"Tell me what happened the day the Ryan girl accused Dwight of molesting her."

"Happened in the vacant lot behind Wanda's. There's some overgrown weeds and privet. The kids call it the cave. Susie Ryan said he unzipped his pants and wanted her to touch him. She got scared and ran to Wanda's. What she told Wanda and her mama and the police are different stories. Trouble was, Dwight also told different stories to the police. His lawyer talked him into pleadin' guilty to get off light."

"Where's the Ryan family live?"

"Off Ruby Street."

"What's the number? I'll need to talk to Susie."

Mrs. Long looked at me as if I were kidding. "You'd have to go to the other world. I wonder Millicent Goddard didn't tell you. She was crossin' the street and got hit and killed on Windom, not long after Dwight went to jail." I, too, wondered why Miss Goddard left that out. But then, I hadn't asked. "No one was ever arrested for running her over."

"This neighborhood seems to have a lot of mysteries," I said, "like the other girls that disappeared."

"People pickin' on them unlucky kids—it just gets my goat."

Her laughable understatement seeped under my skin. "When was the last time Lanny took the Rose girls to the cemetery?"

"Wasn't yesterday, I know. They went to the store after school. Old Bassett's. Maybe Monday, or Tuesday, I can't keep up."

I caught quick movement from the hill. Lake was step-sliding down the muddy slope. A large man followed. For his bulk, he almost danced down the slope.

Mrs. Long said, "There's your Santa Claus."

"What do you think of him?"

"Gives the kids sweet treats, even if they don't have the money. He tells Lanny stories about trains. Gets the boy to havin' the wanderlust."

Lake introduced Cyrus Bassett. He stuck out a big paw and we shook. His hand was sweaty and his face was red, from rosacea and exertion. I was reminded of Miss Goddard and her concern for her heart.

He said, "Call me Cyrus. Too bad we meet like this." He was in his sixties, tall and broad-shouldered. His white hair was thin on top, and his white beard was closely cut to his face. He wore seersucker trousers and a short-sleeved cheap white shirt. His pants were kept up by suspenders—the kind with faux gold snaps.

People in the park shifted to where we stood to catch snatches of our conversation. Although I was certain Lake covered my first question, I nonetheless asked Cyrus, "When was the last time you saw the Rose girls?"

"Yesterday, like I told the lieutenant here. They came to the store with Lanny Long."

"Anybody else with them?"

"No, the three of them."

"They come to the store every day?"

"Nearly. All the kids, they make the rounds. I'm heartbroke about them girls. We got to find them."

Lake turned to me. "Cyrus says the neighborhood kids played in the cemetery frequently."

"The sexton isn't happy about it," Bassett said. "It's historical, and if he had his way, the public would be kept out all the time. But not their money. We in the community believe they poison stray dogs and cats that wander in."

"Kids, too?" I asked.

"They'd probably like to," Bassett said with a smile. "But can't keep kids out of a cemetery. The Confederate Lion was Jessie's favorite. Her daddy that's in prison filled her little head with a bunch of nonsense about their kin. She believed that kinfolk of hers is buried under the Lion—them being a hero of The War. One day I saw the kids all playing with sticks and poles, pretending they were the Rebels and the Yankees. Until the sexton ran them off."

I pictured children reenacting the Uncivil War on the grass by the Lion. Which was probably how an indistinct child's footprint came to be there.

Lake asked Bassett, "Did the girls wander in the neighborhood by themselves?"

"No. Wanda was protective. They had to be with Lanny or in other groups."

"Was it because of the Yates and Patterson girls who disappeared?"

"Could be. Nobody talks about those girls, but it's got to be on your mind. In today's world, there's lots of kooks snatching kids right off the streets in broad daylight."

Lake's body appeared tight as a bowstring. "Was anyone suspected in those disappearances?"

Bassett cleared his throat. "No one arrested I know of."

"But suspected?"

"Nobody particular by me."

I asked, "Is anyone else known as Santa?"

"Like I told the lieutenant here, I'm the kids' Santa at Christmas. I let my beard grow out come September."

"Dottie saw somebody yesterday whom she signed as Santa." I was beginning to sound like a broken record.

Bassett said, "She saw me yesterday, but I wasn't Santa yesterday."

"What does she sign for you?"

He drew his hand down from his chin as Doonan had.

I said, "Tell us about Dwight Judd's problem with the Ryan girl."

"The truth about the mess hasn't been told," he said. "I know Wanda got in the middle of it. Don't know she did either one of them a favor. I always wondered if Wanda didn't see more of what went on than she let out. All she had to do is look out her kitchen window."

"Whose side was Wanda on? Dwight's or Susie's?"

"I never knew."

"What's your gut feeling about it?"

"I got none. You need to talk to Millicent Goddard. She and Wanda were close. If Wanda talked to anybody it would be Millicent. She had a way of getting you to say things you have no intention of saying."

I smiled, having thought the same thing. I turned to Lake. "Back to the beginning."

Bassett said, "I've got to fetch Dwight. I need him at the store. Bad things bring people out of their houses, and they come to the store for a Coke and a hot dog. You stop by, Miss Dru. The treat's on me."

Hot dogs. I scrutinized Lake's mouth. He grinned as his fingers traced the corners. He'd erased the tinge of yellow. The man was a glutton for cheap hot dogs lathered with mustard. Then, as if he were a magician, his hand flashed, and two Hershey's chocolate bars with peanuts appeared. My weakness.

He laughed. "Energy."

He'd made a delicious sensation flow through my body. So who needs chocolate?

Bassett said, "The lieutenant said you two used to be partners before you went private and specialized in looking for kids. Ask me, you're still partners."

As we turned to leave, Lake said to Bassett, "Leave Judd where he is. I need to talk to him some more. Maybe I'll bring him to the store later."

The muscles in Bassett's face stiffened, but he turned away as if to keep himself from blurting something he shouldn't.

TEN

We reviewed what we knew as we tracked back to the vacant lot. "This was a staged abduction," I said. "He killed and hid the dog."

Lake speculated about the car that Judd and Miss Goddard saw. "Likely, it was driven by the kidnapper. It was sighted at two-thirty by Miss Goddard and about six by Judd. The storm begins at two-thirty when Miss Goddard spotted the car. It turns into the alley by the Barnes house. He parked in the vacant lot. He kills the Barneses, snatches the girls, and plants the devices inside the house to ignite by remote control."

I picked up the thread. "But he didn't start the fire right after the abduction because it began pouring rain. It's iffy that a fire will keep burning in a blinding storm."

"Exactly," Lake agreed, jangling change in his pocket. "So after the storm blows over, he drives back to start the fire. He gets to the top of the alley, down the street from Judd, and stops. For some reason, he lit a light before pressing a button."

I said, "Maybe the light was a laptop computer or a cell phone LED."

"Smart girl."

"Learned from the master."

"Anyway, the house goes up, and he takes off to Memorial Drive."

"The storm put a kink in the plan, but he got away with it."

"The chips aren't all in, my love," Lake said.

"Mrs. Long says people are picking on unlucky children."

"Those were her words?"

"Gets her goat."

"But were the Rose girls unlucky? They had the good luck to find a good foster family. They were adapting, according to Portia."

"Maybe the predator didn't know that."

"Then he'd have to be from outside the neighborhood."

"Or new to the neighborhood."

"He has too much knowledge."

"We keep saying *he*, Lake. Mrs. Long said *people* . . ."

"I like neighborly intuition, but what, besides that—as in facts—would make us think more than one person is involved?"

"I suppose one person could snatch two little girls, but . . ."

"Easily, if it was someone they knew."

"Santa." My heart threatened to rip at the seams.

"Let's visit this so-called cave," Lake said, grabbing my waist and giving me a side hug.

The vacant lot had become our bivouac. The quarter-acre parcel hinted it had once been part of a large Southern pine forest with vigorous understory trees. Lake led me through the tangle of bushes into the privet cave. The rubbish was almost ankle deep and soaking wet. The leaves above dripped dark, smoky water. It was a sinister place—a place where happenings were hidden, secret. I thought of Dwight Judd and the dead Susie Ryan. Hugle's image popped into my head. I looked up at the clouds hovering gray above the wisteria-tangled trees. A mental picture of the blond girls floated through my head, of their being thrust into a dark car. A dark seed took root in my spirit, as my world suddenly ebbed. I looked at Lake, who was searching the treetops, maybe listening to his own interior mono-logue. "I hate this . . . this feeling of feeling small," I said. "Like whoever took them . . . did it to show me . . . spite me."

Lake put one hand on my shoulder and, with the other, brushed back strands of my hair. "I had similar thoughts earlier," he said. "About you and this predator, I mean. It happens, as you know. You've become famous in the child-find arena."

"But I wasn't known when the other two were kidnapped from here. And how would he know I'd get this case? I could be in San Francisco if—"

"Because he knows the facts of that case, too."

"Hugle."

"The predator's plan was grandiose from the start—the snatch, the fire to cover his murders, which any simpleton knows, if he watches *CSI*, won't fool Forensics."

"I despise Hugle, but I can't believe he's capable of—"

"Never underestimate what people are capable of." He slipped a hand to the small of my back and, with the other, pressed my face to his chest. I circled my arms around his muscular body as my heart beat fitfully between my breasts. He must have felt the thumping, because he drew back and lifted my chin. "We'll get them back, Dru. You and me."

"Wanda Barnes . . . she knew . . . and Miss Goddard knows, too."

"I think so."

"She's Wanda's friend, a confidante. But why wouldn't these women speak up if they knew who was responsible for snatching kids? It's unthinkable."

"They may not have known. They may have suspected." He smiled confidently. "We'll find him—with or without Miss Goddard's help."

I kissed his chin before our hands slid away from each other. Lake, my Lake. He helps me focus when my inner moorings threaten to break loose.

We left the flora cave and walked to the burned-out house. Facing the cave, Lake said, "Wanda Barnes couldn't see what went on in the cave from her kitchen window. The brush is knocked back now, with all the tramping through it, but even so, she couldn't see what went on—unless she was very near."

Agreeing, I said, "I'm off to grill the spinster again."

"Whistle 'Here Comes Santa Claus.'"

I made my mouth into a whistle circle and sucked in air. I can sing, I can dance, but I can't whistle. While I was making these silly noises, Lake looked beyond my shoulder. I whirled to see Captain Turquin coming toward us. I felt foolish. Lake winked.

"We're about done here," Turquin said. "We'll pull out most of the equipment, but leave a truck in case a hot spot flares up."

"Thanks, C.T.," Lake said. "What's the inspector saying?"

Turquin contemplated the burned house. "It was set with gasoline and other explosives. It burned unevenly. Hotter spots than others. Three points of origin."

I asked, "Could the gasoline have been ignited from a remote control device?"

"You'll have to ask the inspector, but I believe it's possible."

"Thanks," I said and walked away, across the street to Miss Goddard's.

The beveled glass door to Miss Goddard's cottage was slightly ajar, and the screen door was unlatched. I pressed the button and heard the bell ring the familiar tune. I waited, and then rang again, listening for footsteps. None. I pressed the button again. And again. She couldn't be taking a nap. Too much going on for a busybody like her. I drew the screen toward me, pushed the glass door back, and tiptoed into the parlor.

Her shawl lay on the floor. A sliver of ice worked its way down my backbone even before I saw her. In her chair. Dead. As I stepped closer to her, I pressed my lips to keep from whimpering. Her mouth sagged, and the tip of her tongue protruded. Her eyes were half closed; their faded blue irises peeking through lashes. Her left hand, which lay on her lap, curled ceilingward. A pillow kept her head from falling sideways. I didn't know whether to weep or curse her. I scanned the room for an indication of what happened. Nothing to indicate an intruder. The air smelled smoky, but it smelled smoky throughout the neighborhood.

I got my legs moving and ran through the door. Across the street, Captain Turquin was stepping into an SUV. "Captain," I called casually so as not to alert reporters eager for more bad news. Turquin's face froze into a frown.

He crossed the street. "Something the matter?"

I put my hand over my mouth. "It's Miss Goddard. She's dead. Careful of the media."

He walked up the cottage steps as if he were going to tea with her. I looked up the street where Lake talked to his squad, and stared, willing him to glance in my direction. He broke away, and I noticed Doonan standing on his porch watching me. He skipped down his steps and fell in step with Lake. I hoped Lake would tell him to get lost, but he didn't. They came up together. Lake asked, "What's up?"

"She's dead."

He glanced at the reporters and walked up her steps.

I turned to Doonan. His mouth was parted and his face white. He looked plain ol' scared. "You see anyone go in and out of her house?"

"I . . . ?" He arched his shoulders. "Her heart was bad. She took pills."

"I didn't ask that. I asked—"

"She said just the other day—"

"I know she had a heart problem, and she may have had a heart attack, but maybe not." I looked at the Barnes house. "Please answer my question. Did you see . . . ?"

He frowned as if he didn't know whether to lie or tell the truth. It's the kind of look that tells you he's going to be deceptive in some way. "A while ago—I don't know when exactly, because I'm not in the habit of looking at my watch—I saw Conrad Hugle go up the steps. He stayed on the porch for a while and then he let himself in. I noticed because Miss Goddard doesn't like him. It seemed odd, but he came out a few minutes later."

"Did you see Miss Goddard after he came out?"

He shook his head as if to give himself some think-time. "I don't believe I did. No."

"Did you see anyone else enter the house?"

"I can't believe you think somebody killed her. That would be foolhardy, wouldn't it, with all these people—the firemen across the street, the media, and all?"

"Let's go to the back." His feet appeared stubbornly rooted, legs unable to move. "I want you with me as a witness."

Resigned, he said, "Okay."

He followed several steps behind me, over a narrow strip of grass separating the neighbor's house. The neighbor, we'd learned, was on vacation. Miss Goddard's tiny garden was a mass of blooming azaleas. Like Doonan, she'd taken great pride in her flowers and shrubs. Despite a stab of sorrow, I couldn't help saying, "If one has to die, azalea time is as good a time as any."

Doonan's eyelids fluttered.

A little flagstone patio led to four concrete steps. They were painted green to match the shutters. I raised a hand to the knob when someone inside turned the locks. The door had three locks—an ordinary one, a deadbolt, and a chain. Captain Turquin opened the door. He still had on gloves, and I thought about fingerprints. Anyone who could sneak in and kill Miss Goddard was savvy enough to not leave any.

Doonan stayed outside, and I pushed the door closed with the back of my hand. The cottage was eerily quiet. Lake came into the hall. He wore latex gloves, and his lips were pinched in deep thought. He shook his head. "The medical examiner is on the way."

"What do you think?" I asked.

"Could be a heart attack. But her eyes had some petechial hemorrhaging."

"Sure looked like she'd been smothered," Turquin said. "Don't quote me. I'm no ME."

"There's a bruise on her jaw," Lake said. "It looks like a one-handed smother technique. One hand uses the thumb and fore-finger to cut the air to the nose, with the jaws gripped between the heel and fingertips."

"Someone strong," I said.

"Or determined. She could have been napping, and someone sneaked up on her, catching her by surprise if she woke."

"The back door was locked," I said. "Doonan said the only person he saw come inside this house was Hugle."

I followed Lake and Turquin while they checked the other rooms. There was no other entrance. All but the front two win-dows, and one in the kitchen, had been painted shut.

I asked Captain Turquin, "Did you see anyone enter this house?"

"Didn't notice anyone. I wasn't paying attention to this house in particular."

My cell played Mozart. I walked out to the front porch and looked at the cell's LCD.

Portia.

"First let me tell you what's happened," I said.

"You don't sound right."

"Miss Goddard is dead."

"What! Her heart. God, I should have—"

"Lake thinks she was smothered. The ME's on the way."

"Christ!"

"I've talked to neighbors. There were things she could have

told us and didn't. They had to do with Judd, and Wanda's role in his problem."

"Whatever her role, Judd was convicted. He was sent to Middle Georgia and served two years and two months. Here's a kicker: he hung with two men. One was a doper dealer named Miguel Lopez. The other was Timothy Rose. Name ring a bell?"

"Holy moly. Jessie's and Dottie's daddy."

"During the foster proceedings, I had conversations with Timothy Rose. I told him that it was in his daughters' best interests if he'd relinquish his parental rights to the Barneses. He wouldn't, and maybe I don't blame him. His lawyers are trying to get his conviction overturned, saying that the deaths were accidental, even if done in commission of a crime. You never know how appeals can turn out."

"But maybe he believed that you would terminate his parental rights?"

"He may have."

"So what are we to glean from this?"

"It could be that Judd and Rose conspired to kill the Barneses and take the girls."

"Where to?" I asked.

"Rose has a brother. Still lives in the mountains. Name's Thomas Rose. My staff's got calls in to the authorities in that county."

I didn't buy a Judd conspiracy. "I have a problem with Dwight Judd being mixed up in this. You didn't see him. It would be a monumental mental task for a simple mind. And he wears a monitor. His parole officer told Lake that he's been where he should be at the relevant times."

"Okay, so he wasn't out in the middle of the night, but he can arrange the deed."

"Where's Miguel Lopez?" I asked.

"He's out of prison."

"I'll revisit Mr. Judd."

"Get there before somebody kills him," Portia said. "Now let me tell you about the ten-year-old girl that disappeared from the Bolton foster home eight years ago."

"I'm listening."

"It was before dark in November. Bonnie Yates was visiting a friend at the mill apartments." Hugle's face popped into my head. Portia said, "Yep, the mill apartments. She left there to go home, which is a couple of blocks away, and vanished. I remember the case now. CPS and Hugle came in for a rough time, and so did the foster people. They had reported problems with her sneaking out. A four-year-old child told his mother that he saw the girl get into a car with Santa."

My chest puffed like a cobra's hood, and I felt vindicated for fixating on Santa.

"You heard right," Portia said, happy to be imparting unexpected news. "Now it was November, so people glommed on to Cyrus Bassett. But Bassett was in church that night. It was a Wednesday, and he takes up the collection for Wednesday services."

"Funny," I said, "we talked to Bassett. The disappearances were mentioned. He didn't tell us he was suspected in the Yates case."

"Don't blame him for not bringing it up. His alibi is solid. The girl was due home at five-thirty, and Mr. Bassett was at the church by then. It let out at seven, and he was home five minutes later."

"Two kids called that devil Santa," I said. "No coincidences there. What's the name of the child who saw Bonnie Yates get into a car with Santa? He'd be about twelve now."

"He was a juvenile. No name in the police report, or follow-ups. It was pretty much discounted after Bassett was exonerated."

"Anything on the Patterson girl yet?"

"I've just gotten the file. Talk later." Click.

Portia never says goodbye.

ELEVEN

I heard Hugle's voice. "Miss Dru."

He walked up, shepherding a slender young woman by the elbow. She had wild brown hair, almost as windblown as mine. I couldn't tell the color of her eyes from the grief in them, and her long nose looked like it had been stung by a bee. Hugle introduced us. Her name was Lorette Weymouth, and she was a therapist at the Marietta Speech School.

"I can't believe . . ." she said, dabbing her nose with a handkerchief, "that it was Dorthea, and her sister."

"Let's sit on these steps," I said, feeling sure that Miss Goddard wouldn't mind.

Hugle hung back like a wobbly marionette. I asked Lorette, "How long was Dottie a student of yours?"

"She enrolled last summer," she answered, her breathing shallow and quick. "She came . . . in the middle of the session, but . . . I worked with her until school started. She . . . also went to public school."

"How good did she sign?"

She laid her hand on her chest and took a deep breath. "Sorry."

"You're fine," I said. "Take your time."

"Dorthea was coming along nicely. Actually . . . she communicated better in her own way by reading faces, and lips, and body language. We don't try to break those habits." She coughed. "But at some point a child must learn American Sign Language."

"Did you teach her ASL for Santa."

"Santa?"

"A neighbor saw her sign to her sister. He said it was ASL for Santa."

"That would be odd," she said.

"Why?"

"She didn't communicate to her sister in ASL."

"How did she communicate?"

"A mixture of lip-speaking and lip-reading. They'd also developed their own type of signing. But to answer your question, I didn't teach her to sign Santa's name because we don't do religious or quasi-religious words. We're very PC, if you understand what I'm saying. I taught Dottie other simple words like girl." Lorette made a quick L-shaped sign. "And sister." Lorette's thumb moved along the jawbone almost to the chin and her outstretched fingers flashed together. She said, "Dorthea would sign for sorry when she goofed." Her right hand rotated several times above her heart.

Something shifted in my side vision, and I looked behind me. Lake stood above us on Miss Goddard's porch. His jaw bulged with fury.

Lorette said, "It would be my guess Dorthea didn't use ASL. She would have her own word for Santa Claus."

"Thank you for your time," I said, rising and giving her my card.

"It's no use searching here, is it?" Lorette asked, standing.

I shook my head, and she spun away as if to keep me from witnessing tears bursting from her sockets.

I walked to where Hugle stood. "You talked to Miss Goddard a while ago, didn't you?"

He looked offended and didn't answer.

"What did she have to say?" I persisted.

"She had nothing important to impart."

"You talked about something."

"She said she was tired and was going to sleep. Now I've helped you. I think you owe me at least a thank-you for bringing Miss Weymouth to your attention."

"Where did you run across her?"

"She was bawling in the street."

"I'm surprised you didn't run the other way."

"We clearly don't understand each other, Miss Dru."

"I think we do. Why did you pay special attention to Dwight Judd? You visited him in prison a couple of times."

He half closed his eyes, making him look smug. "He's what you might call my pet project. Rehabilitation starts in one's own neighborhood."

"Who is being rehabilitated, Conrad, you or Dwight?"

"I think I've been helpful enough. I'm going home."

TWELVE

Maybe Stephen Doonan and Conrad Hugle and Dwight Judd and the missing kids all tied together to somehow ignite the inferno that killed the Barneses, but I couldn't figure where the threads began, and I was getting knotted up thinking about it.

Doonan and Hugle had the smarts to plan an abduction-murder plot better than the one being played out, but not Dwight Judd. I couldn't help but think Judd was in more danger than he was a danger. Mrs. Long's words about people picking on unlucky kids kept popping into my head. I punched out Webdog's cell number.

"Yo!" he said. "Just about to call with the info on Doonan."

"Speak."

"Doonan's troubles started when he began seducing and stalking his boss."

"What?"

"I got the skinny from three people at his firm—none liked Doonan as you might guess. He was aggressive. The boss's wife was about to come undone from all the hang-up phone calls. She thought they came from women. Finally, the boss got a chance to get rid of the problem. A design flaw in a hotel in Alabama caused the catwalk to collapse injuring five people. Doonan was the architect of record. So long, Stephen."

"His ex-co-workers called him aggressive?"

"Driven. Maniacal."

"Good work. Now you got more to do."

"Bring it on."

Web loved hacking up stuff. "Timothy Rose has a brother. Thomas Rose still lives in the mountains. It's possible the children might be taken there. Also, Cyrus Bassett. He owns Bassett's Grocery on Windom Street. And, last but not least, our old friend Conrad Hugle."

"I've already zeroed in on him," Web said. "I got official and unofficial sites of stuff showing he's a mediocre ass-kisser who gets rewarded with promotions. No stellar academic record, no public accolades or medals of appreciation. But no bad stuff either. Not so much as a speeding ticket. Wife died leaving him a lonely widower."

"Too good to be true. Keep on."

"Gotcha."

I punched END, and caught the thumps of microphones. Lake was to be grilled again. He was frustrated and showing sharp edges, but it was his job as lead investigator to keep the public informed. He said simply that Miss Goddard had a bad heart, and it could have caused her death. He didn't take questions and motioned for me to follow him after he stepped from the mikes.

We cut through Doonan's yard to Miller Street. On the sidewalk in front of Judd's house, a squad car pulled away. From the back seat, Judd's face stared out at us.

"Good," Lake said.

"What's up?" I asked. "Where's he going?"

"City East," he answered. "Parole violation."

City Hall East was APD's second home. It housed the special police units including the Major Crimes Section, and a detention center.

Lake put his hand at my waist and urged me back the way we'd come. "I don't feel sorry for the son-of-a-bitch, but I want him alive. He's got a story to tell, and I'm going to get it out of him, one way or another."

"Dwight is not a killer," I said. "Miss Goddard's death proves it."

"I'm going to have a talk with Hugle. He's like a chimera, pops up and then disappears."

"Miss Goddard knew who Santa was."

Lake looked into the overcast sky, his face veiled in fury, his body taut and brittle. His arm would crack like glass if I tapped it. He said, "Someone slips into a cottage and murders a woman right under our noses because he can, and then thinks we won't figure it out."

"I wonder what Millicent Goddard hoped to accomplish? Was it her intention to talk a pedophile into giving up the kids and turning himself in?"

Lake shook his head. "A pedophile doesn't burn down a house to snatch two kids."

"We need a reliable witness. Someone else must have seen who went into Miss Goddard's house. We know Hugle did, but was he the only one?" An earlier brainchild popped back into my head. "Lake, the cameras in the helicopters."

He grinned, momentarily passing his anger off, and snapped his fingers. "Why didn't I think of that?"

"You already sent for the tapes, didn't you?"

"You can't think of everything."

"Maybe I got cop instinct overload," I said, "but I'm wondering if we aren't being misled."

"By whom?"

"Maybe ourselves."

He said in a level voice, "Go on."

"Let's say a serial abductor is at work here."

"Take it as a given, but an abductor has a reason beyond the act of snatching—he rapes, or he rapes and murders, or murders for the thrill of killing scared little kids, or he snatches for ransom, or selling to the flesh trade."

"The other kids were never found," I said. "Rapists and murderers leave bodies. The hostage-for-ransom is out for obvious reasons, so that leaves . . . ?"

"Slavery." He said the word as if it were the dirtiest in the world. "If that's the case, I'd say this isn't the only neighborhood he targets."

"You're right. This state has a big foster care problem. Big cities across the country, too. A gold mine for predators."

"But if foster children are being snatched regularly in this city or state, Portia would know."

"Therefore," I said, "they aren't."

"Slavers don't act alone," Lake said. "They have rings. In Asia they call the leader the Snakehead. Different rings have different names. One ring might call its leader the Headhunter, another, something else."

"A smart ringleader doesn't snatch enough kids to raise a hue and cry."

"And so?"

"I don't know . . . I don't know . . ." I sighed and shook my head. Inspiration—I needed some in a hurry.

We reached our bivouac. The first thing I noticed was that Lake's car had been moved closer to the privet cave. Lake tipped his head toward the unmarked. "What the f—" He hurried to the car, looked inside, looked at me, and shrugged. "Seems okay." He reached in and snatched the keys from the ignition.

"Mister?"

We turned toward the small voice. It came from the alley street. It had to be Lanny Long, the boy I'd been searching for. He had fat cheeks like his mother.

Lake motioned to the boy, who walked forward. "Lieutenant Lake?" he asked, peering inside the car. His eyes gleamed at the computer and the shotgun.

Lake's angular features were at their mildest. "What is it, son?"

Lanny looked up. "You said nothing was too unimportant to tell."

"That I did," Lake said. "First, tell me your name?"

"Lanny, sir. Lanny Long."

"Lanny," Lake said, and then scratched his cheek in recollection. "I've heard your name. You were friends with Jessie and Dottie."

Lanny nodded and looked at his shoes.

Lake put a hand on Lanny's shoulder. "Keep the faith, boy. We'll find your friends."

When Lanny raised his face again, I saw hope in it. Hope and adoration.

"Where's your daddy?" Lake asked.

"He's dead."

"I'm sorry to hear it. How old are you?"

Lanny stretched his body. I thought I heard joints popping. "I'll be thirteen in June. I take care of things now Mama's a widow."

"I'm sure you do a good job. Now tell me what your unimportant bit of information is?"

Lanny took a deep breath. "Yesterday, after school, Jessie called me up. She and Dottie wanted to go to Mr. Bassett's Grocery. Mrs. Barnes says they're too young to go places by themselves."

"I see. What time did Jessie call?"

"'Bout four, sir."

"And so you walked to the store?"

"No, sir, we rode our bikes."

"Wasn't it raining?"

"It stopped, sir."

"Then what?"

"We got there and was picking out stuff, and then Mr. Barnes comes in."

"Mr. Barnes? Was he looking for Jessie and Dottie?"

"No, sir. He went right up to Mr. Bassett. He was mad."

"Mad? How could you tell?"

"Mr. Barnes was always smiling. But he wasn't smiling."

"Go on."

"Mr. Bassett said to come into the office. It's in the corner of the store. It has windows you can look inside. Mr. Barnes was chewing him out."

"I take it you couldn't hear what was said?"

"No, sir."

"Very good. What happened then?"

"Mr. Barnes came out and came up to us. We were in an aisle, all looking at what was going on. Then Mr. Barnes laughed-like, and said, 'A little misunderstanding is all.' He asked Jessie and Dottie if they wanted to ride home with him, and Jessie said they would ride their bikes home, and he said okay, but come along soon. Then he left."

Lanny stood with his hands hanging at his sides as if Lake was going to say, So? What's the big deal?

Lake said, "That's fine, just fine, Lanny. I'm proud you came forward."

"You think it's important, sir?"

"I can tell you think it's important. So you tell me why you think so."

"Mr. Barnes was mad, sir. And . . . and . . ."

"Mr. Barnes died," Lake finished. "Is that what's on your mind?"

"Yes, sir."

"Do you like Mr. Bassett?"

"Yes, sir. He knows trains really good. I like trains and the yard. But he gets mad sometimes."

"What about?"

"People come in, tramps and stuff, from different places. They steal."

"I'd be mad, too, if someone came in to steal from me. So after you bought your treats, you rode to Jessie and Dottie's house?"

"No, sir. We cut up my street."

"Did you pass Dwight Judd's house?"

"Yes, sir."

"Did you talk to him?"

"Jessie did. She asked about her dog. It disappeared."

"Did she think Dwight stole it?"

"I guess."

"Did you think Dwight had the dog?"

"No, sir. I don't think he took Buster. He's got cats."

"What happened next?"

"We cut through to the side of Mr. Doonan's house. He came out and said we were mashing his flowers. I went home."

Doonan hadn't said anything about a confrontation with the kids.

Lake asked, "Do you remember a girl named Bonnie—"

I heard a whoosh behind me. Turning my head, a blast slammed hot air into my face. Acrid fumes pierced my lungs. My eyes burned.

Lake grabbed Lanny and pulled at my arm.

I coughed and stumbled to the cave. "What . . . was . . . that!"

"Bomb," Lake said. His face was black. Lanny was black-faced, too.

The scream of sirens came at the same time I saw Doonan's house. "Lake, look! It's on fire!"

Suddenly, hoses gushed rockets of water. In no time the flames died to smoldering. The whole thing lasted a minute.

We stood beside Lake's car. The flaring embers had missed it, but the fire hoses hadn't. I studied the Barnes house. The standing remnants from the earlier fire had been leveled. I looked at Doonan's house. "Lucky Stephen. If firemen hadn't stayed behind, his place would be a black hole."

Captain Turquin hurried toward us. "Lieutenant! You folks need help? We got the paramedics."

Lake glanced at me. I shook my head. He asked Lanny, "What about you, son?"

Lanny's pupils were fixed with excitement. "I'm okay, sir."

"Thanks," I told the fire captain. "We're fine."

Lake took my arm. "I'm going with C.T. Please, Dru, take Lanny home. His mama's worried sick by now."

Reluctant me led reluctant Lanny up the alley. He kept looking back to where the action was.

So did I as I rubbed soot from my face.

THIRTEEN

Mrs. Long ran toward us. She grabbed and hugged her son. "Oh thank you, miss. My God, it sounded like a bomb went off."

I told her it was a secondary explosion at the Barnes house. I also told her Lanny was a brave young man. As she stroked his head, I asked her to keep him at home, that the police had asked him questions, but might want to talk to him again. Puffed with importance, Lanny pulled away from his mother and sped away. She laughed and said he was going to tell his friends about helping the police. I asked her again to keep a close eye on him. I was talking to the wind, because she wouldn't know discipline if it bit her on the butt. Before I left, with a face full of proud wonder for her young son, she wiped my face with her apron.

I took off up Miller Street and came to Judd's cottage. The screen door to the porch was unlatched. I used the back of my hand to open it so I wouldn't leave fingerprints. Movement came from inside, shadows through the thin dirty curtain. Someone was in the parlor. I pressed my back against the clapboard by the window frame. Had that someone seen or heard me? Moments passed, and I cautiously turned my head to peer through the window. A figure crouched in front of a stack of magazines. His backside faced me, his jeans so low on his butt the crack showed. He wasn't tall, but his strong shoulders pulled at his yellow muscle shirt. A knife handle protruded from his back pocket. He was busy with his hands, and he wasn't being quiet. All of a sudden, he stood and wheeled. He stared hard. A cold tingle arced across the base of my brain, but I registered his characteristics precisely. Hispanic. Hair curling on forehead. Two black dots for eyes, scowled together by lines in forehead. Pencil mustache, otherwise clean-shaven, pocked cheeks. Bugs Bunny chin.

He grabbed for his knife as he leapt out of sight. Spinning on my heels, I crashed through the screen door and rushed up the sidewalk. Searchers were still in the street and were startled by my mad dash. I spun to face the house, expecting him to come running out. He didn't.

The back door.

I sprinted through the small space separating Judd's house from his neighbor's. In the backyard, I caught sight of his yellow shirt as he disappeared behind a shed. If I had had my gun, I would have chased after him. I made a mental note to get it. I had a feeling I was going to need it again.

Cell phone in hand, I punched Lake's number. "I'm at Judd's. A Hispanic man was in the house. He went through the backyard and down to the creek. He was going toward Boulevard."

"We'll check it out," Lake said quickly. "Don't follow him."

I went back inside Judd's cottage.

The whole place stank of marijuana. In the parlor, I caught

my reflection in the mirror: two big eyes looking out of a smudgy face. I rubbed the streaks left by Mrs. Long and then looked at my hands. If I touched anything it would be as if I'd inked my fingers on a fingerprint pad. On the sofa lay a Baggie of pot. I doubted it was there when the cops came to take Judd in.

Tucking my hands into my pants pockets, I examined the stack of magazines that had interested the intruder. The cover of the top magazine was ripped. Photographs poked from its pages. I couldn't use my hands. I'd have to get an implement. In the tiny abysmal kitchen I thought of Hugle. Why didn't he teach his pet project to clean up after himself? With the insides of my first and second fingers, I picked up a dirty dinner knife by the handle. I pried the photos from the magazine pages until they landed on the floor, then knelt and separated them.

Atrocious kiddie porn, and interspersed were pictures of the Rose girls. Their photos had been snapped in the Green Space while they rode their bicycles down the incline. I'd say they were shot from a telephoto lens. An envelope was with the photographs. I spread it open with the knife. The letter was written in a cramped hand on lined yellow paper, and signed with a T. It read: *You loking out for my grils? Don't let thm Barnes keep thm. Don't let that fukin judge ruun thm, nether. Mak up some stuf. My lawer says I'm geting out soner then later. Frends til the en. T.*

I heard a noise behind me. A surge of adrenaline had me scrambling to my feet. It was Lake. "You snuck up on me."

"He got away. Sorry I frightened you, sugar."

"I about had a stroke."

He looked at the knife between my fingers. "That's a mean weapon you got there."

"It's an investigative tool."

"I see."

"What happened with the Hispanic?"

"Kids saw him running to a dark car. There was a second man apparently waiting for him."

"An accomplice. It's looking less and less like a lone pedophile."

A smile creased his face as he regarded me longer than usual. I felt my face warm as he moved closer and touched my chin, then rubbed at what was apparently a streak of black. "And you're looking more and more like a dirty girl."

I pushed back strands of unruly hair. "I feel like somebody threw smut at me." I touched the photos on the floor with the toe of my shoe. "Look at this."

Lake pulled a pack of latex gloves out of a pocket, ripped it open, and stretched on the gloves. He picked up the prints. "Crude," he said. "Off the Net."

"It was planted by the intruder. I saw him through the window, bending over the magazines. When we were here interviewing Judd, that stuff wasn't there."

"The Rose girls' photos are dated three days ago," he said. "The day the dog went missing. Bassett swears he picks Judd up for work and church and drops him off. And his parole officer says he's been at home when he's supposed to be."

"Maybe Bassett isn't telling the truth. Maybe he lets Judd cruise the neighborhood. Judd wouldn't admit it."

"Maybe," Lake said. "Maybe Bassett has a motive in letting him cruise."

"Can we burn that crap?" I asked, pointing the knife at the photos in his hand.

Lake looked as if he were thinking seriously about doing it. But he shook his head and threw the photos on the floor. "Let's lock up. We'll get a warrant later."

"Not so fast, Lone Ranger. Read the note. It's on the floor."

He picked it up, glanced and snorted. "Prison stationery. The guy couldn't spell cat if he was spotted the c and the a."

"Wait until Portia sees this note. She turn heaven and hell to get the girls away from anyone who penned that garbage. Fukin' judge, indeed."

"I'm sure Portia's used to being called a 'fukin judge,' " Lake said.

I couldn't help but giggle at the literal phrase. Way back in Portia's past, she'd married. It lasted two weeks, but produced a beautiful boy. Other than that . . . even her best friend didn't meddle in her carnal life.

I pointed to the Baggie on the sofa. "Somebody wants Judd to take the fall."

Lake nodded his head at the obvious plant. "Let's get downtown. Get a sketch of the man you saw."

"If it's Lopez, we can do better. He's got a mug somewhere, doesn't he?"

Once we were on the move down Boulevard Avenue, which was a straight shot to City Hall East of maybe ten minutes, I asked, "What caused the explosion?"

"Kerosene and oil and fertilizer apparently."

"Where?"

"Supposedly in the Barnes cellar."

"Isn't that stuff you make a bomb with?"

"Right you are."

"What's Barnes, a pillar of the church, doing with bomb stuff in the cellar?"

"Doonan said Barnes used fertilizer on his lawn, gas and oil for lawn mowers, the kerosene for lamps in winter. You should have seen Doonan. He's beside himself that his little dollhouse is black on one side."

"Bless his heart," I said. "But Lake, doesn't stuff have to be mixed to cause an explosion?"

"Basically, all you have to do is soak a bag of fertilizer in oil or gas and light it. C.T. said you don't have to have a spark. The heat it generates can explode it."

"What produces the heat?"

"Ammonium nitrate. In addition to giving your garden a green glow, it can also produce a lot of gas, because it's unstable. When it mixes with oil or gas, it heats up. When it touches off, the release of gas under pressure causes the explosion. The explosion and fire cause ammonium nitrate to break down into nitrogen and oxygen. The oxygen feeds the flames that burn more oil, thus making more oxygen that burns more oil. Oil is why your face is so dirty." He reached out. "Let's get the spot above your eyebrow."

I waved his hand away. "Why didn't it go up before now? The fire was nearly dead."

"That, my darling, is the question."

"Who was in a position to throw such a bomb?"

"Ever notice how close Doonan's house is to the Barneses'?"

"I'm not blind yet."

"Open a window and toss."

I can't see Doonan destroying his own house."

"Cross and double cross. Remember how we used to think up ways a perp can avoid being caught by being a victim of his own crime. It's a version of the poisoner poisoning himself."

"Yes, but you're talking about a thinking perp. I've never met a smart one yet."

"Doonan's no dummy."

"You think he's our guy?"

"Don't you?" he asked, throwing me a speculative glance.

"What's the point of the explosion?"

"Destroy evidence. Fingerprints on the back door."

"But he and other men tried to open the back door during the blaze."

He pooged out his lips. "Maybe he left his other earring in the kitchen."

"Diamonds don't burn and Doonan would know that."

He tilted his head at me. "You are being very exact today."

He was right; I'd lost my sense of his humor. "Did you see Hugle or Bassett?"

"Bassett was in the street," Lake said. "I didn't see Hugle. Before the explosion, I'd sent a detective to his apartment. He wasn't at home, or wasn't answering his doorbell."

"Taking deep cover," I said. "Did you talk to Bassett?"

"Yep. I asked about the argument he had with Barnes at the store yesterday."

"And?"

"He didn't appear surprised I would know of it. He said he'd made an oversight regarding the church collection money. He says he took up the collection on Wednesday night and put the checks aside in his safe at the store because they were rather large monthly donations. When he gave Barnes the collection money on Thursday, he forgot to include the checks. Simple mistake, he says."

"Lanny didn't say anything about Bassett going to a safe."

"No he didn't, did he? But it's Bassett's word about the argument. The other party is a dead man."

Several questions fought for domination as the squad car descended a long hill. Ahead was a stop light. It had gone from amber to red. But Lake wasn't slowing.

"Lake! Watch it!"

Lake jammed the brake pedal repeatedly, but the car rocketed on. He hit the button for the dashboard's blue light. "Shit!" he yelled as we sailed through the intersection. Cars swerved and brakes squealed. An old pickup banged into a parked car.

We raced on, siren yelping, vehicles scattering.

A block ahead, the light at the intersection turned green, but it didn't matter. Bumper-to-bumper cars carrying people to a ball game were stalled in the intersection. At our speed, sixty miles an hour, we were going to take out a dozen cars. I thought about how I didn't have much time to prepare for the Grim Reaper— not even a prayer of supplication.

"Hold tight, Dru."

Lake jerked the car toward the sidewalk, sideswiping two parked cars. The impact threw me forward, but we'd slowed. The right tires mounted the curb, and the car rammed a bus stop sign, impaling the radiator. Hissing poured from the front as the car ran up a telephone pole. Momentarily it hung on the guy wire. The wire snapped, plunging us to the concrete. The car bounced twice before whirling to a stop, thankfully on all fours. Before I counted myself still among the living, I noticed the stink of rubber.

I punched my air bag aside and looked at Lake. He looked like he'd been dunked in flour. I tried on a smile through rigid lips. Lake grabbed my hand. The feel of warm blood and solid muscle reassured me that we were alive. I fell back on the headrest and told the man with the scythe to come back another day.

Then the tumult reached my ears. Outside, faces with comic-book expressions mashed together against the shattered windows. The door ripped open; hands grabbed and pulled me out. I was in a crushing babble of exuberant thanking and hugging. I hoped the crowd wasn't going to pick me up and bounce me above their heads. I got a glimpse of the intersection and understood. Car doors stood open. The folks smothering us with ecstasy had been spared annihilation by a man with nimble reflexes and the luck of the Irish.

FOURTEEN

A police duty room is not usually a cheerful place, but when cops coddle you, you have to glow inside and out. I had a lump on my forehead the size of a robin's egg and was turning as blue. Cops I'd known when I was on the force—and some I hadn't—pampered me. One had gone for expensive designer coffee and the sweetest filled donuts this side of heaven. Except for candy bars, I hadn't eaten all day and the oozing cream slid down my throat in continuous waves. Cops know comfort food.

The door suddenly thrust open, and Lake banged through it. He held up the photo.

"That's him," I said. "That's the Hispanic in Judd's house."

"Miguel Lopez. It ties him to Dwight Judd and the neighborhood."

I didn't like it. I could see by Lake's face he didn't, either. The abductions and murders weren't the work of two ex-cons. Or if they were, the prisons were graduating geniuses.

Lake handed the photo off to be included with the Amber Alert.

"What happened to your car?" I asked, although the question was unnecessary.

"Some asshole cut the brake lines," he said, and reached for a donut. "The same asshole who moved it so its nose was shoved into the bushes."

I had an idea. "Lanny," I said.

"Lanny?"

"Not that he moved it, but he was there, and he maybe saw who did."

"Let's finish up here," Lake said, needing action so bad he was about to sizzle out of his skin.

"Webdog's on his way here," I said. "He's gone to my house to get my gun."

Lake looked at me. "You're serious."

"As a crutch. Somebody tried to kill us. Maybe just you. But I take it personally, either way."

"Hey, Dru," a cop called. "Your lackey's downstairs."

"His name is Webdog," I said, heading out the door. Lake had gone upstairs to see Dwight Judd in detention.

Webdog had parked in the strip mall across from City Hall East. I got in his car. His blond hair had been shorn so close to his scalp he looked bald, and there was a twinkle in his geeky eyes as he launched into his report on Timothy and Thomas Rose. While he talked, I strapped the Glock onto my right ankle.

"Mountain boys," he said. "Rednecks. They always had trouble with liquor and the law, and fighting, and doing drugs. After Timothy moved to Atlanta, the sheriff said Thomas righted himself and got steady work. The sheriff said he'd keep round-the-clock on Thomas. He's got the Rose girls' pictures plastered throughout the county."

"Find out any more on Conrad Hugle?"

"Zip." It apparently pained Web to admit that.

"What I'm looking for is how an abductor would learn who was in foster homes and where the homes were located, etc."

"When agencies share information, it goes over a network," my able assistant said. "It's called the Web."

"Golly gee, technology's got an up on me." He laughed. "Got anything on the grocery man Bassett?"

"He's sixty-nine," Web said. "Married to the same wife for forty years. No children. Grew up in Manton. Had a little grocery there, but it went bust when the Winn-Dixie came in. Has lived in Cabbagetown twenty-five years. Two DUIs. He has financial problems. The store doesn't cut it, and his savings are dwindling."

"Web, you didn't crack into his bank records, did you?"

"Not crack," Web corrected. "Hack. And no, a neighbor told me about his financial situation." He grinned. "I called a couple places. Said I was an investigator with Child Trace. They heard of you. They saw you in the neighborhood and on TV. I asked about Santa, too, and a lady said Bassett's wife didn't like him playing Santa for the kiddies. He was too fond of the little ones sitting on his lap."

"Uh-oh."

"Right. Oh, and Mrs. Bassett talks all the time about going back home to Manton."

"But there's the problem of money, right?"

"Right. He's had the store for sale on and off. No buyers at any price."

"Thanks, Web, and oh, would you arrange to get my car from Lake's place? Lake and I will probably split at some point. Bring it here, park it right where you are."

"My royal command. A friend's looking to make a few bucks."

"Pay 'im."

"I called your neighbor about your house plants."

"How's Mr. Brown?" Mr. Brown is a homeless cat who camps out in my yard and eats the fauna. His specialty is the titmice that hang out at the bird feeder.

"Neighbor said Mr. Brown was not around."

I held up my hand to high-five Webdog and got out of his car. He took off in the beat-up old thing that has a zillion horses under the hood. Web was a streak before I blinked twice.

Back in the cop shop, I checked the gun at security and rode the elevator to Lake's office.

"Judd's not talking," Lake said glumly. He threw a pen across the desk and watched it skitter to the floor. "He don't know nothin' about nothin'. He don't want to leave here. That's a quote."

"He denied knowing Timothy Rose?"

"He knew a Rosey in the joint, but didn't know his real name. Never got a letter from him. Never knew he was the dad of the Rose girls. Never heard of Miguel Lopez. Never smoked marijuana. Never did nothin' but go to work and come home and drink Coca-by-God-the-real-thing-Cola and eat SpaghettiOs. Now go away nasty policeman, and leave me in here by myself to eat the hot mystery meat and overcooked peas."

"Great."

"So," Lake said, "I went and talked to a couple guys in Vice—their Child Exploitation Detail."

"And?"

"When I laid out a theory, they listened."

"That's good."

"Very, since those animals are territorial. They don't come up with the crime, they don't believe in it. Anyway, you know about the kids that get smuggled into Atlanta from overseas." I nodded, thinking it was probably a matter of time before I got a case. "Vice busted a massage parlor in Midtown. The kids couldn't have been more than twelve. They had no IDs. They said they were there to givee a blowee, and make seventee."

The words hit like raw sewage. "Sad."

"So, if we're right, what we have with the Rose girls is the reverse. It's not new, and it's not rare. There's a lucrative market for white kids, mostly in South American countries. But also in Middle Eastern countries. They don't think about pedophilia the way we do."

"Yuck on them. So how do we start looking for these perps?"

Lake looked sideways at me, and I recognized that look. It was saying: let's start with the phone book at the As.

"Santa," I said. "We've got to find out who he is."

"I'm going back to Cabbagetown," Lake said. "I got three murders there, and the press hollering for updates. Because I have to be there, I've a special assignment for you."

Excitement surged in my blood. Lake never sends me on sissy missions, and, by his expression, I knew this wasn't going to be the first.

"Go to St. Mary's Church. You know where it is, don't you—good Catholic that you are?"

"St. Mary's hasn't seen me in a long, long time, but yes, I know it's on North Avenue."

"A man will sit behind you in the back, so give him a pew or two. Do not look back."

I laughed, "Oh Lake, we're not in a movie."

"Pretend like you are."

FIFTEEN

The downtown cathedral was quiet at nearly noon. I hadn't been in St. Mary's since I was a kid. My parish is Christ the King. Up front, a priest entered from the side door. He busied himself at the altar and ignored me, but I sensed his watchfulness.

After genuflecting, I sat in the second to last row, close to the center aisle, feeling like Ingrid Bergman in a forties intrigue.

I heard the rush of the door, and felt him—or her—genuflect and sit. The priest looked over his shoulder, but quickly turned back to his preparations.

"Moriah Dru?" the man rasped.

"That's me." The impulse to look behind me was hard to resist.

"What you want is information on dem kidnaps this morning, right?" His accent was hoodlum Spanish—"dem kidnaps."

"What do you know?"

"Know? I don't know nothin'. All I know is I heard about that fire and them kids missing from the TV this morning, and I put it together with some stuff I heard last week. I called my narc and told him if this ain't an ordinary snatch to do the dirty on a kid, then maybe I can help. Them girls is fosters, right?"

"They are fosters."

"Fosters are ripe for a snatch. Older ones are easy to talk into going someplace they can be picked up, but young ones, that takes a bit more doing."

"I realize that."

"This particular ring I heard of snatches white boys or girls. You can't do it too often, people get suspicious. But you get these kids, throwaways . . . and bam you can make some bucks if they're virgins."

My eyes went to the statue of the Virgin Mary in her station. "How much for a virgin?" I asked.

"Negotiable."

"Millions?"

"Depends on the goods."

The Rose girls were the goods all right. "Tell me about the organization."

"I mostly work with narcs, but people-peddling ain't much different. It's buying and selling."

"Where are the kids headed?"

"This part of the country—east of the Mississippi—likely for the trade in Mexico, South America and the islands. Probably Costa Rica, where most buyers are. No morality cops."

"How does it work?"

"The Bishops hire a Knight—"

"The Bishops?" I looked up at the priest and thought this church doesn't need any more scandal.

"Yeah, like in chess. The Bishop is the ringleader, the go-between of buyers and sellers for the Pawns—the ones being sold."

"Another brand of organized crime," I said. "I can't believe I haven't heard of this ring."

"They change names."

"So the Bishop hires a Knight. What then?" I knew about slaver rings, but I wanted a step-by-step about this particular one.

"The Knight is the seller. He's got the Pawns or knows where they are. He passes them on to the Rooks. The Rooks are the transportation boys. Some rings out West still call 'em Jockeys." I knew about the Asian ring. The snitch continued. "Rooks take the Pawns to a stash house. Same as in drugs. They also use the same routes in and out, as with drugs."

"Where are these stash houses?"

He snickered. "You could be living next door to a stash house. With this merchandise, though, it can get moved to different houses. Each move gets the Pawns closer to the shipping point. Once they get to the destination, the Rooks stash the Pawns and contact the Bishop. He makes sure everything went as planned and makes delivery to the King—the buyer. Checkmate."

"The Rose girls were taken from their home in Cabbagetown. Where would the stash house be?"

"Stashing people is dicier than drugs or guns. Those don't need food, water, or cry, or go to the toilet."

"So they need a house with amenities."

He snickered again; perhaps the word amenities amused him. He said, "Maybe the Rooks got some dump on Memorial—a cheap motel nobody asks questions."

"How long would they be kept there?"

"Depends."

"Why wouldn't they take them out of town immediately? Why wait and start a fire? Why murder the foster parents?"

"The last two questions I ain't got no answers to, but they used to fly 'em out right away. That was before the Feds got to scrutinizing the private planes going in and out of muni airports like Charlie Brown or PDK. And now since they got the highway child alerts, that route ain't safe either. The Rooks keep close to the scene until they see there's no screwups. With different layers of jobs, you get screwups. If there's a bad screwup, like somebody gets made . . . you won't like this much, but there's another layer to erase the mess. He's called The End Game."

"I think I get it. He kills the girls and leaves their bodies to be found not far from their home."

"He rapes 'em with a dildo first to make it look like your everyday ordinary rape and murder. And he don't leave his DNA."

"Who are these people?"

"The lowest. I got kids myself. I'd kill the mother . . . uh . . . them if I run across one."

"Are they Mafia?" I knew the mob didn't traffic in human flesh.

"Strictly slavers," he said. "They been operating longer than the Mafia—always been buyers and sellers of people."

"So who's the Knight in this operation?"

"If I knew I'd of told my narc. I heard a couple days ago something big was happening in Rooksville."

"Sounds like a community."

"In a way. East of the Mississippi, Rooks're mostly Latinos. Mostly Asians in the West. You don't have black Rooks. They used to be the ones got slave-traded."

Latinos. Lopez. Maybe Lopez was a Rook, but Judd a Knight? Impossible.

I said, "You say you heard something going down in Rooksville. What exactly?"

"A twofer operation, paying big."

"Could be our girls. From the stash places, how will they get the girls out?"

"Probly stolen autos on regular streets. They may pass off ten times. But definitely no innerstates. They'll go up in the air at some point. You got all these dinky airstrips in Georgia and Florida and the Gulf Coast—freelance pilots making runs down to Miami or Mobile. The Rooks know pilots that don't mind taking a couple of Pawns on a ride south. It's an easy fly to the Yucatan where every airstrip is a loading zone for whatever you want loaded."

I had a sinking feeling. "How about by sea?"

"Dicey. Lot of Coast Guard surveillance in South Florida. Better on the Gulf Coast, but I'd bet they're going out by air from some Podunk runway."

"How would they treat the kids?"

"Like the finest coke. No spoiling the merchandise. Not like when they bring the South Americans or Asians into this country when they get breakers on 'em."

I knew what breakers were. Gang rapers to break the spirits of the unwilling.

The snitch said, "But these two white kids, if they got stolen to be sold, they won't get that. You see, they're already bought by some rich boy who wants virgins."

"He's a sicko."

He grunted. "One of thousands. Supply meets demand."

When I looked at her, the Virgin Mary appeared to weep. "Where would you start if you were me?"

"I'm giving you my best guess, okay?"

"Yes," I said, hoping for something concrete.

"You got dogs, I see on TV. Old warehouse buildings are everywhere. Find an airstrip in Nowheresville."

The sinking feeling hit bottom. "Even with dogs, it's a needle in a haystack."

"Amen, sister. I wish you good hunting. I hear pedophiles in Costa Rica can rent a six-year-old Pawn for five thou a day. Once the King gets his jollies, the kid goes to the tourist trade. These kids are money machines."

I didn't think I could get much sicker. "How do the Bishops get word a buyer wants to buy and a seller wants to sell?"

"Like any businessman—cold calls to likelies, word of mouth, repeat business, the Web. There's even blogs."

"Got any names?"

He was fond of snickering. "You're getting help on this, right?"

"The APD."

"You'll need 'em. You're up against a well-oiled machine, not a one-man show."

"You volunteering to help?"

"I'm helping here now."

"Have you ever come across a Miguel Lopez?"

"Where'd you pick up on him?"

"Prison. He's out."

"He's a Latino street ape."

"Would he know the Rooks and the routes?"

"Maybe overheard something. Probly know some drug routes."

"Could he be in contact with the Bishop?"

"Eh, not likely. The Bishop's a businessman who wouldn't

dirty his eyeballs looking at shit, excuse, por favor, a punk like that. But, yeah, I'd go to Lopez. You know the old saying, you get more'n one person knowing or doing something and soon lots of people know about it."

"Like you."

"Yeah, like me."

"How do these chess pieces communicate?"

"How does everybody communicate? E-mail."

Another job for the Webdog.

SIXTEEN

I found a place to park by the Green Space. Odd, how quiet the park was. Although the girls weren't going to be found by the searchers, the collective neighborhood didn't know it. So where was everybody?

As I bustled across streets and through yards, I caught the scream of car horns. I ran toward the cacophony and came to Bassett's store. The single person inside was a woman at an old-fashioned metal cash register. "Are you Mrs. Bassett?" I said, a little out of breath.

"Yes," she said, scrutinizing me. "You're the child expert. I saw you on the television."

"What's with the honking?"

"Somebody got hit in the tunnel."

I left the store and hurried to the intersection. A Grady Memorial Hospital ambulance weaved through a line of cars, down the hill, toward the Krog Tunnel, the viaduct beneath the train yard. I looked up at the boxcars sitting on the tracks overhead.

Trains. Of course.

My legs tried to outrun my body as I raced down the hill toward the yellow tape surrounding official vehicles. Grumbling drivers—stuck with nowhere to turn—were out of their cars. I checked up and called to a young man, "What happened?"

"Kid hit on a bike."

Something greasy sank into my bone marrow: Lanny's gone. And I knew why. Son-of-a-bitch Knight (at least I had a handle for him) stayed a step ahead of us. I rushed toward the emergency vehicles and heard a woman call out, "Miss . . . miss!" It was Lanny's mom. "My boy!"

She slammed into my arms, and I held her while she sobbed. After a while, she raised her head. Her swollen face looked like a cold night's moon. I took her aside and brushed her hair from her eyes. "What happened, Mrs. Long?"

"He's been hit. My Lanny's been run over. They got him in the ambulance. They won't let me ride with him. Not enough room, they say."

"What was Lanny doing here?"

"He must of been going to the train yard."

When I looked toward the scene, I saw Lake. Regret shone in his dark eyes. "Excuse me just a minute, Mrs. Long," I said and extricated myself from her embrace. By the time I got to the yellow tape, the ambulance had pulled away. Mrs. Long was behind me and grabbed my arm. Lake came up and hugged her and told her how sorry he was, making her cry harder. He called to a uniform and told him to see that Mrs. Long got to the hospital.

He took my elbow and urged me under the crime tape. Pointing to the bicycle at the base of a rampart, he spoke in a voice that rasped like radio static. *"Looks* like an accident."

Lanny hadn't reached the tunnel lanes, which were divided by concrete supports painted with colorful graffiti. He'd hit a rampart before the lanes dipped into the darkness. "Looks?"

"No rub-off paint on the bike where a car might have hit it. Only real damage is a bent handlebar. Appears Lanny laid it down suddenly and caught his head on the cement." He pointed to where I could see a patch of blood. "Paramedics don't know if he'll make it." He waved a hand at the pavement. "Fresh rubber on the roadway. A vehicle could have cut in front of the bike before entering the tunnel."

I stepped back and looked up at the boxcars sitting on tracks in the switching yard. The same tracks running by the cemetery half a mile away. "Where was he going?"

"Don't know. Yet."

"Bet I do."

I went back to the crowd of people milling on the sidewalk. As I raised my hand, they quieted. "Who was with Lanny?" I called out. A collective murmur rose, then a man pushed through with his hands on the shoulders of a boy about Lanny's age.

"My son and Lanny were together until Lanny decided to go into the tunnel," the man said.

Holding out my ID, I introduced myself. "I'd like to ask your son a few questions, if it's all right."

"I don't see why not," he said. He looked at the boy. "If he's up to it. Son?"

The boy's beagle eyes blinked up at me. I asked gently, "You are Lanny's friend?"

"Yes, ma'am. Me and Lanny, we're in the same grade."

"What happened here?"

His eyes shifted to his dad. "Lanny must of fell off his bike."

"Tell the lady, son," his dad said.

I asked, "Did you see it happen?"

He shook his head no. "I heard."

"Where were you when it happened?"

"Up the street. I can't go under the tunnel without Mama or Daddy." He looked up at his father, who nodded at that established fact.

"Did you see any vehicles go by?"

"Yes, ma'am."

I was thinking dark blue sedan. "What kind?"

"A van went by, fast."

"What color?"

"Gray."

"Did you hear a crash?"

"No, ma'am."

"Did Lanny say where he was going when he got to the other side of the tunnel?"

"The train yard. Lanny knew a way to get in."

"He say why he wanted to go to the train yard?"

"Find Jessie and Dottie."

A quarter mile of earth and concrete separated the community and the switching yard, so why did Lanny think the girls might have taken refuge there? If only the damned bomb hadn't blown up when it did. I asked the boy, "Did Lanny tell you why he thought Jessie and Dottie might be in the train yard?"

"No, ma'am."

"Did he tell you he talked to a policeman this morning?"

"Yes, ma'am."

"What did he say he told the policeman?"

"He told the lieutenant about the argument Mr. Barnes had with Mr. Bassett."

"Did he say anything about Lieutenant Lake's car?"

"The police car?" he asked, glancing at his dad for encouragement.

I said, "Yes, it had been parked in the vacant lot behind the Barnes house. Someone moved it. Lieutenant Lake wondered who moved it."

"A fireman moved it."

"Which fireman? The captain?"

His young brow wrinkled, and he shrugged. "Dr. Hugle told a fireman he should move it because it was in the way. Then Dr. Hugle got in it."

The boy's father made an impatient sound, which I took to be disapproval of Dr. Hugle. I asked the boy, "What did Dr. Hugle do in the car?"

"Lanny said he sat in it for a while, then he got out and went to Miss Goddard's house, and then he went out the door, sneaky-like, and then the police went in and . . . she was dead. Then the Barnes house blew up again."

The father asked me, "Where does Hugle come into this?"

"He lives in the community, and—"

"Yeah," the man interrupted. "He's head of the agency that oversees foster children. No wonder the agency's in trouble."

The boy said, "Dr. Hugle told Lanny to go home, but he didn't."

The father said, "This neighborhood's gone to hell ever since that jackass moved in. Him and Stephen Doonan should go take a flyin' leap to my way of thinking."

I asked the dad, "How long have you lived here?"

"Moved here fifteen years ago."

"Then you knew about the Patterson and Yates cases?"

"Yeah. People here are making assumptions they're connected with this Barnes thing. I, myself, don't think so. In the other cases, no one got murdered, no houses got torched. This was pure spite against the Barneses. They were good people, they got the kids they always wanted, and some jealous bastard took his anger out on them. That's my way of thinking."

"Miss Goddard didn't agree."

"Miss Goddard has, had, her own axes to grind." He looked at his son. "Let's go home, boy. Mama will be worried."

The boy lifted his hand in goodbye, backed away, turned, and shot away like a bullet.

Television cameras and microphones crowded Lake. He looked like he wanted to snarl at every question fired at him, but reporters have thick skins.

A woman reporter: "Is he alive?"

Lake: "As I've said, he was when he went into the ambulance."

"What caused the accident?"

Lake: "We're gathering facts."

"Who caused the accident?"

Lake: "It's early yet."

"Lieutenant! Here! What were his injuries like?"

Lake: "You've asked a question for a medical professional."

"Will he live?"

Lake: "That's a medical question, too."

"Is he unconscious?"

Lake: "Last I saw, yes."

"Who called nine-one-one?"

Lake: "Several callers."

"Did a car hit him?"

Lake: "Not clear yet."

"You haven't given us much!"

Lake: "I've given you what I know for a fact."

"Is there a connection to the house fire this morning?"

Lake spread his arms: "Ladies and gentlemen of Atlanta's esteemed press corps, and those who have come to our city to broadcast our tragedy to the nation and the world, please give us some time. We'll get the full story, and when we do, we'll give it to you."

A woman reporter: "Was he a witness?"

Lake: "To what?"

"Was he a friend of the Rose girls?"

Lake thought a moment: "They went to school together. That's all I can say at this point. We will, I assure you, have a press conference shortly to bring you up to date on the progress of our efforts. Thank you for all you do."

I walked away, and Lake fell in step, up the hill toward Bassett's store. I stopped and faced the way we'd come. "He's moving his Pawns to keep from getting cornered. The Knight is beginning to make desperation moves." When I saw the confusion lining Lake's face, I realized I hadn't told him what the snitch said.

When I finished my report, his eyes no longer focused on me, but into the middle distance as if thinking about the implications. "A slave ring with chess piece names. I used to play with Daddy when he got home early enough."

"Wait until Portia hears. She's some kind of master."

"She'll rip the Bishop's heart out."

"I'll rip out something he values more."

Lake winced.

I pointed at the overpass. "The train yard. Lanny was headed there."

Lake unhooked his radio. "I'll get the dogs back."

SEVENTEEN

The stout yardmaster led us past tankers, grain carriers, and reliable old boxcars covered in graffiti. "I heard on the news," he said. "I had those girls in mind when I came on and checked out the yard, but I can't see little girls comin' here in the middle of the night, gettin' up in boxcars."

Lake hit his fist on a car. "If they're in one of these, somebody put them there."

The yardmaster raised an upper lip as if he figured some idiot would do something like that. He said, "You can't get in the train yard through the neighborhoods."

I looked toward Cabbagetown. The only building I saw was the old mill, now condos, across the mounds of earth and high and wide concrete ramparts.

The yardmaster went on, "It was in the sixties they built the barrier to the neighborhood, then the mass transit come through, and they reinforced it and built all those fences. To get to the yard now, you got to come under the tunnel to Decatur Street, and through the parking lot, like you did."

My eyes swept Decatur Street where the fences separating it from the yard appeared new and strong, but toward the east, where the main track led out of the yard, the fences were in bad repair. Trees had fallen on them. Gully washers eroded holes under them. Access was not a problem for the older, more adventurous kids—kids whose mamas' had a cavalier attitude about their comings and goings.

"Can someone get in the yard by Oakland Cemetery?" I asked.

"A wire fence runs along the line to keep people off the tracks, and there's a gate at the end of Oakland Avenue. It's padlocked, but I guess anyone could cut the lock off or cut through the fencing."

"Anything odd occur during the night?" Lake asked, his eyes roaming the cranes and stackers.

"Storm throwed us off schedule. Had to reroute the mail from downtown."

While we waited for the dogs, the yardmaster told us his yard was primarily intermodal, which meant placing containers on flatcars and off-loading them. "Not much goes on after midnight here."

We trudged along a line of cars that needed repairs. I knocked on a black one. The iron side rang. "Soundproof?"

"Not those."

"Kids play in the boxcars?" I asked.

"Not supposed to, but can't keep boys from trains." His laugh was a hee-hee.

"Who writes the graffiti?"

"The 'boes," he said. "Although they ain't called hoboes no more. They're boxcar tourists." Hee-hee.

"When you catch them, do you toss them out?"

"Naw, we kinda ignore them, specially if we know them. Homeland Security isn't happy about it, but we ain't got time to police these yards, and they ain't got the manpower."

"I haven't thought of hoboes in a long time," I said, as two squad cars pulled into the yard's parking lot. "So yesteryear."

"Nope. Still bedeviling us. From old pros to fun-ride types." Hee-hee. "Camp out near the yard till the cars are coupled, watch for the empties or half loads on the short lines. Some of the young, quick ones jump the hotshots." Hee-hee. "They slow a little, but it's dangerous to hop one that's balling the jack. We had a death last month. Slipped, went under. Cut his legs off. Bled to death before we found him." Hee-hee.

The sound of dogs reached us. The yardmaster had agreed to halt all movement in the yard while the police dogs searched.

Buddy, the German shepherd, loped toward us, head in the air, weaving his way through the cars. The black Lab was on a lead, with his nose to the track. He disappeared between a line of flatbeds on a side track, then popped back into view by a diesel engine on another track.

The yardmaster said, "I'm a dog man, myself. Love to watch 'em, but can't stand here all day. You need anything else, I'll be in the tower." He walked away, hee-heeing.

Jed, the trailer Lab, wagged along, sniffing at tracks, and ties, at diesel engine wheels, at a torn bag with a wine bottle in it. Buddy, the air-scent, had a tougher time—first going against the wind, then with it. Once or twice, he dashed back the way he'd come.

His handler came up. "Buddy's telling us something. Don't know what yet. Jed's got the scent, it looks like."

I hoped so. I was out of guesses if this one didn't pan out.

The dogs worked for another fifteen minutes before Jed made a beeline for a red boxcar with a wheel missing. His tail wagged vigorously. He jumped up and pawed at the corner. Up the track, Buddy made a U-turn and zigzagged back toward us. He halted and barked, his tail flashing at the partially open sliding door. Jed's master reached to widen it, but Lake said, "Careful."

The officers pulled their dogs back. I reached to my ankle for my automatic, and lay back against the car. Lake drew his gun from its paddle holster. Facing the metal handle, he rammed the door and stood aside. The door creaked back. Lake gave it another ram and it slammed open. The car looked empty, but I sensed someone was in there.

"Police!" Lake yelled.

No answer.

"Police! Come out. Hands in the air."

"Comin'," a weak voice said.

A man with a cigarette dangling from his lips came into the light, blinking and wrinkling his nose. "What?" he said, shielding his eyes with a hand.

"You the only one in there?" Lake asked.

"Me and him," the man said. A boy appeared, maybe thirteen.

"What you doing in there, boy?" Lake asked.

"Visitin' with my pop."

"Hop on down, both of you."

It was a slow hop for the man, who looked seventy, but was probably forty. His eyes were bright blue, and bloodshot. You couldn't not think of the Fourth of July. Lake holstered his pistol, but I held mine pointing at the ground.

The man and boy were wary of the dogs. "They won't harm you," Lake said. "Don't touch them, and don't run."

"No runnin' in these legs, mister," the man said.

Lake told the handlers to continue the search of cars as he reached in a coat pocket and brought out a packet of gloves. He climbed onto the boxcar and disappeared inside. The man, the boy, and I shared several silent moments before Lake came into the opening carrying a small doll. It was new-looking. "This yours?" he asked.

The man cackled. The boy looked chagrined. "Naw, sir."

"Didn't think so." Lake jumped down and stuffed the doll in my backpack. I holstered my gun. "Let's talk," Lake said.

"Okay by me, but I don't know nothin' 'bout no doll," the man said. "I ain't no thief."

"So it was already in there when you climbed in?" Lake asked.

"Tell you the truth, I didn't notice it."

"What about you, boy?"

"It was there. I noticed."

"What time did you hop this car?" Lake asked the man.

"Right 'fore shift change, 'bout."

"What time's that?"

"Eight's shift change."

"Where did you ride in from?"

"Birmingham," he said. (The seven o'clock this morning, Engineer Number Two on the horn.) The man leaned his head toward his son. "Came to meet up with my boy."

"Did you see the fire across the way?" Lake asked.

"Smelled it."

"You, son," Lake said, "when did you get to the yard?"

" 'Fore sunup."

"You been in this car, waiting for your daddy?"

"No, I waited in the underpass, then I came up when the crew changed and the rain let up."

"You see anything?"

The boy looked at his daddy.

"You can tell 'em, son, we done nothin' wrong here."

The boy said, "I seen two men and two little kids get out of this here boxcar." He pointed across the track. "I was behind the coal car. They left the door open and when they were gone, I got in here myself and waited till I saw Daddy moseyin' along the tracks."

"Were the kids boys or girls?"

"Couldn't tell. They all had on ponchos. Like t' scared me. Looked like black ghosts sneakin' cross the track."

"How tall were the men?"

"Short-like."

"Did you see faces?"

"One little kid bent to the ground. They pulled it up quick-like and went on. When I saw the doll in there, I guess it belonged to the kid—so must of been a girl."

"Was she upset?" I asked. "The child that bent to the ground?"

"I couldn't tell ya."

"Did the kids go willingly or were they forced?"

"I kind of think one was jerked."

"They go toward town, or away from town?"

"Away." He looked down the main track toward the east.

"Did you hear their voices?"

"I didn't hear nothin'."

"Where do you live, young man?" Lake asked the boy. "You stay with your mama?"

"No, with my aunt in Grant Park."

"That's quite a hike to see your daddy here."

"Me'n Pop's close."

Lake pulled his wallet from his pocket, took out a card and some money. "Go to Bassett's Grocery. Get yourself a drink and a treat. If you remember anything else, call me, or have Mr. Bassett get in touch with me. Two little girls were kidnapped from their Cabbagetown home."

The man and the boy stared at each other. The man spat, "Sons-a-bitches."

Lake turned to the kid. "Son, you go to school, don't you?" The kid got interested in his shoes. Lake said, "I'm not a truant officer."

The kid bobbed his head and shoved his chin at his father. "One day I'm leavin' with him. But he won't let me till I get out of school."

"By then, you'll be edjucated," the man said. "Too durn smart to ride them rails."

Lake looked at the man who wanted a future for his son. He said, "You need help, you got my number."

EIGHTEEN

The dogs had cleared the switching yard and rambled down the main track. As we followed, they left the track and segued to a gash in the chain link fence. They turned to wait for us, their tails wagging for us to hurry. (Like I can read dogs' minds.) When we caught up, they angled through the opening and scrambled down the bank and jumped a drainage ditch. I landed funny when I tried it. Fortunately, Lake was there to catch my elbow. "Careful," he said, "I'd have to put you down if you break your ankles, and get me a new partner."

"Younger, too, I bet," I said, loping alongside him.

"Older, with stouter ankles."

I heard my anonymous caller's voice in my head. I doubt she had stout ankles.

The dogs led us with an easy, assured lope, heading east.

"The Rose girls gave off a powerful scent," I said. There was no doubt in my mind as we followed their invisible wake.

"Look at ol' Buddy with his nose in the air," Lake said. "Innocence stands out in this reeking decay."

Trash tumbled down Decatur Street, which was lined with boarded-up warehouses, a café, and a couple of ironworks yards. All excellent stash houses. We came to the rapid transit station. Up the block, a couple of homeless men camped in a recessed doorway. One stared at us. The other was curled in a fetal position, apparently asleep. I waved at the sitting man and pointed my finger, meaning, I'll be back to you. The way he waved back, I think he understood.

"I don't get it, Lake," I said. "Why would the Rooks expose themselves on a city street?"

"Necessity. But it's dark and lonely here in the middle of the night. Not even drug dealers or hookers hang out here. No buyers. The Rooks merely had to worry about a patrol cop spotting them. They were probably on the lookout to see one pass before they took off up the street."

Buddy and Jed turned up an avenue leading into Inman Park, a community much bigger than Cabbagetown. In its heyday, it was on the right side of the tracks. The dogs got livelier when we approached a large Queen Anne set back in its grounds. An ornamental iron fence surrounded the large oaks and dogwoods in the garden. We stood on the sidewalk across from the house because the dogs had paused, Jed's tail pointing skyward and Buddy's nose quivering. The handlers urged them up the street, but after meandering for a block or so, the dogs lost interest and turned back.

Jed's handler said, "The trail ends here. Probably they got into a vehicle."

A scraping noise caught my attention. I looked toward the Queen Anne to see a side door open. A man rushed down wooden steps, and Lake and I crossed the street. The man carried a red drink. Bloody Mary. It could have been plain tomato juice, but the celery and ice were a giveaway. That, and his gray eyes looked ready to weep blood. He had on shorts and a sweatshirt, both wrinkled, and his brown hair stood on end. He unlatched the gate with one hand.

His first words were, "I knew something wasn't right. You're cops, aren't you?"

We showed our IDs. He said his name was Tom Davis. "When I saw you and those dogs out here, I knew."

"Knew what?" Lake asked.

"My girlfriend turned on the television this morning. I was dead to the world. Finally, she got me awake. The fire in Cabbagetown's all over the news. I saw the pictures of the little girls." He shivered, the ice in his glass rattled. "We've been talking about what to do."

"We're listening," Lake said. I hoped he didn't get too huffy.

"Last night I went to a bachelor party for a buddy about to get married. Got home about five-thirty this morning. It's a couple blocks away, and I made it home, Lord knows how. Had a lot to drink as you might expect. I let out my dog to do his duty and sat on the steps. I saw some people cross Decatur Street and head up this way. Two men and two kids—one was a girl, I'm pretty sure. Her hood slid back."

"Describe the men," Lake said.

"I didn't see their faces, but I saw their hands. They were dark men."

"Tall, short?"

"Small, thin. Hispanics is my impression."

"What did the girl look like?"

"Only caught a glimpse when the hood slid back. Blond. A man grabbed it and pushed it up. When I saw the pictures on television, I saw the resemblance. Maybe my imagination."

"Go on."

He pointed a shaky arm to where the dogs stood. "They stopped right there. Not a minute later, a van pulled up. Everybody got in the back. My dog started barking, and the driver stared at me. Jesus, he looked mean as a snake. I called my dog. The driver kept looking at me as if he wanted to jump out and strangle me. Then he pulled away."

"Why didn't you call the police?" Lake asked.

His bleary eyes widened as much as they could. "This is Atlanta, man. Weird things happen all the time that turn out to be normal. I convinced myself it was probably my imagination. I mean I had a lot to drink."

Brushing open his coat, Lake wrapped his thumb and forefinger on his hip, a telltale sign of aggravation. "Besides being mean-looking, what else can you tell us about the driver's face?"

"Not much. His face was distorted. He was older, heavier than the men with the kids. Sorry I can't do better."

"How did the kids seem?"

He shrugged. "They didn't look kidnapped, like yelling and thrashing about."

"Describe the van."

"It was pretty new. Panel body, commercial type. Like a painter would use. It had a top rack for ladders, or whatever."

"Color?"

"Gray, but these vapor streetlights don't show true color."

"Did you get a tag number?"

"Gee, no."

"Any individual marks on the van?"

"Yeah, it had a yellow light on the top at the back."

At this point, I slipped away.

On Decatur Street again, I jogged back to the homeless men. One still slept, or was passed out. The other sat hunched, legs folded under him. Then I saw he had no legs, and his torso rested on a wheeled platform.

"Hello," I said.

He looked up kindly. He was much younger than at first glance. "Ma'am," he replied softly. In another life, he might have been a Southern gentleman sweeping a bow at a cotillion.

"I need your help. What's your name?"

"Billy," he said. "How can I help you? I saw you go by a while ago with the cops and the dogs."

"We're looking for children who disappeared after their house burned down during the night."

"I saw kids last night. Didn't belong to those men. Light kids, dark men."

"You were awake then?"

"Yes, ma'am. I pretended to be asleep. Didn't like their looks, and I got to be here to protect Moses." His head motioned to the man asleep. "He's not got long."

"I'm sorry to hear it."

"Yes, ma'am. He's a vet like me."

"Did you see the fire across the tracks this morning?"

"Smelled the smoke. Heard the fire engines go out."

"Before it started, were you awake?"

"Yes, ma'am."

"Do you watch traffic?"

"All there is to watch. All I got to do."

"Before dawn, did you see a gray van go by shortly after seeing the men and kids?"

"I did. It's not usually out that time of a night."

"You've seen it before?"

"Yes, ma'am."

"You know who it belongs to?"

"Mexicans. They've been fixing up houses hereabouts."

"Do you pay attention to tag numbers?"

"We used to play the tag game when my mama and daddy took us kids to Florida. I learned the knack."

I drew in a hopeful breath. "You know the van's number?"

"VAN 582."

"Bless you, Billy!"

"You a police lady?"

"Used to be. Now I'm a child finder."

"If I had my legs, I'd help you."

His words split my heart at the stitches. "Thanks," I said, handing him a business card I'd taken from my backpack. Plus, a twenty dollar bill.

"You don't have to do this," he said, offering the twenty back. "I got means."

"What war did you fight?"

"The first Gulf," he said.

"Give it to the veterans of that war."

"They'll thank you. I'll be on the lookout for the van and those creeps. I can get in touch with you. Down at the mission, they have a phone."

As I hurried back to join Lake and the dogs, an approaching

dark car caught my attention. It was a dark blue Buick without a front tag. The chrome strip on the passenger side was missing. The glass was darkly tinted. I couldn't make out the driver, but I felt his malignant eyes.

Suddenly, the car engine revved. With a burst of speed, he drove straight at me. My back slammed against the brick wall at the exact moment the car roared past, its two tires on the sidewalk. A foot closer, he would have gotten my knees and toes. The car caromed back onto the roadway and streaked away. No chance to see the driver. With blood hammering my veins, I bent for my gun, thinking to blow out a tire. No use. Half a block away, he screeched around the corner, but not before I saw he had no back tag.

I ran back to Billy. "You recognize the car?"

"No, ma'am. You must be getting on to him, trying to run you down like that."

"I hope so."

"Watch yourself. Hate to see a good girl get taken out."

I drew air deep into my lungs. "The police will take you and Moses to the mission."

Billy shook his head. "Moses won't go, so I can't."

"The bad guy saw me talking to you. You and Moses are in danger until we catch him."

Billy looked up, his eyes admitting the truth. He reached and put his arm gently on his buddy and shook him. "Get it together, partner. We got to go."

I called Lake on my cell.

"What's wrong with your voice?" he said.

"Absolutely nothing. I still have it."

"What?"

I briefed him on Billy's observations, recited the tag number of the gray van, and then told him a blue Buick tried to run me down.

"Goddamn fucking son-of-a-bitch."

"Your language is deteriorating."

"That's not all. I'll be there in a minute."

"Don't sprint ahead of the dogs," I said. "They don't like to be outrun, and they'll bite you in the butt." I felt giddy, like my whole day had been leading up to this moment, one where I felt like screaming with joy. We were going to get him. He was getting vengeful, which meant he'd get sloppy.

I reached down to help Billy rouse Moses and soon heard a squad car race up and brake. Two cops and I got Moses to his feet as the paddy wagon arrived. I heard the dogs coming closer. They were followed by Lake and the handlers.

Despite his dash, Lake looked pale. "Jesus, Dru. Are you all right?"

I spread my arms and did a three-sixty. "See, nothing's broken."

His fingers slid inside mine. "This business. It's aged me ten years in two minutes. God, nothing can happen to you."

He always could set fire to my nervous system. "I'm fine, honest. He missed. His intention was to frighten me. When he was coming up the street, I don't think he expected to see me. His move was impulsive."

"Poor bastard, doesn't know he's up against a mind-reader."

The officers closed the door of the paddy wagon and drove away. The dog handlers led their dogs back up Decatur Street to the squad cars in the train yard.

"I got a feeling we'll be seeing them again," I said, looking after the dogs. "But not the blue car, nor the gray van."

Lake said, "I got a call. The brass is coming to the crime scene for a press conference."

"Wonderful."

NINETEEN

The men who wore the brass were puffed with importance. The cameras caught their pre-conference gravity as they stood in a tight circle and spoke somberly. The pantheon included the police chief, the fire chief, the FBI agent in charge, and the Georgia Bureau of Investigation—GBI—task force honcho. Lake and Captain Turquin were to stand in the background and furnish the facts of the case. Lake said Hugle was supposed to be here, but I didn't see him.

When I'd shown up with Lake, the men were polite, but detached, especially the GBI and FBI agents. Their testosterone hung heavily on the air, which put my back up because this investigation could spiral away from me if I caved to their condescension. That wasn't going to happen. When I was a cop, the federal and state agents treated me like a fellow cop, and, when I formed my agency, they were quick to throw out the red carpet when I took on runaway children or parental abduction messes every agent hates. But to this august assemblage, on this spectacular investigation, I was not welcome. I could read it in their eyes: *This is real police work.*

Miffed, and determined to let them know I was an integral part of this investigation, I shoved closer to them.

Then Lake came up beside me. "You have me, don't forget."

Those five words dispelled the resentment that might have led me to say some really rotten things. I touched his arm. "Thank you for reminding me I'm on the hunt for two little girls, not on an ego trip."

He told me the GBI had sent a team to quiz Timothy Rose, and the FBI was scouring the city for Miguel Lopez. Tips from the public were pouring in by the hundreds. He said, "Nothing worthwhile so far; nothing coming out of the neighborhoods in the vicinity of Cabbagetown."

When the show finally got underway, I left to see Dwight Judd. Since Lake had gotten on his wrong side, maybe I could get on his right side.

On the way, my mind churned on the monstrous crime—how it had been carried out and by whom. But mostly I thought about the Rose girls. At times I felt like I could reach out and touch them, and if I strained my brain I would know who had stolen them. A ring headed by a Bishop—could I ever play chess again?— was responsible for their abduction. The crime was carried out by a Knight-abductor whose brazenness was breathtaking. Eight years ago, he'd snatched a ten-year-old foster girl. Three and a half years ago he'd taken a troubled eleven-year-old. Last night he'd taken two little girls. He'd been patient enough to let time go by between the abductions. This time, maybe if he'd taken one child, and hadn't had the bad luck of stormy weather, he may have gotten away with another mystery disappearance in a transitional neighborhood. But he'd taken two kids, and I wondered why. Greed? Opportunity? Both? Why didn't he anticipate this crime would become a news sensation?

Then a thought struck—as one sometimes will—and blazed with insight. What if he didn't care if the crime captured the public's attention? Why would he not care? Because this was to be his finale. I reveled in my epiphany for a brief moment before I wondered how the hell it was going to help me find the girls.

Large raindrops spotted my windshield. The low, cumulus black-bottoms churned like my brain. Who was the Knight? The Bishop might be some go-between scumbag in Miami, but the Knight knew the neighborhood too well to not be part of it.

Was he Stephen Doonan? Doonan would need money for his ambitious dream of restoring old neighborhoods. Did he sell little girls to fund his dreams? The Barneses' dog was killed so it wouldn't bark when the operation went down. Doonan had said nothing about the dog until we found it dead in his tenant's cellar. Doonan had been reluctant for us to search the house. On the other hand, Doonan had told the truth about the dark Buick. I'd seen it for myself, up close. And he'd told us about Santa. But the argument against Doonan was I couldn't see a finale in him. He was a young man, full of verve and ideas, and if he was selling flesh to finance them, he'd need to keep himself in the game.

Then there was Cyrus Bassett—Santa. Bassett knew trains and he needed money. But if he abducted and sold two girls before, where was the money from the sales? So far no tales of high living or gambling came into his picture. But didn't Webdog say the Bassetts were looking to retire? That's a finale. He could have a bank account in the islands, or he could be keeping the plunder under his mattress. Did I think that likely? No.

Conrad Hugle as the Knight? He was cold and arrogant and had the inside track on foster children. But would he prey in his own neighborhood? Was he the type of egomaniac who thought he could play a dual role and no one was smart enough to figure him out? I thought so. Under extreme pressure to clean up CPS—a lot coming from Portia and me—I could see him staging a finale, and then flying off to Argentina, or wherever, to retire with his blood money.

Finally, where did Dwight Judd fit in? Could I get him to tell me the truth?

I was nearing City East when the radio news reader came on: "The press conference about the sensational fire that killed a foster couple and saw the disappearance of two girls is underway. The FBI report tips have flooded in from people throughout the Southeast. The Rose girls have been spotted from Louisville to Miami. Agents say each tip will be followed up. Captain Turquin with the AFD said the multiple explosions were likely caused by a gasoline-rigged bomb. Let's listen in for a moment to the reporters' Q&A."

A female reporter asked: "Could you repeat the license plate number of the van?"

Lake: "VAN 582. It's out with the Amber Alert."

Reporter: "When and where was the van last spotted?"

Lake: "I'm going to keep that part of the investigation confidential for now."

"It might help finding it, Lieutenant."

Lake: "It might further jeopardize the Rose girls."

A male reporter's voice asked, "Lieutenant Lake, why have you arrested Dwight Judd? Is he a suspect?"

Lake: "Mr. Judd is not a suspect. Mr. Judd is in detention for violating his parole."

"What did he do to violate his parole?"

Lake: "An illegal substance was found in his home."

"Did he leave his house at times when he was not authorized to?"

Lake: "Not according to his parole officer."

A female reporter asked, "Do you believe Lanny Long's injuries were from an accident?"

I sat straighter at the wheel. It was *her* voice.

Lake: "There's no reason not to at this time."

"What is your theory of why the girls were abducted?"

It was her voice.

Lake: "I deal in facts, not theories."

"C'mon, Ricky."

My heart raced like an Indy car. My anonymous caller went on. "You're a cop who follows his instincts, plays his theories, you've told me so."

I knew the established reporters in the city. She had to be new.

Lake: "I formulate theories based on facts. I don't have all the facts yet. Next questioner."

"Ricky . . ."

A male voice hollered louder than her teasing voice. "How many kidnappers do you believe were involved?"

Lake: "That would be guesswork."

"Where is Moriah Dru?" Deep Voice shouted.

The male voice overrode her again. "Lieutenant Lake, we've heard the FBI is involved because the girls could possibly be out of the area. Do you believe they've been taken out of Atlanta already?"

I heard Lake's hesitation. Did he want the chess pieces to believe they were safe enough to move down the trade route, or did he want them to believe the cops were closing in? Either way, it was dangerous for the girls. Lake answered, "From the facts we've gathered, it's impossible for me to say."

"Is Moriah Dru investigating with the APD?" Deep Voice persisted.

Lake: "Miss Dru is working with the Juvenile Court."

"Where is she? Can we hear from her?"

You'll hear from me, broad.

Lake's voice sounded harsh. "Fine by me."

A man's voice shouted, "Lieutenant, two other girls have disappeared from this same neighborhood. Is there any connection?"

Lake: "That's part of the investigation."

Another reporter: "Would the FBI agent answer that question. Are the crimes similar? Do they fit a profile?"

The FBI agent: "They might."

The news reader broke in. "The conference is continuing and we will bring you highlights in the next half hour. Meanwhile, the race is on to find the Rose girls before . . . what? What fate awaits two beautiful blond children? Now, for a look at your weather."

Wouldn't be long now I'd know the name of the woman who was harassing me, who claimed Lake was going to leave me for her, who had the gall to play coy with him at a press conference as serious as this. I looked at the speedometer. I was going sixty-five

156

down Ponce de Leon, had blown through a yellow-turning-red light, only two blocks from City East. But the rain had let up.

Judd sat at the end of a long metal table, his cuffed hands moving restlessly atop it. The orange jumpsuit he wore had to be at least two sizes too big. I sat in a metal jail chair across from him, looking up to see a guard's outline in the two-way mirror. Anyone who ever watched a cop show knows a mirror in a jail means a clear window on the opposite side, so why not cut the deception and use plain glass? Judd mirrored my thoughts by saying, "He's watchin' me, ain't he?"

"And me," I said. A grin blossomed from Judd, showing off his square yellow teeth. "How're they treating you?" I asked.

"Fine, Miss Dru. I got a cell by myself. I don't like sharin' with strangers."

"Food good?"

"Very tasty."

"What do you miss?"

"You know . . ."

"You haven't made a connection yet?" We were talking marijuana.

"You wearin' a wire?"

"Smart man," I said, and held up a hand. "No, I promise."

"I'm smarter than most think, you know. I watch TV and I seen you and the cop ain't found Jessie and Dottie."

"That's why we need your help."

"I said all I can."

"Our investigation turned up that you knew Timothy Rose in the Middle Georgia Correctional Institution."

He shrugged. "We called a boy Rosey. Don't know it's the same one."

"He was."

"Maybe."

"Did he have a family?"

"Maybe."

"Did he talk about his girls?"

"Maybe."

"Maybe you can tell me what he said."

"He wanted them back."

"Where were they?"

"With the Barneses."

"Did he ask you to keep an eye on them?"

"Maybe."

"Would he hire someone to kill the Barneses?"

"If they took his girls away."

"Who would he hire?"

It occurred to him he might be the *who* I was asking about. He said, "Weren't me."

"Let's talk about Miguel Lopez."

"Don't know him."

"He was a friend of Rose's."

"Rosey had lots of friends."

"Did he want his friends to help get his girls away from the Barneses?"

"Maybe. I ain't saying no more, so don't ask."

"Did you like Miss Goddard?"

"She was all right."

"You know Miss Goddard died this morning, don't you?"

"I heard. I'm real sorry."

"She stuck up for you, didn't she?"

His eyes blanked as if he didn't understand. He said, "I did stuff for her, in her garden and all. She gave me money."

"Did you do work for Wanda and Ed Barnes?"

He hesitated. "They don't need my help, she said."

"Did you like Wanda?"

"She got me in . . . she was okay."

"Timothy Rose told you she wanted to take his children, didn't he?"

"She oughten've done that. She knew they had a daddy."

"They needed a home when Timothy went to jail. The Barneses were foster parents, not real parents. They couldn't take Timothy Rose's rights away."

"That judge could."

"She wasn't going to. Timothy Rose knew that."

"No, he didn't."

"Did Miguel Lopez ask you to help him with Timothy Rose's problem with the Barneses?" He looked away. "Mr. Judd, please answer me."

"Miguel didn't do nothing to Jessie and Dottie."

"What did Miguel ask you to do?"

"Nothing, he asked me to keep an eye out for what was happenin'."

"What did you tell him?"

"That the girls was doing okay was all."

"He gave you marijuana, didn't he?"

"I can't say."

"I know he did, Mr. Judd. I saw a new bag in your house, and I saw Lopez in your house after the police took you away."

"He oughten been there."

"He left some pornographic photos in your house, too."

"He did not."

"I saw the pictures, Mr. Judd. Are they yours?"

"Don't like porn. Grandaddy would stripe me looking at ugly pitchers."

"Did you attend Cyrus Bassett's church?"

That coming-from-nowhere question fuddled him for a second. "Sure."

"Did he take up the collection on Wednesdays when Ed Barnes couldn't?"

"I helped, too."

"At the last collection, did a couple of people give big checks?"

Judd laughed as if I'd ask him if he'd given a big check. "Nobody gives checks in the plate."

"At work, did you hear an argument between Ed Barnes and Mr. Bassett?"

"Once. Mr. Barnes came in."

"When was this?"

"Right after Christmastime."

"What was the talk about?"

"Mr. Bassett givin' the girls a ride home. Mr. Barnes didn't like it. He said Lanny walked with them, and they didn't need no ride home."

"Mr. Barnes didn't like Mr. Bassett's attentions to the girls, did he?"

"Mr. Bassett said he didn't mean nobody no harm."

The more I talked to Judd, the more certain I was he didn't molest Susie Ryan. The community had known it instinctively, but why did they let him be railroaded into prison? I asked, "What really happened with Susie Ryan?"

His mouth clamped tight. "I done my time. I'm not sayin' no more."

"Dr. Hugle came to see you in prison, didn't he?"

"Many times," he said, puffing his chest.

"You like Conrad, don't you?"

"He's my friend."

"How did you meet him?"

"He walks in the neighborhood. He asked me to walk with him before I got in trouble."

"What did you talk about?"

"Things."

"People?"

"Sometimes."

"Susie Ryan?"

"Don't go mentionin' her name to me."

"But she was your friend, wasn't she?"

"Up till . . . no."

"Susie and Dr. Hugle were friends, too, weren't they?"

"I don't know 'bout that."

"But you saw them walking together, didn't you?"

"I don't want to talk about Susie no more."

"You know she was killed right after you went to jail, don't you?"

He raised his shoulders, then dropped them low. "I was mighty sorry to hear it."

"There's a lot of disappearing and death in your neighborhood, isn't there, Mr. Judd?"

"There's death all over. Fact of life."

"Did it occur to you there is a connection?"

"Connection? Like what?"

"Let's say Miss Goddard was killed and Lanny injured because they learned something that would lead to the kidnapper of the girls. What do you think that could be?"

To ask such a question of someone with limited reasoning was asking a lot, but then I wondered how limited his reasoning really was. He could have developed a habit suitable for protecting himself. He'd said he was smarter than people thought and I was beginning to believe it.

He said, "They both were always pokin' into other people's business, weren't they?"

"Did you poke into other people's business?"

"I didn't look in no windows."

Maybe he'd given me the answer. He fidgeted and leaned forward as if to rise.

But I wasn't quite ready for him to go. "Did Dr. Hugle look in windows?" He snorted as if the mental image was funny. "Do you know anyone who drives a gray cargo van with ladders on top?"

His mouth curved in in a version of a smile. "Stephen's Mexicans. Has a yellow light on it. They flash it when they run the streets, like they're important or somethin'."

The guard thumped the glass.

I held up a finger and mouthed, "One more minute."

The guard nodded.

I asked Judd, "When you'd leave the grocery store with Mr. Bassett, did you go other places besides your house?"

He shook his head no.

"Never to get an ice cream, or a burger?"

"Maybe. But that ain't a violation."

"Whenever you took a detour on your way home, did you tell your parole officer?"

"None of his business if I'm home at the time I'm supposed to be and Mr. Bassett owns up for me."

"Did you ever go to the Green Space?"

"Once, but not with Mr. Bassett. Stephen took me home from the store. Mr. Bassett was busy. Stephen wanted to take some pictures."

"Of whom?"

"The Green Space. He wants to tear it up and build houses."

"Did he take pictures of people there?"

"I guess."

"Kids?"

"They was there."

"Dottie and Jessie?"

"I guess, if they was there."

"You ever see the photos he took?"

"No."

I heard the guard at the door. "What can I get for you while you're in here? You'll probably be out in a couple of days."

"Nope. I'm going back to Middle Georgia."

Damned if he didn't look happy about it.

TWENTY

It was still misting when I stepped outside. I headed for my office, which was not far from the jail. I parked my old Bentley—how I came by it is a long story for another time—in my assigned spot in Atlanta's Underground parking lot near Georgia State University and rode the elevator to the fifteenth floor.

Web was geeking away at his computer. When he saw me he grinned, guaranteed to bolster my spirit. "What you got for me? I'm on my way back to Cabbagetown."

"Rush, rush," Web said, playing his keyboard like piano ivories.

"This is a rushing business. You got me some good stuff on the slave trade?"

He hit ENTER. "How long did that take?" he asked.

"One second."

"Piece of cake to track this stuff." He rolled his desk chair to a straight-leg chair and lifted green computer boards from it. He tossed them on top of a tangle of cords on a desk and scooted the straight-leg up to his monitor. I sat on it. He said, "Here's a search site for pedophile procurers—but they don't advertise as such."

I read down the list, pointed to a site, and Web downloaded it.

It began: "I clap my hands and my blue-eyed slaves appear to please me. I welcome those to my side who are willing to participate in the pleasure of the flesh."

Another "buyer" advertised, "We do not recognize pedophilia—that is an American barbarism. It is America's backward thinking that blights the pleasures of youthful flesh. Beauty of any age is its own reward."

"Rationalization for depravity," I said. "My snitch thinks the Rose girls are heading for South America, or the islands."

"Makes sense from Georgia."

"Okay, you got me the procurer's sites. What about the sellers?"

"Now you're talking self-incrimination. Jail time. Sting operation fall guys. No ring's advertising on the Web, but they use the lists to troll for buyers. There are contact codes in some of the ads. One has an embedded e-mail address in it."

"I bet you're going to decode them."

"I ran the alphabet on the script kiddies who do the routine codex of using numbers and characters for the alphabet, and the routine hacker prefixes, suffixes, and equivalencies."

"Dandy."

"I found one e-mail series that's interesting. I finally figured out what crypt they're using. It's a Perl-Crypt-Enigma simulator."

"Which is?"

"It's an application of the Enigma machine used by the Germans in World War Two."

"You mean you use World War Two technology to crack an e-mail code?"

"Exactly. The platform is based on actual Enigma values, which is pretty simple when you understand how Enigma works."

Web inclined his head, and I toned down my impatience. Although I never take Web for granted, at times I give him short shift when he launches into details. Afterward, I get the guilts because he is, first, a fine human being, and, second, he has a passion for justice not usually found in geniuses.

He said, "Ever see an Enigma machine?"

"I've seen them in old movies. Looks like a klunky typewriter."

"It's a rotor scrambler with a keyboard."

"How does it work? In layman's terms, please."

Grinning, he said, "Letters are scrambled by a set of wired rotor wheels."

My head felt like a block of wood as he explained about successive letters showing in windows, plug-ins, and ring orders. When he halted, I said, "So, how does the person receiving the message know how to decode it?"

"The guy getting the coded message has already set his scrambler according to prearranged settings that are supposed to be changed daily. Want to know more about these intricacies?"

"No."

Web stretched back in his chair. "Alan Turing, who is the brains behind the first computer, cracked the code because the Germans got sloppy and left their prearranged settings on letters like AAA or XYZ. Default settings will get you every time."

"Is that what's going to get the Knight?"

"Hope so. He uses the same settings twice, he's cooked."

He leaned into the keyboard, his fingers flying, and up popped a screen with boxes to fill in. He rubbed his hands like a kid. "Let's have some fun and crypt a message."

"I'll leave the fun stuff to you. So our Knight and Bishop communicate like the Nazis?"

"Something like."

Web handed me the photos I'd requested of Doonan, Hugle, Judd, and Bassett, and so I scooted on down to my car, thinking about the bank of computers in Doonan's home office, and geniuses.

The mist was turning into a shower when I rang the bell at the Queen Anne's gate. The man with the big hangover pulled the curtain aside. He looked as if he couldn't believe his eyes. I was holding a newspaper above my head against the drizzle. It wasn't doing a good job.

Tom Davis dropped the curtain, flipped the locks, and drew back the door. I apologized for dripping in his laundry room, and he gave me a large towel from the dryer.

"I caught the press conference," he said, as he led me through the kitchen. "I thought y'all might say something about the van."

"Cops don't tell all they know," I said, "even at press conferences with the bigwigs." I reached inside my backpack and took out an envelope.

"I haven't seen the van again," he said, guiding me into a gloomy living room with dark oak floors. It was sparsely furnished, masculine.

I sat in a black leather armchair in front of a dead fireplace. He sat in a twin chair opposite.

"I have some pictures," I said. "I'd like you to take a look."

He didn't look eager to see them. "I'm not going to get burned out for helping you, am I?"

His face was lined with drama, and apprehension. I was honest with him. "I can't guarantee anything. But let me say this, these abductors—murderers—are part of an organization that kidnaps with a purpose. I don't see you fitting into their purpose."

"I saw the guy's face. I like my house."

I opened the envelope and pulled out the photos. "Setting fire to your house would be risking the operation. For what? They probably know we've talked to you about what you saw. They'd figure you already described the driver to us."

"People get mad. I told you the dude looked mean."

"I believe you."

"That kid's accident." He shook his head. His hands shook, too. "So soon after the fire, the kidnapping."

Since he didn't bring it up, I wouldn't talk about Miss Goddard's sudden death. "I'd like you to look at these pictures," I said, proffering them. "See if the man resembles the driver."

Resigned, he held out his hand to study photos of Stephen Doonan, Conrad Hugle, Dwight Judd, and Cyrus Bassett.

He shook his head until he came to the last photo. "Maybe," he drummed an index finger on it. "The beard, though. I don't remember facial hair. But then, I'd been drinking."

He held up the photograph of Stephen Doonan. "I know this guy. He's the architect, isn't he? He does stuff in the neighborhood. Comes to NPU meetings about restoration."

168

"One and the same."

"He a suspect?"

"Was he driving the van?"

"Not unless he wore a mask."

That was that. At the porch door, he opened it. "I probably won't sleep tonight," he said.

"I won't either," I replied.

The rain sprayed my face. He said, "Hey, I got a rain jacket you can have."

"I'm waterproof," I said.

"No, really. Somebody left it here a long time ago. Throw it away when you get done with it."

The tag at the neck said Rain Shadow. Fitting name. It felt feather light. "I have a feeling I'll keep it—as a memento—when I find the girls."

"God bless your determination," he said, shutting the door with a look of desolation.

TWENTY-ONE

Nobody had bothered to lock Miss Goddard's front door. I took off the Rain Shadow and hung it on the hat rack.

In the cool parlor, I contemplated the platform rocker. I saw her as she'd been the last time I was here—sitting with her head drooped, her faded blue eyes showing through the fringe of her half-closed eyelids. On reflection, she'd been at peace. I bent and picked up her shawl and held it close to my nose. It smelled of lavender water and musty lace like she had, but also it smelled smoky. The Barnes fire had imbued it with its essence.

I knew I was going to mess with the scene's forensics, but it was vital to get information that could lead me to the Rose girls. It would be this evening before we'd get an autopsy report on Miss Goddard, and there was no guarantee the medical examiner would conclude murder. I knew she was murdered. Lake knew she was. That's all I needed to look into her life.

I scrutinized the parlor. *What exactly am I looking for?* It was cramped with decades of artifacts to comfort Miss Goddard as she grew older. I fingered through her knitting bag. Nothing.

A secretary occupied a corner near the window. It was a neat old thing, made of pine. It hadn't been expensive in its day, but now would fetch a high price in an antique shop. I removed the four-volume leather-bound set of Shakespeare, set it on the sofa, and lifted the desk lid. There were six pigeonholes, all stuffed with the mundane papers that kept her life in order, or gave meaning to it. A few bills, some circulars, catalogues, coupons, the current community news pamphlet, greeting cards she'd received in the last year. She probably gathered the cards at the end of a year, strung ribbon around the stack and lovingly put them with the previous year's in a box under her bed. Like my mama, she never intended to look at them again, but it reassured her to know they were there, that they represented people who'd taken an interest in her.

The long drawer under the pigeonholes held her checkbook and insurance papers. A will and the deed to her house were in the back of the drawer. The beneficiary on one life insurance policy was the Church of the Living Lord. It got five thousand dollars. The other beneficiary was Dwight Judd. He got twenty-five thousand smackers. Strange. What about relatives? Didn't she have kin?

I slipped the will from its jacket. After the usual instructions about funeral arrangements and debts, she bequeathed her household contents to Wanda Barnes. What about the house itself?

When I saw the names on the warranty deed, I felt the air being pulled from my lungs. The house was the property of Millicent Burdette Goddard and Stephen Alvin Doonan, joint tenants with right of survivorship.

I was so mad I couldn't see straight. It was all I could do to keep myself from running across the street and setting Doonan's house on fire, and watching it burn to the ground. And if it wasn't for the fact the deed was recorded in county records, I'd have ripped it up then and there. Thank God these impulses pass quickly.

How had he made her do it?

I opened her checkbook. The balance in the account was $237.13. She had a savings book. I opened it—$510.30. Unless there was another financial center in the house, her worldly total was $747.43.

I flipped through two bank statements. It appeared that every fifteenth of the month her checking account received a credit from the Dependents of the Railroad Crewmen of America for $90. She got a $213 a month disability benefit from the Social Security Administration.

I found myself staring into space thinking of my mother after my father lost his business, and then died. Always a worrier, Mama's mind fixed on growing old with little money, even though I assured her I'd take care of her. A year has passed and she doesn't know me. She plays patty-cake with the round-the-clock nurses I hire when I can't be with her.

I came back to the present and shoved the papers back in the secretary. Next, I contemplated the bookcases. The middle shelf of one case was paneled, and it had a keyhole. After a thirty-second search, I found the key in a vase, unlocked the panel, and rolled it upward, like a rolltop desk. Diaries were lined up like soldiers. Ah, ha. Spinsters, especially those who read a lot, write in diaries. I didn't have time to read them word for word, but I'm a fast skimmer.

The writings began when Miss Goddard was twelve years old. Her handwriting was upright and neat, like she was. Inevitably, each entry began, *DEAR DIARY.* Some things stick in the throat. I swallowed, and read on,

Mama taught me a new knitting stitch this morning. Daddy came home for lunch. We had chicken noodle soup and sour dough bread. I hung out the clothes on the line. I don't like it that she makes me hang up my underpants. The boys cut through the yard and tease me at school. Goddy, Goddy pants are roddy.

Cheerless though I was, I still smiled. When Miss Goddard was eighteen she had a boyfriend. His name was Henry. Then Henry broke off the "understanding" and married Bertha.

Miss Goddard wrote:

Some are born never to marry. For my part, I knew I never felt about men the way some girls did. Mama took to calling me an old maid before I was twenty.

Miss Goddard wrote in short simple sentences. Some entries contained a few lines. It was easy to flash through the pages, and on to another book.

Some years ago there was a mystery man in her life.

HE begged that I never mention his name, so I won't write it. One day, HE said, the way would be clear and we would be together forever. Thankfully, he understands my nature.

Later, she wrote:

HIS wife died. I find it hard to reconcile a guilty feeling of glad-ness with the death of another human being. But HE says when mourning is over, we will make our mutual admiration public.

Then:

HE came this morning. HE had blood on his trousers. I asked him why. He'd had to put down a dog. I asked HIM how. "I slit its

throat," he said. *I could never look at HIM fondly again, even though the dog was old and sick.*

In later volumes, Miss Goddard writes of her joy when her friend Wanda talked her husband into being foster parents. The distrusting spinster had cautioned them, however, on the adoption issue:

I told them it would never happen. Even fathers in jail for life don't give up their kids, and judges don't take custody away. It was a sad fact, but life is sad for those who don't deserve it.

Of Doonan she wrote:

He was unbearable at this evening's meeting. He has no kindness in him. He wants the children of the community to scrub the graffiti off the Krog Car Tunnel. We gave them permission last year to do their art on the pillars. It is colorful and adds to our community. Stephen said it was tacky.

Another Doonan comment:

He would like to own Cabbagetown and turn it into a doll house village for tourists to pay by the head. That's not historic, that's make-believe.

She also wrote:

I can't pay Stephen for seeing to the repairs of the termite damage. Daddy always said spreading creosote would keep the insects away. He was wrong. The three-by-sixes are rotten. Stephen says soon the porch roof will cave in. What can I do?

A month ago, her mystery lover reappears:

HE was all charm and grace. Then he got to the real reason he'd come. HE wanted me to convince Wanda and Ed to give up the Rose girls. "What," I said! "It would tear their hearts out." HE said, "It's not good for them to be so attached. They will go back to their father if he wins his appeal." I told HIM we prayed Tim Rose stayed in jail for the rest of his life. I might be hard-hearted, but when a man does illegal things and blows up his wife and son, then he deserves the fate he has.

HE said over and over, "I hate to see Ed and Wanda hurt."

HE left. I don't want to see HIM again.

I pored through the references to identify HIM when I discovered she never mentions Hugle in her diary. Or had she?

Footsteps pounded up the porch steps. When no one knocked, I looked outside. Doonan stood with his hands in his pockets. Then he reached out and tried the screen door. I had locked it.

At the screen, I asked, "Mr. Doonan, can I help you?"

"Uh . . . well . . . uh . . . I thought I'd best come and see . . . uh . . . what's what."

I knew why the son-of-a-bitch had come. "I'm seeing to what's what right now."

"Uh, you see, uh . . ." His hand went to the screen again. "Miss Goddard put me on the deed in case anything happened to her."

"Are you a straw party for someone?"

"Uh, no. The house is mine."

"Didn't Miss Goddard have relatives?"

"Actually . . . no. Some cousins in South Carolina, but they never came to see her."

"And you did."

"I fixed up the house for her. It was only . . ." He looked away.

"Fair . . . right?"

The line of his jaw bulged. "I don't understand your attitude."

"Mr. Doonan, it doesn't matter to me who gets this house. It would only matter if I got it. However, right now, you can't take possession." I wasn't sure of my legal ground, but I bluffed like I was.

"And why not?"

"Because until the cause of Miss Goddard's death is determined, things in here will have to remain as they are."

"She had a heart attack."

"If she didn't, then this is a crime scene."

"You know it's a bunch of hooey. Miss Goddard had a bad heart. She was always complaining. I took her to her doctor at least three times in the last month."

"The cause of her death will be determined by the medical examiner, not you. Now if you'll—"

"Why are you in . . . my house?"

"I'm an investigator."

"Not a cop though."

"Juvenile Court investigator."

"So, why aren't you out finding the kids?"

At that moment, a familiar hat moved across the laurels in front of the house. In seconds, Lake sprinted up the steps.

Doonan turned and made a rude noise. He brushed past Lake. Lake called after him, "Wait a minute, Mr. Doonan."

Doonan spun to face him. "More harassment?"

Lake didn't glare as I expected. "I want to know about a van registered to your professional corporation."

"What about my van?"

"Is it a gray cargo van with ladder supports and a yellow light on the top?" Doonan looked like he didn't know whether to say yes or head for the hills. Lake said, "Tag number VAN 582?"

176

"I think that's the tag. What about it?"

"Where is it?"

"I don't know at the moment. I never drive it. The corporation bought it for my hirelings."

"Who drives it and where is it kept?"

Doonan clearly did not like the tenor of Lake's voice. "My foreman, Ramon Torres, keeps it in a shed at his house. He picks up the workers in the morning. After work, he takes them home. Why are you asking?"

"Where is he working today?"

Doonan's face reddened. "I asked why you want to know."

"Where is he working today?" Lake repeated.

Doonan had the good sense to reply. "We don't work on Saturdays unless clients pay double time."

"Where does Torres work on workdays?"

"A Victorian in Inman Park. I have two there."

"Call him."

Doonan flattened his hands against his thighs. "My cell's in my car." He bolted down the steps.

I unlatched the screen. Lake rushed in as if he were going to take me in his arms. But with Deep Voice's words resounding in my brain, I turned away and went to the antique desk. I kept my voice steady. "Web thinks he's on to the Knight."

"No surprise," Lake said, standing close behind me. "Dru . . ."

When I faced him, he looked spurned—a lovely word, one I picked up from Miss Goddard's diaries—but when I launched into the highlights of my conversation with Webdog, he grinned. "Excellent."

I showed him Miss Goddard's checkbook, her will, and the warranty deed. "Greedy scum!" he said.

"I don't think he abducted the girls."

His eyes, like two frowning holes, roamed my face. "You take up for him."

"Not—"

He interrupted, mocking Doonan's voice: "You need your house fixed, you don't have any money, put me on the deed, I'll fix it for you. For me. You need a ride when your friend Wanda can't take you to the doctor, I'll drive you. For a price."

Had I caused his unprofessional cynicism? "Does that make him a killer?" I asked.

"How else could he get his hands on the Barnes place? They weren't going to sell."

"Lake . . . you're not jumping to conclusions, you're leaping tall buildings."

He pressed the lines in his brow with his fingertips, as if to ease an ache. "Aren't you the one who made the comment about him waiting for their house to burn down? Now you don't think so?"

"Okay, I shot off my mouth. There's no proof."

"You stick up for him even after you saw the deed, read those pages?"

"I didn't say I like him, nor that I'm sticking up for him. I'm saying there's no proof."

"You might also want to consider this. The Feds are looking into Doonan's money affairs. Where'd he get the jack to begin with? It takes seed money, and a lot of it, to become a developer. Eight years ago, maybe Doonan saw a way to get some cash by selling a foster kid, or tipping the sellers—for a piece of the price. He needs more cash, the second girl's an easy score, too. Mom's no good, Dad's nowhere in sight. The kid's turning promiscuous."

"Would he use his own truck?"

"Sure, lay the blame on the Mexicans. But we'll see how clever he really is. A GBI guy went to Middle Georgia and interviewed Timothy Rose. He's pretty cut up about the girls being gone. Threatened to sue everybody he could name."

"Rose might start with himself for landing them in foster care," I said. "Does Rose realize he's under suspicion for their abduction because of his association with Judd and Lopez?"

"Rose denies having anything to do with the abduction, even volunteered to take a lie detector. He said he sought out Judd in prison when the scuttlebutt went around Judd lived in Cabbagetown. He also admitted when Judd was released from prison, he'd asked him to keep an eye on his girls."

"What about Lopez?"

"Rose clammed on knowing Miguel Lopez."

"I'm getting an idea of what the deal was between Rose and Lopez."

"What?"

"Planting evidence to get the kids away from the Barneses. Eventually Judd's marijuana use was going to come to the attention of his parole officer or the police. An anonymous call would do the trick. The cops would search his house, find the porn with the photos of the Rose girls, and before you can say Jack Robinson, the girls are out of Cabbagetown."

"I see your point. Rose knows Child Protective Services is in a mess and it was Judge Portia Devon who put the girls in the same neighborhood with a convicted molester. Another judge might consider placing the children with their uncle, since it appears he's cleaned up his act."

"Portia would have something to say about that."

"I'd hate to try and outmaneuver her."

"Poor Dwight. A born dupe."

"We got the search warrant on his house."

The doorbell rang "Georgia on My Mind" and Lake opened the door.

Doonan came in and scanned the parlor as if determining what antiques I'd made off with.

"The van?" Lake asked.

Doonan's complexion paled. He turned his palms up. "It's been stolen."

"When?"

"Ramon says it must have been stolen sometime in the night."

"Why didn't he let you know earlier?"

"He just found out."

"Where was it, to get stolen?"

"He said last night he was playing pool with friends on Ponce at a taquería. He got too drunk to drive home and left the van parked in the back lot and got a ride. When his sister drove him to get it an hour ago, the van was gone. He has his set of keys."

"Why didn't he call the police?"

Doonan looked out the window. "I couldn't say."

"Ramon's illegal, isn't he?"

"When I hired him he provided a driver's license and a Social Security card. He speaks English."

"But he's illegal."

"It's not up to me to do Immigration's job."

"Where's Ramon live?"

"Norcross. Now can I ask you what this is all about? I'm asking nice. What does it have to do with all . . . all that's happened?"

"Maybe nothing."

"Do the police have my van?"

"No."

"How'd you know the tag number and its description?"

"We need to take a look at those Victorian houses you're renovating. Anyone live in them?"

"No."

"You own them."

"One of them."

Taking his radio from his belt, Lake stepped outside.

Doonan said, "It can't get any worse than this, can it?"

"Sure it can," I said.

"My house is ruined." He threw his hands in the air. "I'm under suspicion for God knows what-all." He tried looking sincere. "I'm telling you the truth, Miss Dru."

"I want to ask you something."

"Okay."

"Who were Miss Goddard's . . . uh . . . gentlemen callers?"

He let out a caw, reminding me of a crow. "Gentlemen callers!"

I could have smacked him upside the jaw. "Okay, special men friends."

"Sorry, but the very idea . . ." The caw again.

"Give the idea serious thought."

Maybe he remembered she was dead, because he said with something like atonement, "Ask anyone that question, and you'll get the same reaction. I'll tell you what I observed in the few years I've lived here. A lot of people looked in on her—men and women. She didn't drive, and we took turns taking her places where she needed to go. You might say I was a regular gentleman caller in that regard."

"In her diaries, she writes of a secret lover. This man's wife had died. I don't think she was writing fiction, and I believe it's important to find him."

He scratched the back of his neck. "Millicent Goddard having a secret lover is far-fetched, but if I had to guess it'd be Conrad Hugle."

"Why?"

"The dead wife thing. Conrad moved to the mill right afterward. He said he wasn't interested in remarrying, but I don't think he became a monk, if you know what I mean. You know, Miss Goddard was a very pretty woman in her day."

"I can't see Conrad Hugle as Miss Goddard's paramour."

"Goddard would like that word—paramour," he said. "You're right, though, Conrad's too sleazy to be anyone's paramour. Besides they bickered constantly at NPU meetings."

"I understand you bickered, too."

He nodded. "Revitalization doesn't suit everyone."

Lake came back with two detectives. He said to Doonan, "Detectives Howard and Allen will go with you to check out the Inman Park houses."

Walking between the detectives, Doonan turned his head and looked at me like I'd charged five thousand dollars on his credit card account without him knowing.

I grabbed the borrowed raincoat and locked the door.

TWENTY-TWO

I went to see Mrs. Long in a waiting room at Grady Hospital. It was a hard visit to make. She hadn't stopped crying and her eyelids had swollen into blotchy red mounds. "He's still in Operating," she told me.

Lanny's siblings—all four of them—had taken charge of the room. Their stupendous racket made conversation impossible, so we took the elevator to the cafeteria. Mrs. Long sat hugging a box of Kleenex while I sipped strong coffee.

"Sorry, Miss Dru. I can't take it in. The nurses don't know or won't say what's going on with him. Never thought I'd be buryin' that boy one day." She shook her head and snuffled into the tissue.

"You won't bury Lanny."

"For all his young years, he watched out for us."

"How long have you lived in Cabbagetown, Mrs. Long?"

"All my life."

"What happened to Mr. Long?"

"He got the cancer, asbestos, and died."

"Are you all right financially?"

"We got the settlement benefits and Social Security, so we make do."

"If you need help with Lanny's expenses I think the Good Samaritans of the community might help. The banks set up accounts—"

"Oh, miss . . ." A torrent of tears came, and she rubbed her cheeks, "they say he skidded on the concrete. Lanny was a good rider. I don't know . . ."

"Did Lanny hang out on the railroad tracks?"

"He weren't supposed to. All the young'uns did. Liked to play in the boxcars they was fixing."

"The Rose girls didn't go there, did they?"

"My heavens, no. Mrs. Barnes would raise the roof if Lanny even thought of taking them girls to the trains."

"Did Lanny go there this week?"

She thought a minute. "He got run off by a mean man, he said. This Mexican had a knife on his belt, and he told Lanny to get lost. Lanny don't like being told nothing."

"What was the Mexican doing?"

"Going along opening up cars, looking in. He put a concrete block in one so the door wouldn't close."

"Lanny say anything else about him?"

She shook her head, scattering tears. I tilted back to avoid the spray. "You know everyone in Cabbagetown, don't you?"

She grunted. "You can't help it if you wanted to."

"A long time ago, Miss Goddard was engaged to be married. Who was Miss Goddard's fiancé?"

The question surprised her. "Miss Goddard's? My, my, you must mean Henry. She and he had an understanding is all. That was a long time ago, when I was a babe."

"What's Henry's last name?"

"Judd. Henry Judd, Dwight's granddaddy."

"But he married Bertha, why?"

"Bertha was quite different than Millicent," she said, blowing her nose harshly. "A jolly one, for sure. Bertha came with her parents a few years before she broke Henry and Millicent apart. My mama told me, and she always knew the truth about going's on. Poor Millicent, she was awful blue for a long while after. Never talked to Henry or Bertha again."

"Why, then, would Miss Goddard leave life insurance to Dwight Judd, Bertha and Henry's grandson?"

Blinking, she sat back. "Didn't know she did." She reached for a Kleenex, but her red eyes had dried as we talked. "Now I think about it, I remember Wanda saying she suspected Millicent felt responsible for Dwight."

"I don't understand."

"I do, in a way. If she'd been different, I mean, if Millicent Goddard had been different, then Henry would have married her instead of Bertha and then poor ol' Dwight wouldn't have been born into the world."

I understood, I think. "A few years back, Miss Goddard had another gentleman in her life, do you know who he was?"

"Millicent had another gentleman?"

"The question is, who was he?"

"I'd sure like to know."

"It was a secret affair apparently."

"Must have been real secret. Nothing stays secret long." An idea struck her. "She kept books. Surely, she put his name in her diary."

"She didn't. I thought maybe it was Conrad."

She grunted. "She's ten times too old for Conrad."

"This secret affair lasted for a while, and then ended abruptly. Did any man in the neighborhood lose his wife a few years ago?"

"I'll have to think on that. So many moved away about the time you're asking about. Revitalization was raising the taxes."

"Do you know of a man who'd slit his dog's throat because it was old?"

She blew her nose into a Kleenex. "Lanny said something once, but I don't remember a name."

"Call me if you think of anything," I said. "You have my card."

"I surely will, but I can't think . . . what's it got to do with . . . ?"

"Maybe nothing, but I have a feeling it might have something to do with her death."

"Oh, miss, don't you know? She had heart."

I got up to go. "Keep a close eye on your other children."

She looked at the box of Kleenex and then back up at me. Her head tilted forward; she sighed and kneaded the wad of tissue in her hands, looking as though she wondered what Lanny had to do with anything we talked about.

I turned to walk away. She called, "Oh, miss." I faced her. "You asked me this morning about Santa, a man named Santa?"

I held my breath. "Yes?"

"I couldn't recall right off because of all the happenings, but then I remembered. When the Boltons' foster girl went missing, Lanny was a little thing then, but he wandered away that evening, and we found him two streets over. Later, when we learned the foster girl was gone, he said he saw her go in a car with Santa. Poor ol' Bassett came in for some trouble, but he was in church they said."

"They said? You don't believe it?"

"Oh, he was in church all right, but the matter is, what time did the girl go missing?"

"What time did you find Lanny on the street?"

"Wasn't after dark like they said. He said he saw the Boltons' foster go in the car. You can't see a man in a red hat when you're four years old unless it's daylight, now can you?"

According to the railway schedule Webdog e-mailed me, the through freight from Montgomery was about to reach Atlanta.

Mr. and Mrs. Bassett worked the counters in their store. Mrs. Bassett waited on a line of exhausted customers. Cyrus stood at another register selling lottery tickets while his eyes roamed the aisles. A shoplifter would have to be very quick.

Recognizing me, he waved, sold another ticket, and motioned for me to join him at the coffee urns. Cups full, we went into his corner office. The office was glass after the first four feet from the floor. A sign on the glass read: "The safe contains less than twenty dollars."

The antique blue Mosler could be seen by customers. Lanny would have been able to see Bassett open the safe and give Mr. Barnes the checks he alleged he'd taken in the church collection. I didn't think the argument was about the phantom checks, but about the Rose girls.

"Nice safe," I said.

"Eighteen-nineties. My great-grandaddy's. Always been in a grocery store."

"But not this store?"

"No. We're from Manton. Little town south of here in Meriwether County."

"Ever think of going back?"

There was something odd in the way he contemplated me. Perhaps word had gotten back to him about Web's queries to his neighbors. He said, "Eventually. When we retire."

He peered through the glass to watch his wife ring up little purchases for the line of people taking a break from disaster, and I cocked my head to listen for a train. Bassett said, "The police, and the media, and all the rubberneckers from other neighborhoods are good for business. It's all over cable news." He waved toward a corner of his office where people on the small screen mouthed inaudible reports. Next to the TV sat a personal computer, with a printer, scanner, and a few other attachments I couldn't identify. He continued, "The cable news folks were here, getting food and Cokes, asking questions I wish I had the answers to." He put his thumbs in his suspenders. "See the two women, just came in?" He motioned with his head.

The big brassy blonde went to a soft drink case. I'd seen her before in media bars. The slim redhead went for a bag of popcorn. I'd never seen her before. The two stepped to the cashier line, where colleagues let them go to the front.

Bassett said, "The blonde's a field producer. Runs the show, she said. The little redhead is a reporter. She was here earlier, asking a lot of questions about you and the lieutenant."

Oh? "Like what?"

"Where you were. What questions you asked me. Wha'd the police ask. Buncha stuff."

"And what did you tell her?"

"Nothing. Lieutenant asked me not to tell, so I didn't."

"Good." The blonde opened the door, and the redhead went outside first. "Excuse me a minute," I said and hurried out of the office. I cut through the line and dashed out the door. The newswomen walked casually up the street. As I closed in, I said, "Pardon me." They turned. The blonde smiled. The redhead's blue eyes were like marbles. "I'm Moriah Dru. I heard you were looking for me."

The blonde stuck out her hand. "We've met, Miss Dru. Jan Morrison, remember? Producer for cable news?" We shook. She turned to her colleague. "This is Jennifer Dawson."

I waited for Dawson to speak. She smiled with her lips closed.

"Miss Dawson," I said, "are you new? I don't recognize you."

"Ummm-hmmmm."

The producer said, "Jennifer's our new police reporter. Jen, get Miss Dru here for an interview. She hangs out with Ricky Lake."

Jennifer looked at her producer, and mouthed, "You ask."

I said, "Jennifer, where are you from?"

"Denver." Her voice sounded whiny.

"Work for a network there?"

She shook her head no. "Local."

"You've taken a step up in your career." Her chin jutted, the pert nose went up, and she sucked in her breath. I said, "Welcome to Atlanta. Were you at the press conference earlier?"

She bobbed her head yes and turned to walk away.

I got beside her. "Are you the one who asked where I was, and if I was working with the APD?"

Her mouth parted like she wanted to speak, then she clamped it shut.

"Jen?" the producer said, looking perplexed. "You need to get an interview."

Jen looked at me. "So, what if I did?"

The producer looked startled, and no wonder. Jennifer had pitched her voice higher than its timbre allowed.

Morrison asked me, "You going to give us an interview?"

"No, just wanted to listen to what you had to say."

With that I made an about-face and hurried back inside Bassett's store.

Bassett was still in his office. Before we could thread a conversation, I heard the chug-rumble of a distant train and a bell clanging wildly at the crossing. Seconds later, the train thundered past, its horn an earsplitting cry. The building shook as if a low-grade earthquake was stirring the mud below the cement. "Engineer Number Six," I shouted. "His horn sounds like a cat with a bad hangover."

Bassett laughed. After the train rumbled on down the line, he asked, "How'd you get to know air horns?"

"I hang out on Castleberry Hill."

"That horn's a Leslie S-5T, tuned to B Major 9th. Older horn."

"It's a yowler."

Oh boy did I have his interest. He went into rhapsodies. "The differing sounds come from different horns with different chords. Another old horn CSX and Norfolk Southern uses is the Leslie S-3K. The 3 means the horn has three bells. It's throatier than the S-5T. The most popular horn is the K-3LA with three chords: B D# A. And its five-chime counterpart the K-5LA."

What in heck was he going on about? But I listened to the man who knew railroads, and horns, and other things of interest.

He continued, "Also the individual horns get fouled and will clog a horn chord. Sometimes engineers are known for their missing chords."

"So that's why some horns lament, and some howl, and some chortle."

"Chortle?" Bassett beamed with delight.

"Those are the short toots. Toot-toot-toot—toot-toot-toot."

"When you hear three short toots, the train's backing up. Engineers are supposed to blast and toot in regulation train talk. For instance, when our hotshot just came through the yard, he blasted his way in—a single long blast, like is called for in the regs. Now further down the track, when he comes to a grade crossing, which is a road going across the track, he goes blast, blast, toot, blast."

"I recognize the blast, blast, toot, blast. But some engineers blast longer and some toot more than once."

"Sure, they have individual styles, but not like the days of the steam whistle when the engineers could play songs to their lady love as they rolled by."

"I don't understand how the engineers get away with roaring through an urban area."

"Tch. They sure do. Once every five years a yard spokesman comes to neighborhood meetings to take complaints. They promise, but nothing changes."

"Where do the trains branch off from the Cabbagetown switching yard?"

"Different places. Coming east, they go to Savannah and on down to Florida and up to D.C. The other way—west—they go to Alabama and Tennessee, down to New Orleans."

"As you can tell, I love trains. I believe I was a hobo in my last life."

"You'd remember in this life. It's a hard one, believe me. Times have changed for them."

"Not many left, I guess."

"More'n you might think. Different class of hobo today, though."

"You get them here?"

"They sleep under the viaduct waiting for a hop."

"You know any?"

"A few regulars come in for the train schedules I print from the Internet. I give free coffee and a cigarette. It's a neighborhood tradition. Give the tramp a drink and a sandwich to hoe your garden. But some today—I wouldn't turn my back on them."

"Illegals?"

His jaw clamped. "I don't know of any illegals."

"Someone told me the illegal problem is growing on the railroads."

"I never heard of anything." He was clearly lying.

"It's a good way to transport stolen goods."

He shook his head negatively. "I don't know I credit that." I gave him a moment while I stared at him with my mouth twitching. He drew his hands apart. "The cars today, you know, they make them hobo-proof as much as they can. Before you jump on, you know, you better know what you're doing. In those piggybacks and grainers, the load shifts and you got a ton of junk on you. Don't even know you're in there sometimes until they off-load. Whew!"

"Hoboes should stick to boxcars."

"Boxcars are used mostly for short lines."

"Short lines?"

"Longer than locals, but shorter than going to, say, New Orleans. They'd go to Athens or down to Waycross."

"So if you want a safe ride to Waycross, you'd hang out until a boxcar is going to be coupled onto the train bound for Waycross?"

From his expression, he expected a trap. Wish I had one. Then the Mozart concerto played from my backpack, and he noticeably relaxed. Talk about saved by the cell. I excused myself and left the store, saying hello to Lake, and thought of the little redhead who'd pitched her voice so high it shocked her producer.

TWENTY-THREE

"I'm at City East," Lake said. "The GBI called when they brought in Miguel Lopez."

"Where'd they find him?" I asked, striding down the street with the cell plugged into my ear.

"At his mother's house."

"Doesn't sound like he was hiding. Is he talking?"

"Not much, but he will."

"You sound sure."

"Let's say Mama Lopez must have had a passel of enemies. She had a shotgun, two high-powered rifles, three forty-fives, and a twenty-five automatic."

"Ah, so."

"Parole violations galore."

"What's Lopez saying?"

"Says he hasn't been in contact with Timothy Rose and never saw Judd since he's been out. He doesn't know anything about slave rings. He doesn't know what a Rook is, or a Knight. He was good with the phrase *no entiendo.*"

"He want his lawyer?"

"Not yet. I think he's thinking about a deal."

"Find anything besides porn and photos of the Rose girls in Judd's house?"

"Old dead tokes and Dead Head records. Judd is interested in trains, too. He's got books and stuff with Cyrus Bassett's name stamped on them."

After a short goodbye, with no sweet tags at the end of it, I hiked down to the viaduct where Lanny was hit. The two-lane tunnel was short. On entering, I could see the end of it. The dim light cast shadows that gave me the willies. There were no pedestrians or street people loitering, but a few cars drove through as I made my way up a sidewalk that split the lanes. I roamed between the colorful columns painted by children. Adult graffiti writers had left the kids' art unscribbled upon, but along the concrete walls people advertised themselves with a variety of paints and markers. Most of it was gang insignia, but a couple were by lovers who'd painted their initials inside hearts.

A doggerel, painted in black, stood out.

Georgia Peach was here and near.
Georgia Peach be goin the beech.
Georgia Peach be out of reech.

A hobo?

Then there was an ominous doodle done in red spray paint.

Wach out for Senor Shiv. He be a hotshot rider.

A Hispanic man with a knife. Could he be the man who'd run Lanny out of the yard a couple of days ago?

I went back to my car, which was parked on Cotton Street, made sure it was locked, and walked the short way to the mill apartments where Conrad Hugle lived. To no one's surprise, he'd been a no-show for the joint news conference, clearly dodging questions about a connection between Cabbagetown's previous disappearances and the Rose girls.

In the lobby, a cop I knew chatted with the concierge. He told me he was keeping an eye out for Conrad, who lived on the fourth floor. The cop said Conrad wasn't opening the door for anyone, but I went upstairs anyway. I rapped my knuckles and pressed my thumb on the bell button. I called to him. "It's me, Moriah Dru." Minutes went by, no answer.

I walked back out into the drizzle—cheerless, and aware of something preternaturally dreadful just around the corner.

Inside the Union Mission, Billy played gin rummy with three down-and-outers who sat on the floor, at eye level with him. He smiled big at seeing me, and a rush of fondness spread like connecting dots through my soft spots.

"Where's Moses?" I asked.

"In the hospital," he said, blinking up at me. "He's bad."

He laid down gin, wrote numbers on a pad, and wheeled his platform away. I followed him to a corner where folding metal chairs rested against a wall. I took a nearby plastic footstool and sat almost level with him. His eyes probed my face. "I recognize you're a kind lady, but you didn't come to ask about Moses."

"You're right. I'm still trying to find the two little girls. After I do, I'll come solely to see how Moses is."

He bobbed his head and smiled. "You got more questions about what I saw?"

"I do."

"I thought more on the van. But I can't think of anything I haven't told you."

"We know who owns the van," I said. "An architect named Stephen Doonan. He renovates houses in the old historic neighborhoods."

"Ah . . ."

"You know him?"

"Not by name. Blond thin fellow. Runs."

"That's him."

"He in trouble?"

"He interests me because he lived next door to the little girls. But how he fits in, I don't know. Ever speak to him?"

"To say thank you and God bless. He gives Moses and me a five dollar bill every now and again when he passes on our side. He gave Moses a coat last fall."

No use fishing in that empty hole. "I'd like to ask you about hoboes and trains."

The unexpected question made him smile. "I'll tell you what I know."

"How many hotshots go through the Cabbagetown train yard in a day?"

"Four, five roar through. They're the mail and passenger priorities."

"What about trains that aren't priority?"

"They're freights. Most times, they stop and back up and go onto different tracks to swap out."

"Taking on other cars?"

"They make a racket when they do."

"Do they couple and uncouple the cars at night?"

"Yard's quiet after dark, usually."

"Trains keep to schedule?"

"You never know about train schedules. Only thing you can count on are the hotshots going through at about the same time, otherwise—"

"So there isn't a particular time that a freight train comes in, takes on more cars, and then leaves?"

"Yes and no. See, what I'm saying is that trains have a mind of their own. 'Course you know they're at the mercy of the tracks."

That phrase rang a bell, or more appropriately, a horn. "What goes on in the Cabbagetown yard on Friday nights, or in the early hours of Saturday morning?"

He looked canny. "You mean like last night?"

"Yeah, but I'm looking for a routine. Something you can count on every Friday night, say, past midnight."

He thought a second or two. "A slow one going east comes along and stops. It gets shunted onto another track because the mail going west is due."

"What time?"

"Three, about."

"Think back to last night. Was the usual routine happening at the yard?"

He paused for several more seconds. "Can't say's it did. The storm kept me awake. Tried to keep Moses from getting soaked.

I never saw the slow freight come into the yard. Come to think of it, no mail train went through, either."

"Now let's talk about hoboes."

Grinning, he said, "Got more in common with hoboes than trains."

"You know a Georgia Peach?"

His smile was beatific. The man was clearly bound for angelhood. "Georgia Peach. My gosh. Where'd you hear about him?" His eyes shifted into worry. "He's not in trouble, is he?"

"I came across his name on the Krog Tunnel wall. It was a bit of rhyme—by him, I presume."

"Peach is a poet. The newspaper printed some poetry he wrote. Simple stuff, but he was real proud. Kept the article in his bindle. Then some jackass went and stole it."

"Have you seen him lately?"

"He's retired."

"Retired?"

"Not for long, probably. He gets wander in his soul like all of them. Him and Moses were friends going way back. Last time Peach came, he told Moses he'd got some poetry published and he was retiring to Florida. He even got himself a Web site."

More for the Webdog. "Did Peach ever say anything about smuggling on the trains?"

"It went on all the time."

"Drugs?"

"You name it. Every kind of contraband, guns, drugs, people from across the border. Peach tells of once in Texas, he was in this switching yard and a dog comes with the Border Patrol. They're looking for Mexicans. The dog goes nuts and they check out the boxcar. Nothing. But the dog keeps carrying on, and then they notice the car's insides are not as long as the outside. What the smugglers had done is welded a metal piece across the front and back of the car and hid their stash of pot inside—and two Mexican illegals."

"I'd think the new sides would be obvious."

"Naw, beat them to look old."

"What can you tell me about a hobo named Senor Shiv?"

"What were we talking about?"

"Smuggling. Drugs and people."

"Stay away from him. If I knew where to find him, I wouldn't tell you."

"At least tell me about him."

"His name tells you all you need to know."

TWENTY-FOUR

Lake and I were to meet at the train yard parking lot. Not seeing Lake's car, I drove to the firehouse. I had a few questions for
Captain Turquin. Despite having a horrific start to their day, the
men in the firehouse were in a festive mood. Perhaps that's
what happens when you're accustomed to death and disaster. A
few balloons floated against the ceiling, and a young fireman
came into the small waiting room eating a cupcake. He told me
Captain Turquin wasn't in the house. "He's out with the chief
about the fire this morning."

He offered to get me a Coke and returned with a half dozen
chocolate chip cookies, too. The sugar surge felt good. Thanking him, I left munching and drove to the train yard. Lake still
wasn't there.

I called Webdog. "What's the word?"

"The blogs are crowded with speculation the little girls are
bound for Costa Rica . . . going to slavers operating out of there."

"Horrid blogs," I said, swallowing Coke and biting a cookie.

"Hey, that's my communication network."

"That, and your hacking software."

"Our bad guy reads the blogs, bet on it. He's never far from his laptop."

"I don't like the Knight knowing we've figured out what he's up to."

"Inevitable."

"Were you able to Enigma your way into our bad guy's e-mails?"

"It took a while since e-mails don't sequence, and senders change IP addresses and do some rudimentary IP spoofing."

"Web, cut to the chase."

"Unless we're on to the wrong bad guys, I've gotten hold of two e-mails that look like they're between our Knight and Bishop. Here's the first e-mail decrypted: *The pieces were checked. We began the match anew, but heat is stepping up. Haste.*

"Haste?" I said, licking chocolate from a finger. "A signature, or a command to hurry up?"

"Hurry. They're not signing off with sigs."

"Any clue when the new match is on?"

"None."

"Same match, you think?"

"Like chess, you start from the same squares."

"It wouldn't be at the same time, or station."

"Maybe black becomes white."

"The Knight becomes a Rook?"

"To be virtual is to morph."

"Let's stay in the real world."

"Gotcha. Here's the other e-mail: *Omni to POD. V119. 10 miles north of county. NDB. Fix position.*"

"I thought you said it was decrypted."

His chuckle echoed in my ear. "It's simple to figure."

"Explaina me, Webby."

"To anyone in Atlanta, the Omni was the name of the building before it became the CNN Center. I reckon POD means point of departure. V119 is an airplane airway designation—low altitude. NDB means nondirectional beacon. It's a low-power radio transmitter that broadcasts its call sign in Morse code. They emit their call signs at fixed intervals. Although they're called nondirectional, their signals can be picked up from all directions by pilots or anyone listening to their shortwave. Fix position means a pilot should triangulate his point in the sky with the beacon in order to land. NDBs are an old-fashioned way of homing on to airports with no instrument approaches. Definitely not your modern GPS station."

"I see. These are stations? Not radios?"

"Some transmitters are portable. But the more sophisticated the antennae, the less interference. These NDBs can be hazardous if pilots depend solely on them, especially in bad weather."

"A private airstrip would have a stationary radio antenna, wouldn't it?"

"Most do. So do lots of things that use beacons, like lighthouses and oil platforms."

"So what does ten miles north of county mean?"

"Probably county refers to the county airport."

"Which county?"

"I don't have all the answers."

"And what do I pay you those big bucks for?"

"Mea culpa. I'll forgo a month's salary and eat steak instead of lobster."

"Where were the e-mails coming from, can you tell?"

"I have to get through the spoofing."

"Get spoofing, then. Oh, and get me a railroad schedule. Bassett says he gets the schedules off the Internet."

"I can do better than schedules."

"Thought so."

"I can gather all you'll ever want to know, or need to know—whether the trains are mail, freight, passenger, short line, local, and how they link up with other types of transportation, like the ports of Savannah or New Orleans—anything."

"Airports?"

"On the maps are plane logos where the airports are located. But that wouldn't include the small private strips."

"E-mail all, and get a list of all the private airstrips in the Georgia counties along the tracks. I think your decoded e-mail refers to a county east of Atlanta. That's where the Rooks were headed last night before the storm messed up their plans."

"Will do."

"And Web, a hobo named Georgia Peach has a Web site. Find it for me. Probably has links. Check it out, will you? See if he has an e-mail address."

Web laughed. "A hobo with a Web site. I like it."

"Keep on hacking, Web."

Pressing END, I dreaded the day I would lose Webdog. When he graduates college, he'll be snatched up by some confidential agency or major corporation to work in its deep underground, cracking codes and dreaming up platforms for national security or beating up on the competition.

————

Lake knocked on the Bentley's glass, which was wet with mist. I hadn't seen him pull into the train yard. He had on his raincoat, which made him look rather Dick Tracyish. Instantly, I pictured the small redhead at his side and felt my core temperature rise.

He held up a videotape as I got out. "From the choppers this morning," he said. "I haven't reviewed it yet. It came as I was leaving. We'll cadge a VCR from someone." He threw it onto the back seat, and then he looked at me with questions in his eyes—perhaps because I had questions in mine, I don't know.

While we crossed the switching yard toward the yardmaster's tower, I briefed Lake on what I'd learned since we'd last talked, including my interview of Tom Davis. In turn, he radioed those facts to the task force headquarters.

"They must be wondering where you're getting all this information," I said.

"They know you're going in a different direction than they are, but they'll follow up. I imagine someone from the GBI's on the way to talk to Billy right now."

"What's the FBI/GBI/APD focus now?"

"The gang of three: Lopez, Judd, and Timothy Rose."

"Waste of time."

"It's one of many avenues. The boys are also storming the massage parlors and taking hookers off the street. Anyone in the sex trade is busy answering questions. Other snitches have added information on the Latinos. We got a million sightings of dark cars. Dark men with light children are being stopped across the state. Two at one rest stop in Chattanooga."

"The Rooks and the girls are under our noses, Lake."

He looked like he believed me. When we were partners on the beat, we didn't have the same gut feelings. We were joined at the heart, but not necessarily at the brain. I said, "I see the shrewdness in moving the girls across the state in a boxcar. No witnesses, and the riders who do see something unusual don't talk to cops."

The afternoon sky threatened to turn the mist into real rain. I could go back to Davis and hug him for the Rain Shadow. The yardmaster invited us into his large, windowed office overlooking the train yard. The circular area looked like a war room. The maps, the rail lines, and terminology were fascinating. A 3-D moon phase calendar hung from a hook in the ceiling. Last night's moon was a new moon. No illumination whatsoever.

Lake asked the yardmaster, "Last night, between midnight and dawn this morning, did you keep to schedule?"

"Like I told you this morning, I come on at eight. I found out why the trains were held up. The wind blew a roof off a house in Stone Mountain, landed on the tracks. I finally got back on sked." Hee-hee.

"What do you do when tracks are obstructed?"

"We reroute the high-ballers, but the regular mixed freight stays put until the tracks get cleared and fixed. The mail got through, you can bet on it." Hee-hee.

I asked, "So the slow freight train that pulled into the station about three o'clock last night didn't leave?"

"Never got to the station. Stayed at Marietta where they got the word about the roof."

We thanked him and left. I was treading on white clouds. There's no feeling like following a hunch that's paying off . . . until at the end, when it doesn't. "Did you see the lunar mobile?" I asked as we trekked the tracks to our cars.

"Is that what fascinated you so much?"

"Yep. Women are at the mercy of the moon."

"Is this where I say something about lunatics?"

I quoted: *"The lunatic, the lover and the poet are of imagination all compact.* Shakespeare."

"We're all nuts, in other words."

"Anyway, there was no moon last night, or light from it. The Knight planned the abduction on the darkest night in the month, and the cloud cover was a bonus, except it brought wind and rain. That was the first unexpected screwup."

"Mother Nature abhors a monster."

"The Knight arrives at the Barnes house. He gets in and grabs the girls. But he can't set the house on fire because the storm will blow it out. After the snatch, at about two-thirty, he takes the girls to the cemetery and passes them to the Rooks, who get access to the tracks by way of the Oakland Avenue gate. You said your men found evidence of lock tampering."

"True. And then?"

"The Rooks take the girls to the boxcar to wait until the slow freight arrives. The Knight hangs out until the rain stops, then he blows up the house using a cell phone as a remote control, or maybe a radio transmitter. Getting back to the Rooks in the boxcar, no slow freight arrives, and it's getting on for daybreak. They had cell phones to keep in touch with the Knight. Before dawn, Plan B kicks in. They take the girls off the boxcar and meet up with the van driven by the Knight. As Web forecasted, the Knight morphed into a Rook."

"Huh?"

"You got to speak Web's language."

"I'd have to have his mind first. Why didn't the Knight pick up the Rooks and the girls inside Krog Tunnel?"

"My guess is there were hoboes and homeless in there. As I've found out, simply because they're homeless doesn't mean they don't see things."

"The Knight was scrambling," he said. "He stole a van on Ponce, which coincidentally belonged to Stephen Doonan."

"You no more believe in coincidences than I," I said. "It was stolen purposely. If it was spotted it would lead to Stephen, or to his workers who usually drive it. When the Knight got the call that the train never got to the yard, he knew where to find Doonan's van."

"If all fails, he wants us to believe this is a routine kidnapping and Doonan or his workers are the suspects."

"And it gives the Knight some wiggle room if we homed in on them. To say nothing of homing in on your jailed trio: Lopez, Judd, and Rose."

"There may still be a connection."

One thing about Lake, he liked to keep the scenario broad. I liked to winnow out the highly unlikely, cut the unlikely, and fasten on to the likely. When we reached our cars, I leaned on mine and folded my arms across my chest. "Is Doonan in or out as a suspect?"

"He's definitely in," he said, his hands on his hips. "Triple cross. The poisoner poisons himself and then shoots himself for good measure." I grinned, and he continued, "Then there's Bassett. Remember, you told me the witness Davis thought the driver could be Bassett?"

"Davis wasn't certain. He had doubts about the beard, but then he'd been drinking heavily."

"Just our luck, the best witness is nine-eyed-goat drunk."

"On the other hand, Bassett knows everything you ever

wanted to know about trains, their horns, their hobo-proof cars, their time schedules, where they're bound for."

"Plus," Lake said, "don't forget, Bassett is also Santa."

Santa.

He haunts me. He sits on the edge of my mind. But he's not jolly old St. Nick. Our Santa's a peddler of children. Who is he? He eludes me—for now.

Lake said, "And then there's Hugle."

Hugle's smug face floated into my head, and I got the damp dreads again. "I think he's immoral. But I can't see him snatching children from the streets or from their beds in the middle of the night."

"Men are good at keeping their quirks secret. How many times have we busted upstanding men in sin dens with garter belts and bras on?"

"Sorry, partner, but I see Conrad in a garter belt before I see him scurrying in the middle of the night when plans start going wrong."

"Have you thought maybe there's two Knights, a planner and an operational guy? Say Doonan and someone we don't know?"

"Possible, yes, but this has the earmark of one extremely ego-puffed maniac."

"How many ego-puffed maniacs have you come across in your life?"

I thought of Deep Voice, the redhead, but now was not the time . . . "Too many."

Lake looked away as though he knew my words were double-edged and personal.

TWENTY-FIVE

I was to follow Lake under the viaduct to Cabbagetown to dredge for more evidence. I'd just cranked my car when Lake's horn blew. There was urgency in the blast. I jerked my head. He was waving for me. I turned the ignition off and pulled the door handle. He flung the squad car's passenger door open. I jumped in. "What is it?"

He pressed the gas. The wheels spewed gravel. The siren screamed. I looked at the computer display screen. It told me what the rush was about. My breathing amped up. "VAN 582. Stephen's van. Stephen's Victorian."

"I never bet against you, haven't I said that before?" He drove the maze of Inman Park streets like a sixteen-year-old with a new driver's license. He angled his head toward me. "Since they've abandoned the van, they're going to need another set of wheels. Ask Dispatch for a listing of all cars stolen in the area after midnight."

I swung the computer screen toward me and typed, trying to keep steady in the rocking and rolling cruiser. When Lake braked at a curb in front of a large house, I massaged my neck muscles, hoping they wouldn't ache in the morning.

I love and hate Victorian architecture. A pretty gingerbread house with roses and sunflowers in bloom has its allure. Our objective was a brooding eyesore. Two squad cars pulled behind us and discharged our new partners, Buddy and Jed. Buddy's handler said, "Saw the call go out. Figured you'd need some help here."

Lake looked at the dogs. "Steak dinners for the elite among us."

Detective Howard walked up to Lake. "Right before dawn, neighbor across the street, walking her dog, saw the van drive by and circle the block. She went inside her house but saw the van pull into the driveway. Right after that, she saw a kid in the yard, and two Latinos. She said Latinos are working on the house, and she knows Stephen Doonan and his van, although not its tag number. But when she heard the latest Amber, she remembered the kid and called."

Some forty feet behind the house, a shed sagged and leaned into a couple of oaks. Its wide door was open revealing the gray van with the right tag number. The dogs sniffed at bicycle helmets and got interested in the van. Jed, the Lab tracker, stuck his nose to the ground and circled it. Buddy, the air-scent, lifted his nose and pranced away from the shed, toward bushes bordering the property. His handler called for him to halt. Air-scents know no boundaries and neighbors aren't thrilled when big dogs burst into their yards.

Lake put on gloves and booties and stepped up through the van's back door. I headed for the back of the house. Stephen Doonan looked like a statue standing on the brick patio, facing away, as if contemplating the overgrown thicket at the back edge of the lot.

"Mr. Doonan?"

He half turned and looked over his shoulder. Had he been crying or smoking dope?

"Is this the house you own?" I asked.

His nod indicated yes. "You were right," he said. "Something worse is happening. It gets worse every minute. I'm ruined."

"Not if we get those girls back."

"What makes you think you'll get them back alive?"

"I know I'll get them back alive."

"If you don't, I might as well check into the jail."

I sympathized. If the children weren't found and the case solved, he'd always be suspected.

He looked toward the shed. "I didn't touch the girls. I don't do those things. I'm not like that."

"I don't believe you're a pedophile, Mr. Doonan. But there are other reasons to abduct children."

"Ransom, you mean?"

"Or selling to the sex trade."

"God. You think I could do that?"

Lake and the two detectives came onto the patio. Lake told Doonan to wait where he was. Doonan flung himself in a rusty metal lawn chair, and Lake led the way into the back hall of the house. In the old days, the occupants would have used it to keep milk and eggs in the wintertime. In the kitchen, remodeling was underway. New cabinets were hung, but they hadn't been painted or stained. Granite countertops were in place. Doonan had kept the original brick floor. Across the room, a bay window overlooked the garden outside. I could see Doonan sulking in the chair. On the brick floor, underneath the window, lay a blanket. It had been spread out as if for a picnic. Two empty half-pint milk cartons lay on it as well as a box of Krispy Kreme donuts. One donut was left.

"Looks like the girls had breakfast," Lake said.

Detectives used prongs to lift the cartons and put them into evidence bags.

I said, "The Rooks didn't bother to hide the fact they were here."

"They expect to keep a jump or two ahead of us."

"Serving up Doonan as prime suspect," I said.

Lake bent and tweezed a cigarette butt off the floor. He held it up. "Might be a perp's, or a workman's."

"Doonan doesn't smoke."

Lake shook his head. I guess he was resigned to my defending Doonan. The irony of it was I didn't know why I felt compelled to.

"Anything interesting in the van?" I asked.

I heard a dog bark in the distance. Buddy with his nose in the air?

Lake answered my question. "Half the van's full of paint cans, carpenter's tools, that kind of stuff. But there were some blond hairs on the rug. The children had been lying down. I didn't see any signs of blood, or bodily fluids. Looks like the van picked the girls and the Rooks up in front of Davis's house, drove the few blocks, and parked in the shed." He gestured toward the window. "They came in here with a bag of food and sat down to eat."

"They probably had it with them to eat on the train before their plans changed."

"They never planned to be in this house, but they came here—to Doonan's house."

"Besides you," I asked, "who hates Doonan that much?"

"I have a completely open mind," Lake said—touchily so, I thought. "So, if he's being served up to us, the real question is who *knows* Doonan that much?"

Buddy's handler came in looking excited. "Buddy's alerted."

We took off down the steps and across the yard to where a gate hung on a broken hinge. On the other side of it, a path led through overgrown wisteria. I heard something behind me and looked back to see Jed tracking toward us.

Ahead, Buddy was on his haunches about two yards from the gate. When I got nearer, I saw the black poncho. The sight curled my intestines. The small stiff poncho lay on soggy green grass. I rubbed my midsection.

Lake took my arm. "You okay?"

"No."

"It's all right."

"No it's not."

"Don't give up."

Was reality catching up with me? The assuring words I said to Doonan about finding the girls alive were doing na-na-na-na-nanas in my head.

Suddenly, Jed flashed past and plunged into the shrubbery. I held my breath while the dog rustled through the tangle of shrubs. No one moved. And then I recalled Doonan had been staring toward this spot when I found him on the patio. I turned to see him watching us, looking pale and spellbound.

Jed jumped out of the bushes and went to his handler, his tail between his legs.

The handler shook his head. "Nothing in there."

I could breathe again.

Lake asked the handler. "What made him go in the bushes?"

"At the end of a track, Jed'll sometimes go ahead, see if the scent was interrupted by a cross track, maybe a raccoon or cat. He didn't get anything in there, so I believe this is where she last stopped."

The other handler said, "Appears she left her coat here and went back the way she came."

"Not of her own accord," Lake said. "She ran away from her abductor. That's when the neighbor lady saw her. The kidnapper caught up with her, grabbed her by the coat, and it came off. He took her back inside, overlooking the coat. Hopefully we can lift some prints. Everybody step easy. Look before you put a foot down."

The dogs backed away and played with their handlers. Detectives Howard and Allen searched the bushes and Lake and I stepped lightly, searching the ground. The grass was sparse. There were scrapes in the soft muddy patches, as if someone was dragged backward. I kept the sick feeling at bay by thanking God there wasn't any blood.

Lake's radio crackled. I straightened to listen. He said, "On Elizabeth. Got it. Put it with the Amber. Out." He clicked off, and turned to me. "Car reported stolen a couple blocks from here. A silver, late-model Camry. They took the tag off and threw it in the street."

Jed's handler walked up and listened, Jed by his side.

"Why throw a tag in the street?" I asked Lake.

"Why are crooks idiots?"

"It wasn't the Knight," I said. "It was one of the Rooks."

"Which means?"

"The Knight's not with them any longer. He left them here . . . he had business elsewhere. How many silver Camrys in this city?"

Lake's lip curled. "Two hundred in Inman Park alone."

Jed's handler said, "I got an idea. Let me take Jed to the tag. Give him a sniff. Maybe he can pick up the bad guy's scent. He caught it in the van. These dogs don't want to quit till they find who they're after."

"Do it," Lake said. To the other handler, he asked, "Take Buddy to the van, get him a good whiff of the driver's area, and bring him inside the house."

"Will do. Can't promise anything. There'll be a lot of scents, different drivers."

"Worth a try," Lake said.

A forensic team wearing overalls arrived. Uniformed officers ringed the area with yellow tape.

Things were happening too fast. I looked at Lake. "We're squeezing them. They got a call from the Knight to move out of here. They're stealing cars on the fly, making mistakes. They're going to do something stupid to those girls. I told you about The End Game, didn't I?"

"Don't think of it. They're still trying to get out of town."

His eyes deepened into liquid pools of compassion. "I don't think they're going to dump a million bucks until they get in a corner they can't get out of."

Lake followed the dog inside the house. I hung back with the heavy-legged feeling that accompanies not knowing which way to turn. Where are the Rooks? What is their timetable? When do they have to meet their connections? What does the Omni have to do with anything? In which county is the POD? Is Web right about the airway? How desperate are they? More than anything, I was obsessed by the impression I should know who the Knight is.

More crime scene techs streaked by, jolting me out of apprehension. They carried oversized canvas bags containing forensic tools. I went to the patio to talk to Doonan, but he was gone. Inside the house, I heard action on the second floor and climbed the steps. I followed the CSIs, having quick looks in rooms going off the hall. In an empty room at the front of the house, I glanced out a window and saw the news van. TV was here. I heard dog whines. Buddy alerting.

Lake yelled, "Everybody get back."

I nearly turned my ankle racing to where men crowded around a door. I squeezed past them and walked into a long, narrow room. It had no basin, tub, nor toilet—simply a hole in the floor where the toilet would stand.

The user had been careful not to drip urine on the floor, or if he had, he'd cleaned it up, but Buddy smelled it in the hole. His tail beat like a metronome.

"The driver of the van," Lake said.

I was happy for Buddy's victory, but my heart was a piece of lead struggling to beat. By the time DNA identified the Knight—if it was the Knight's DNA—the girls would be out of reach. Out of this world. Gone for good. The End Game, either way.

"Dru?"

Lake had shaken me back to the moment.

"You okay?" he asked.

"Sure."

"Yes, it will take hours to get a profile, but in the meantime, we're closing in."

I chewed on my lower lip—hope swirling, draining, like water in a bathtub. His arm circled my waist, and he whispered close to my ear, "What did you do with my never-say-die partner?"

He had a special knack of snapping me back to business. I poked him gently in the ribs with an elbow. "I'm going to let her back out."

My cell played Mozart. Webdog.

I walked out of the bathroom. "Yeah, Web."

"Your hobo? The Georgia Peach with the Web site?"

"Yes?"

"I got an e-mail from him. Look at his site. He wants you to contact him."

"Will do."

"Also, I e-mailed the railway maps and the private airstrip info."

"A million thanks."

"My pleasure."

I felt irrationally giddy as I ran to an adjoining room. A piece of plywood was stretched over two saw horses. Setting aside an electric saw, I fished the mini-PC out of my backpack. It's about the size of a trade paperback and weighs about a pound. The display is small, the keyboard smaller—the numbers and letters are sized to hunt and peck. Having fingernails helps. The wireless network is supposed to connect from any location. Maybe the reason it doesn't always is because it belongs to a techno-dolt.

But today, in the heart of the big city, I got lucky.

TWENTY-SIX

I wasn't prepared to appreciate Georgia Peach's Web site. His introduction goes on about the hobo's place in America—a rosy-eyed view of the hobo as a true American adventurer. I wondered who his editor was on the sophisticated intro, because his poetry was of the cornpone variety.

> *Regular frieght comes round the bend*
> *The engine whistle calls*
> *Nearer she slows and rattles her end*
> *I beat her before she stalls*

Most of his pages are blogs, and it appears he chronicles each day.

The first piece began:

Why I became a hobo.

My first job was at McDonald's. I needed spending money.

The first minute of the first day, I knew working wasn't for me . . . I was desperate to be free . . . As Jack Kerouac said, "The problem with work is you're doing someone else's."

Slingin' at the diner
Gettin' sumpin' finer
Loadin' up the liner
'Bo-ing off to Chiner.

After that, I dashed off an e-mail.

Hey, Georgia Peach. I'm Moriah Dru. Webdog said I should
   contact you. I need info on a problem I have here in Atlanta.
   Are you there now? Moriah.

Minutes later his e-mail came in:

Never met a woman named Moriah. I don't know I could tame
   a Moriah. Peach.
Me: I bet you could. Cool website. Poetry's nice, graphics great.
   Where in Florida did you retire?
Peach: *Tampa.*
Me: You miss the rails?
Peach: *Like mad.*
Me: I need to pick your brain.
Peach: *It's old and wrinkled, but shoot, girl.*
Me: Who is Senor Shiv?
Peach: *You're starting at the bottom of the pit, girl. He's a killer*
   like his name says. He wears his knife so you don't mistake him
   for a Sunday school teacher.

Me: I'll try not to be fooled.

Peach: *After the 70s, which I consider the personal heyday of the modern hobo, before de-reg, and before the slicks—I don't call them spics, too un-PC—came to the South, there was a bond between everybody who rode the rails. No matter if you were black or white, you rode the train, you got everybody's respect. People like SS changed all that. They came, they had knives, they'd slit your throat for your bindle. Throw you off the train going seventy miles an hour. Old boes like me, we quit before we caught the Westbound—means died.*

Me: Was SS part of a gang like the Train Riders of America?

Peach: *He's not part of TRA, but I hear he has a gang connection of some kind. Muling, mostly.*

Me: I'm on a case involving kidnapped children. Would he mule kids?

Peach: *Is there money in it?*

Me: Lots.

Peach: *There's your answer.*

Me: I've never hopped a train. How easy is it with two small kids with you?

Peach: *You wouldn't grab a moving train, but there's always boxcars sitting open. Whole families used to, in the old days. Remember I told you it's dangerous to ride alone. Nobody does no more. But today riders band together for safety. I met a group in Nashville a few years ago. Six people—three boes, three bims, three dogs. They carried tent—three for the couples and one for the dogs. It's sure SS wouldn't get on a double stack or a grainer with two kids, but boxcars are always open. Easy to hide—easy to ride.*

Me: What if he was on a tight schedule?

Peach: *Shouldn't be trying to run away on a train.*

Me: You familiar with Atlanta's train yards?

Peach: *I used to catch the Norfolk and Southern freight to Birmingham from the Marietta Yard. You wander around for a couple of miles up and down the track. There's trains all over the place. They don't travel more than walking speed. You pick out your ride on the spur of the moment or you've got a schedule. Watch for the bulls, but they're easy to spot. You don't look too suspicious, the yard crew don't pay attention. Otherwise you hear steps on the gravel and you look up and see a bull in your face. But that won't happen to SS. Everybody knows him, everybody stays clear.*

Me: Thanks, Peach. Can we talk later?

Peach: *Anytime, Moriah. Next time I get to Atlanta, we meet girl. Deal?*

Me: Deal. Can't wait.

Peach: *I'm asking a favor in return.*

Me: Just ask.

Peach: *Let me know when Moses catches the Westbound.*

While I Web-chatted with Peach, I was aware Lake had come into the room. When I closed the e-mail window and looked up, I saw a brooding man with a clenched jaw standing in the middle of the room staring at me. His eyes were so murky, I could sink like a stone without knowing why they were scolding me. On impulse, I averted my eyes to the window. The sun lowered in the west, casting weird shadows across the walls. I jumped off the board. "What's going on?"

"I . . ." His tone made me wary. He shook his head to indicate he wasn't going to speak his thought. Instead, he said, "We may have gotten lucky. Buddy's on a scent. The Camry was parked in vomit. Apparently some drunk retched in the street and the Camry came along and parked in it. Buddy's handler said scent like that will stay on those tires for a long time."

I brushed sawdust from the seat of my slacks and packed the laptop. As I did, I reported what I'd learned from the Georgia Peach.

"Okay," Lake said, "so we assume the Shiv's got the kids."

"Dear God, hope not," I said, slipping on the backpack.

"The dogs are tracking on Decatur Street, toward downtown, away from the Cabbagetown yard."

"The Marietta yard is west of downtown. The Rooks aren't leaving from the Cabbagetown yard. They'd be stupid to."

"But they may not be leaving by train. They may be driving."

"Too dangerous with every cop and sheriff looking for them. Besides, the e-mail said the match would start anew. Same pieces, same squares. I've studied the map Web sent. There're several county airports near the railroad tracks—all the way to Savannah. There are three major switching yards and several smaller ones where the train will slow enough to get off. Web identified several private strips close to the county airports."

"So you think they're heading for the Marietta yard?" Lake said. "There are several other yards west of the city. And south. And north."

"Marietta," I said, feeling stubborn.

"I won't bet against you." Even though he looked ill at ease, he grinned, once again splitting my heart at the seams.

Lake reported in to headquarters. He told Commander Haskell the SAR dogs were tracking the suspects in the stolen Camry toward downtown. He hit the high points of my conversation with Peach. Lastly, he outlined our conclusions and asked for a stakeout at the switching yards, especially Marietta.

While Lake listened to Haskell's words, he paced. I could hear Haskell's voice and it didn't sound upbeat.

Lake spoke: "I know, but it's more than a hunch. We also need to stake out those other yards, too." He listened, his gloom deepening. "I know, I know. They're big yards. Lots of trains. Lots of empty boxcars. Lots of . . ." He sighed. "I want to give it a try, Commander."

Lake hung up and slapped his thigh in disgust. "He's not convinced. All he'll do is alert the bulls at the yards that the Rose girls could be in a boxcar. He reminded me security has tightened in the yards and airstrips since Homeland."

I thought of all the guns and knives and box cutters filling bins at airport checkpoints and didn't have a good feeling about security anywhere. "According to Peach, the bulls and yard crew know Senor Shiv, and they don't confront him."

Lake's cell rang. "Yes, Commander." Lake listened, then said, "On my way." He slipped the cell in its case on his waist. "Lopez is cracking. I'm going to the shop."

"I'll come, too. You got a VCR somewhere in the old building, don't you?"

"I requisitioned one."

"When we find Santa, you can ask him to drop one down the chimney just for you."

"Ho. Ho. Ho."

It was a less than jolly sound.

TWENTY-SEVEN

I hung the Rain Shadow on the back of a straight chair to drip-dry and settled into Lake's leather chair. It was not city issue; he'd bought it, and it smelled like him—like the smell of intelligence and kindness and loyalty. The last word came to mind unexpectedly and lingered on it for a moment.

Since the advent of DVDs, I hadn't worked a VCR, but at last I got it going. The news cameraman—or woman—in the helicopter did an excellent job of recording the disaster. But as for the people, I might as well be watching a movie with all the action filmed above the actors. Sometimes the camera caught a face, but not often.

We'd been given an edited copy. The opening scene had the house fully engulfed with jets of water snuffing the flames. The editors had snipped out the shots of the dogs working the yards. The angles of many shots made identifying people difficult because of the trees. The oak tree at the corner of the Barnes lot covered half the yard and met up with another large oak across the street at Miss Goddard's. I picked out Captain Turquin crossing the street once the fire was out. He spoke to his crew, and then he went toward Miss Goddard's cottage. He stood in the street for a moment, and then spread his hands apart as if answering an unanswerable question.

There was an obvious break in the tape.

A car with a blue light flashing from the windshield moved through the crowd. That was Lake and me arriving. The camera got a shot of Lake and the dog handlers conferring. I came into view, studying the disaster. I remembered my thoughts and the smell of gasoline. I wished I could see the look on my face. The vacant lot behind the Barnes house was obscured by trees, and the camera followed Captain Turquin until he disappeared beneath them.

Lake, Turquin, and I walked to the front of the house. The camera hovered above Miss Goddard's house, but I couldn't see her standing on her porch. A few frames later, I made out Hugle leaving his gated condo. A boy—Lanny Long—ran up to him. Hugle listened, his gestures impatient, then he shooed the kid away. The camera followed Hugle as he walked down the hill. I saw myself look at him coming toward me.

I fast-forwarded through the scenes I was in, to where a man strode from between two houses up the street from the Barnes. Doonan in his baseball cap. He ducked when he saw the detectives huddled together. Talk about furtive. The trees kept me from seeing where Doonan went.

The camera swung back to the Barnes house. Turquin talked to his men, but broke away from his crew and hurried to where Doonan had disappeared. Both men came back into view and the fire captain motioned to a man—Lake. Doonan's arms were stiff at his side and I could easily read his body language. The fire captain backed away, crossed the Barnes yard, and disappeared into the vacant lot.

The camera didn't show Lake, Portia, and me go inside Doonan's house. But at approximately the time we talked with him, Cyrus Bassett walked up Cotton Street and stopped at Miss Goddard's house. She came down the steps. He held out his arms as if to hug her, but she backed away. He continued to hold out his arms in what looked like appeal, but she shook her cane at him and climbed up her steps.

It was fascinating to see things happen I hadn't experienced.

The camera swung away to the firemen. Captain Turquin stood in the middle of the street, apparently interested in what went on between Miss Goddard and Bassett. A woman approached and talked to Turquin with some animation; then she left. The speech therapist. Throughout I saw shots of the media pack.

Fast-forwarding, I got to the ME's entrance on the scene. Authorities can screen the ugliness of death from the folks on the ground, but not from the air. The lens zoomed onto the two blackened bodies. My finger prepared to fast-forward, but revulsion kept me staring at the remains of once vibrant humans—lovely humans who wanted to adopt two little girls who, until a year ago, they hadn't known existed.

Fast-forward past more of my scenes. The camera came back to Cotton Street, catching a young boy poking along. Lanny again. Suddenly he dashed under the yellow tape. Captain Turquin waved him away. Lanny ran to the side of Miss Goddard's house and looked in a window. What a little snoop. We apparently hadn't asked him the right questions.

The camera lingered on Captain Turquin and his men as they milled uneasily, apparently waiting for something to happen. Then Turquin went to his station wagon, reached inside, and pulled out a radio or cell phone. The chopper ranged above the oaks as officials and citizens dashed under them and then back out. I couldn't tell who they were.

The next time the camera zoomed in on anything significant, Lake had begun the first press conference while I sat on Miss Goddard's steps. I could make out the red-haired CNN reporter. Afterward, Lake and I left to interview Judd. We hadn't known at the time Bassett watched us go inside Judd's house while lingering behind a line of foliage.

In the next scene, the camera focused above the Barnes house. The excitement had died down. Not much happened at the burned-out house, except I could make out two people standing in the leafy shadows of the oak. Suddenly, as if pushed, Hugle stumbled into the camera shot. He ran across the street and up Goddard's steps. The other figure stayed beneath the tree. The camera panned away, toward the Green Space, and then came back to catch Lanny running underneath the oak. At the same time, Doonan came out of his cottage.

Hugle came down the steps of Miss Goddard's cottage and circled toward her backyard. How strange. Someone, maybe the figure under the oak tree, called out to him, because he turned abruptly, retraced his steps to cross Cotton Street.

What was that all about? And who was that figure under the tree?

Rewinding and replaying didn't answer the question.

More fast-forwards and I saw myself walk across Cotton Street and up the steps of Miss Goddard's house for the third time.

Hugle, the fire captain, and a woman—the speech therapist— watched me go inside. Seconds later, I came out. I'd just found Miss Goddard dead. Captain Turquin was getting into his SUV. He paused, looked my way, closed the car door, crossed the street. Lake and Doonan met in the street and walked up. Doonan and I went to the backyard. When Turquin let me in the back door, Doonan lit out like the proverbial bat from hell. Lanny, lingering in Miss Goddard's backyard, watched Doonan, then followed him. I hadn't noticed Lanny there—maybe because I was too caught up in the azaleas and thoughts of my own mortality.

Fast-forwarding again. The camera swept across the Barnes house. The chopper was too close for what came next. I held my breath. The cameraman caught the flare streaking through the air from the back of Doonan's house. The explosion blossomed into bright yellow shooting flames which licked the side of his house and caught the window shutters on fire. The chopper leaped skyward.

No more video.

It had taken me fifteen minutes to look at the edited tape. What had they edited out? Could the missing parts prove who murdered Miss Goddard? I couldn't see any proof on this copy; however, the camera captured some interesting moves made by a couple of people, one in particular. I wasn't going to fasten my mind on the person yet. I hate to fasten a suspicion firmly in my head, because it takes a different approach to unfasten it. I pulled my mini-PC from the backpack.

Lake came into his office, smiling, upbeat. I was happy to see that his doldrums had lifted. He threw his hat on the desk. I got up from his chair and went to rewind the tape. He said, "Lopez wants to cut a deal."

"I bet."

"He admitted he and Timothy Rose communicated after he got out of prison and he's been to see Dwight Judd several times." He threw sheets of paper onto his desk and slipped off his jacket. He draped it across the back of his chair and sat. "Lopez said he supplied Judd with grass, but he swears he and Judd never discussed burning the Barneses' house down and stealing the kids. But . . ." Lake paused for effect, and I gave him an expectant glance. "He thinks he might know somebody who might know something . . ." Rearing back in his chair, he lifted his feet to his desktop and crossed them at the ankles.

"He knows the Rooks?"

"No, he knows an amigo, who knows an amigo, who knows an amigo. You get the picture. He's not about to finger anyone, but he knows what Rooks are. He calls them mules."

"So can we assume this amigo is a Rook?"

"Or an amigo of a Rook."

"My head hurts."

"Lopez says he met this amigo once shooting pool and drinking at a taquería, which happens to be the same taquería where Doogan's van was stolen from. This amigo's name is Juan—no last name. On this particular night, Juan drank too much and told of this business deal."

"A business deal, huh?" I said, pressing the STOP button on the VCR.

"Juan is a businessman himself, Lopez said. But his amigo—that's Juan's amigo—is in the export business."

"Clear as a cloudy day."

"Juan wants in on his amigo's twofer, but his amigo already has a partner, another amigo."

"Twofer?"

"An export deal worth twice its weight in dollars."

"Good ol' heavy greenbacks."

"Juan told Lopez the goods were going to the coast in two nights and if he could get himself cut in, he would get half of ten grand."

"Or all of it, if he cut his amigo's throat."

"You're mighty bloodthirsty, my love."

"Wouldn't you cut your amigo's throat for half that?"

"Anything more than ten percent, he—or she's—headless," Lake said and winked. "Anyway, the same night, this gringo comes into the taquería and signals to Juan. They leave."

"Does Lopez know the gringo?"

"Nope. The gringo stayed at the door, in shadows, and had on a droopy hat. He was a large man, looking very angry. Lopez didn't recognize the photos of our favorite persons of interest. I sent a man to the taquería. Maybe the owner or waiters can identify him, or give a better description."

"Did Lopez admit to knowing Senor Shiv?"

"Nope. He said, 'I don't want to know nobody with a shiv in his name.'"

"Did Juan have a knife, did Lopez say?"

"Didn't see one. But he says Juan was good at hopping trains."

"What do you think?"

"Juan could be our Senor Shiv—or Lopez is full of it."

"Want to see the tape?" I asked.

"Anything useful?" he asked, checking his watch.

I lifted a shoulder slightly. "See for yourself."

His feet came off the desk, he sat forward, and his hands folded expectantly. "Does it show Hugle coming out of Miss Goddard's cottage with gloves on his hands?"

"No."

"Bassett dressed in a Santa suit?"

"No."

"Doonan throwing a bomb?"

I laughed.

"So?"

I pressed PLAY. "Take a look."

TWENTY-EIGHT

I rewound and fast-forwarded until I thought the tape would break. Lake sat back, his eyes contemplative. "It might be. Thin, though."

"Just an idea."

The phone on his desk rang. He snatched the receiver. "Yeah." He stood abruptly. "Okay. Yeah. On Fairlie, back of the newspaper building. Gotcha."

He cradled the receiver and grabbed his jacket. I reached for the Rain Shadow. "Let's go. They found the Camry. The dogs tracked it to the parking lot behind the newspaper building."

My heart felt like it would leap out of my chest. "That's back by the railroad tracks!"

"Bingo, love," he said, slapping the panama on his head. "The very tracks that leave the Marietta yard a mile to the west. I love it when you're right."

First though, we had a videotape to deliver to the brass.

I paced the lobby of the top floor of City Hall East. When Lake came out, I asked, "What'd they say?"

"Haskell was playing it before I closed the door. He'll get an officer on it. He reminded me again of how thin we're stretched, even with the agents. It ought to be a felony for people to report false information."

As the elevator doors opened, I asked, "But they believe it's possible?"

"I don't know about that," Lake said, pushing the button for the basement. "But with you in the investigation, as an independent voice to be reckoned with, they have to look into it."

"Cornpone-batter-for-brains."

"Darlin', they're politicians. God knows what they're saying in there now, but I shocked the shit out of them."

"Nothing should shock them anymore. When they find out you're right, they'll come out looking like geniuses."

The elevator door opened into the garage. "We'll make them look like geniuses," he said, and pinched my arm. "I made sure they knew you reviewed the tape first."

"Setting me up for the fall, huh?"

"You'd do it gracefully."

We hurried to the squad car. In seconds, Lake had the tires squealing on the concrete ramps. Outside, dark clouds were gathering strength for the oncoming downpour. We raced down Ponce, swerved onto Peachtree, and careened onto Marietta Street. At the newspaper office, we made a left into a narrow side street and flew down the hill to the railroad track. The car leapt the track and came down hard, skidding into a parking lot lit by sodium lamps.

The asphalt lot reached into Underground, Atlanta's "City Beneath the Streets." After the Civil War, railroads were at the heart of Atlanta's growth. By the 1920s traffic clogged street arteries, making Atlanta's traffic problems today look like a pleasant drive on a Sunday morning. The city fathers had a brainstorm—probably borrowed from a big city up north, although they wouldn't admit it—and constructed a series of viaducts to free up clots of traffic. Businesses on the ground near the tracks moved to the elevated viaduct streets, leaving their old storefronts to the vagrants and rats. Thus Underground Atlanta was born on two fronts. In between the viaduct streets existed a railroad valley until sometime in the forties, when a plaza park was constructed over most, but not all, of it. Trains run beneath these viaducts and the park and through the valley. I remember in the sixties when the area became an historic district. When Stephen Doonan trips over to Underground today, he most likely drools over the marble and granite, iron pilasters, zigzagging bricks, and rich wooden panels. The city fathers had another brainstorm. Let's open those old shops and businesses, have us a regular entertainment center. It was an instant hit, but went into decline, and the city fathers decided to construct a rapid rail system known as MARTA. In the late eighties, masses of money had the shops at the eastern end of Underground open again. Today crime threatens its existence.

The western section of Underground, where Lake was headed, had never been developed. It's mostly used as a parking lot, if you're brave enough to leave your car and walk through darkness and whatever sticks to your shoes. Lake was driving into Underground's bowels, which looked deserted, but in its sinister, stinking corners, lowlifes hung out, doing drugs or knifing each other.

This evening, the unusual cop activity would drive them deeper into their lairs.

The car rocked across the uneven asphalt pavement lining the railroad tracks. Suddenly light emanated from a thick concrete support in a far corner. The dogs and their handlers rested by a graffiti-smeared rampart near the Camry. Each handler held bike helmets and flashlights.

Alighting from the cruiser, I saw the Camry's trunk lid up. Lake handed me a flashlight and we drew on latex gloves. He searched through the trunk's contents. Golf stuff, mostly. Inside the car's interior, he shined the high-powered LED across the front seats. Cigarette butts and Coke cans littered the console. On the back seat, he tweezered a couple of blond hairs and two candy bar wrappers and slipped them in separate bags.

Lake motioned for the dog handlers to bring the dogs. Lake pointed inside the car. "One more job to do."

Buddy and Jed had been working since dawn. They'd followed the scent of vomit for three miles, but they looked eager to tackle the trash inside the car. I knew who my candidates for cop-heroes-of-the-year were.

Jed's handler said, "They're familiar with the girls' scent. All they need is a refresher."

It took no more than a split second's sniff at the bike helmet before Jed was tracking down Underground's asphalt street, parallel to the train tracks, Buddy on his tail.

Lake tried his radio, then his cell phone. "Nothing," he said with a groan. "Too much concrete."

The dogs tracked west, toward the Techwood Viaduct. In the distance, I saw the pinpoint lights beneath it.

Three train tracks run through Underground where we were.

On one track, an engine looked as if it had rusted into the rails. Another track ended at a concrete fortification. The third track was the main.

A hundred feet to our right, a subway train whooshed by, coming from the Omni station.

Omni. Web, you genius.

The dogs veered off into a dark recess behind a concrete abutment. When we caught up, they were hovering above a child's shoe on the pavement. Their handlers urged them up the street by the track while we waited by the shoe. I heard excited whines, but the dogs weren't gone long before they came back to the shoe.

Buddy's handler said, "What the K-9s are saying is, the kids may have been in several places, but their strongest scent is with this shoe."

"So where are the girls now?" Lake said, his voice tight.

Looking beat, the handler shook his head.

Lake's eyes roamed Underground, eerie by flashlights. "Sons-a-bitches could be anywhere."

The handler said, "Since the K-9s are fixed on the shoe, I'd hazard a guess the perps left it here for the dogs, and wrapped the girls in their own clothes, or plastic bags, and carried them to . . . wherever . . ."

"They know they're being hounded," I said.

"And how K-9s work," Lake said. "Let's to the Marietta yard."

We got back to the K-9 cruisers. Buddy's handler reached into the car for a Frisbee and threw it. Buddy launched himself and caught it. I looked over to see Jed and his handler playing tug with a sock.

Lake told the handlers, "I'll radio in. Thanks for all you've done."

Jed's handler said, "At least they got the car and the shoe. They wouldn't be happy if they were called off before they got something."

The dogs weren't fooled they'd achieved their goal. Buddy didn't want to go into his car. He lifted his head and his black nose quivered.

Finally, though, they were on their way out of Underground.

We'd started for Lake's squad car when, up the main track, a dot of light pierced the darkness. It was growing larger, and the sound of wheel on rail echoed off the concrete, the familiar chug-rumble growing louder. We walked toward the light.

"It's under the World Congress Center now," Lake said.

The light blinded as it came closer, but I made out the two yellow engines pulling a long line of cars. With a loud pssshh-hhtttt, the train slowed to a stop. The engineer stuck his hand out the window and waved. "Cain't . . . long," he shouted down, his arm resting along the outside of the window. Because of the shadows, all I could make out was a round white face under an engineer's cap. His glasses glinted when he moved his head. "Y'all . . . trouble?" he called, his South Georgia voice mixing with the rumbling diesels.

"Atlanta Police," Lake called up. We held out our IDs, and the engineer waved them away. Lake asked, "You see any people along these tracks?"

"Nope," the engineer answered. "Mighty . . . heah." I had a

hard time hearing him for the train belching. "Folks don't want seen . . . don't trouble . . . glarr a my light."

Lake said, "We're looking for two, three men and two female children."

The engineer nodded understanding. "Heared . . . news."

"Could they have hopped your freight?"

"No one's . . . my straaaang, bet your . . . dollah."

"You ever heard of Senor Shiv?"

"Can't . . . has. New . . . here."

"Where you headed?"

"Savanner."

"You going straight through to Savannah?"

"No . . . mixed straaaang. Be pickin' . . . droppin' off."

I looked down the line of cars. "You got empty boxcars?" I yelled up.

"Surely . . . ma'am. Sidetrackin' fer loads . . . built back in . . . when I . . . tomorrow."

"Thanks," I said. Lake waved. Suddenly the train's air brake filled with a whooshshshshsssss. The wheels began to turn and the line of cars quaked and clashed.

"What's a straaang?" I yelled at Lake.

"String. String of cars."

"You understand what he said?"

"Some. He'll be dropping off cars, taking on cars, coming back tomorrow with more empties in his string."

Lake walked away, and I watched the engineer's mixed string. It was made up of grainers, containers, tankers, gondolas, coal cars, piggybacks, boxcars, and some I didn't know the names for. I counted seventy-five cars before I had a feeling about this train. I looked to where Lake was, or had been. Where was he now?

Then two boxcars passed, their doors wide open.

Open doors.

My mind swept back to my childhood when we would see men standing in the open doorways of boxcars at train crossings, waving at us kids.

I heard crossing bells and then the train's air horn. The engineer had cleared Underground and was at the grade crossing in the parking lot. The air horn bellowed something I'd never heard before. Three toots, four toots—five—six—seven. What kind of horn talk was that? Didn't Bassett say short toots were for backing? Was the train going to back up? How could it, it wasn't even stopped? It was building speed. Then I wondered why the engineer didn't know Senor Shiv. But then, didn't he mention he was new?

He didn't know the wily Senor, and the wily Senor probably knew that, or maybe Senor got lucky if he chose this train. But somehow I thought the Knight was probably the one who chose the train, and the Knight would acquaint himself with engineers and how vigilant they were. Another thought: how could the new engineer be sure there were no riders on his string? I couldn't see the end of it yet, so it had to be at least a hundred cars long.

This is the train. This is where the dogs led us. They've been right so far. I believe in them.

I glanced behind me, up and down the line. *Lake, where the hell are you?* I jogged closer to the cars. The last of the boxcars went by and a piggyback came parallel. I noticed the Mercedes emblems on the cars. I let go of the flashlight.

I spied the ladder. Pumping my legs faster, I got alongside the ladder. In a split second, I lifted my foot up to the first rung and swept my other onto the rung above. Facing the car, I braced to jump onto the flatbed. When I landed, I hit a knee. Ouch. No time for pain. I grabbed the trailer's under-rim and pulled myself underneath the eighteen-wheeler.

Flipping on my stomach, I clutched on to a rod on the belly of the trailer and looked up the line for Lake. He came from a recess. I reached out and waved.

His eyes grew impossibly wide, as did his mouth. "Dru!"

He about-faced and ran alongside the train, which was rolling a little faster. My piggyback slipped by him. He sped up and gathered himself to grab the rungs of a grainer two cars back. He swooped up and disappeared on its porch—the V indent at the back of the car.

As the train gathered speed, my car cleared Underground, chugged through the outside parking lot, and ran into another Underground tunnel in a rhythmic cadence of steel rolling on steel. When the train cleared the tunnel, a rush of black air slapped my face and I thought my hair would fly off my scalp.

I got settled under the trailer's back wheels, mindful of the axle.

The air horn sent two long blasts, a short one, and then another long one vibrating through the air. Okay, the engineer does know train talk.

We rushed past Georgia State University. I savored the night air, but in no time the windchill settled into my marrow. My fingers were like cold sticks. The train rounded a curve and dove into another tunnel. The heat was welcome, but didn't last long. The cars surfaced and sped along Decatur Street before rocketing through a narrow corridor of kudzu. This was one roller-coaster ride I'd never forget, if I lived to tell about it.

TWENTY-NINE

Not long, we'd be in the Cabbagetown yard. I imagined the contingent of law enforcement waiting for us, because once Lake got settled, he'd have radioed in. We blew past Oakland Cemetery and approached the switching yard like Casey Jones with his banshee whistles screaming in the night. Roaring past reach stackers and gantry cranes—man—we were on a tear. What in God's name was the engineer doing? I heard his accent again: "Mixed straaaang. Be pickin' . . . droppin' off."

So where would we be picking up and dropping off?

With Cabbagetown yard behind us, I looked out from the wheels of the trailer and saw the line of automobiles stream along Ponce de Leon. The fine mist against the streetlights made them shine. The train swept around a wide curve. All at once, its air brakes screeched as the train reduced speed. We lurched past one crossing after another, the engineer playing the horn like a kid with a new toy. At the crossings, the striped barrier arms were scarcely lowered before we were rollicking past. I knew it was a matter of time before we hit some hapless Jack on the track.

The burbs were behind us now, and we raced through banks of brush and scrub pines. I took deep breaths and exhaled steady ribbons of night air to keep adrenaline from exploding from my pores. Was it velocity like this that lured hoboes to the rails? They could have it.

What time was it? I couldn't see the face of my watch. Cops opt for nonilluminated faces. Once upon a time—don't remember when or where—a cop's watch gave away a stake-out position. The bullet caught his illuminated crystal, glanced off, and hit his partner. They teach you that kind of stuff at the Academy. I wrestled my backpack off and reached for my cell. Bracing the backpack next to a wheel, I used it as a pillow anchor. The cell's LED glowed faintly. I pressed buttons by the Braille method and prayed. If I hit the right numbers, and if there was an operable signal floating on the ether, and if it wasn't disturbed by the swirling gale, maybe I'd get through to Webdog. I wouldn't be able to hear, and I got no texts back, but I kept pressing numbers to clue him something was wrong. I gave up and put the instrument back in the pack.

The train flat hauled through the countryside. We'd be in Savannah before the crow, as she flies. Just as I was settling down, the cars above rocked the flatbed. Tons of expensive autos threatened to crush me. *Don't panic.* Holding the axle, I squirmed forward and stuck my head from under the trailer. The ground below was a white streak from the gravel lining the trestle. Looking up, I saw stark blackness, and considered where we might be. No stars, no dippers to get a direction, but my internal compass had us going east. After a while, the car rocking tapered to a tolerable sway, and I settled to watch an indistinct landscape of fields and farmhouses whiz past. I became conscious my fingers were no longer icicles, which meant we were going south—south and east.

Abruptly, the train lost speed. The air horn screamed one long yowl, and the air brakes hisssssshed. Seconds later, the line of rail cars yanked and clanked, the sudden jolt ripping my hand from the axle. I slid halfway across the flatbed, pawing to grab hold of something. I caught a rung on the trailer, and pain shot through my shoulder. My right foot slipped off the car. As we decelerated, my ankle holster beat against the side of the flatbed. With a long creeeeeeech, the train bucked. *Forget what's above you. Concentrate on getting a foothold.* My right leg beat against a zillion pounds of steel force until the sole of my shoe hit against the iron bar at the edge of the flatbed. I thrust my body forward and belly-crawled beneath the car hauler.

The train slowed more, my rail car rocked, but I could raise myself to half-push-up position. I glanced left, toward the engines, when a sudden movement from the right came into my side vision. Lake ran alongside the train, pulling his gun from its holster.

He hand-signaled *come off.* On my knees now, I reached for my backpack, which had stayed wedged in the wheel. I tossed it to the ground, climbed on the ladder, and descended to the last rung. As Lake scooped up the backpack, the string of cars groaned and I jumped. I stumbled, but caught myself and kept running until I could stop without toppling. The train hissed to a halt. I bent and pulled my automatic from its holster.

A quick glance around the terrain told me we were on the back side of a farm-to-market town. Rows of shops lined the track. The train was on a curve, and ahead I couldn't see the locomotives.

Lake handed me the backpack. "Have you figured out where we are?" he asked.

"We came south and east. But I have no idea how far."

"I think we're paralleling I-16. A while back, a water tower had a sign. Barronton, or something like that. Is there a Barronton on your map?"

"Yeah, tiny place." Barronton was a town on Web's railroad map, west of Onion City. Thankfully I have a good memory for diagrams and maps. "I'd guess we're at the Onion City depot. According to the map, it's a passenger station."

"If this is a passenger depot, why are we stopped?"

"Good question. There's a GBI office in Onion City. I remember the symbol on the map."

"I signaled for backup in Atlanta," Lake said. "Something's wrong with my radio." He grabbed the radio from his belt and tried it again. No signal. He threw it on the gravel. This wasn't the first time a police radio failed to get through on a call for help.

Next, Lake tried his cell phone. One of technology's ironies is that cells are the reason for the static failures of police radios. Too many devices vying for low frequencies.

"Dead spot, no squares showing," he said disgustedly. "It's us, kid. If the Rooks are on this train . . ."

"If?" The word hurt. "Do you doubt the Rooks are on this train?"

"No," he said without overwhelming conviction. He motioned down the line. "You check out the cars on this side, I'll go to the other side. You see a flashing knife, shoot the son-of-a-bitch."

He sprung between the cars.

"Lake you can't cross those couplers!"

He jumped and caught the ladder, and then made a suicidal

leap over the coupler to the other side. He turned and waved before he swept off the car. I ran alongside a piggyback and saw his hips running on the other side of the trailer. Blood hammered through my veins, my lungs blistered, but all I could think about was . . . *If the rooks are on this train . . .*

I'd been so certain. Something about the engineer being new, and his voice, and the horn. But now . . . ? *If?*

There was no if. The dogs were right, even if they couldn't find the girls. The Rooks had hidden them in Underground to wait for the boxcars to glide by. Whatever maneuverings they planned to get the girls onboard, we'd aided them by stopping the train and talking to the engineer.

Lake's voice yelled from the other side of the train. "Dru! You with me?"

"Here!" I shouted. We were aligned between the cars.

"One . . . two . . . three," he shouted.

Metronome pacing was our way of staying up with one another without actually being in eyeshot. We raced up the train, past a line of boxcars to the chain of gondolas. No one in their right mind hides in a gondola.

At the apex of the curve, the air brakes sweeeeeshed, and the wheels started turning. The train bolted forward, sending an iron crescendo down the line.

An open boxcar approached. Goddamn backpack. I hadn't put it on when I had the chance. I threw it to the ground and the gun went into the small of my back. As the car drew alongside, I ran straight for it, leaping up and grabbing the door track. I kept my legs straight and hoisted my body through the door and onto the floor. Breathing hard, I looked up to see Lake lying in the same position in the opposite door. We vaulted to our feet and grabbed for our weapons. I sprang left. He went right. This practiced routine once saved our lives.

Instinct said the black interior was empty. Lake called out, "Police! Identify yourself!" I swept the gun right, then left. A quick walk to the end of my half, and I called to Lake, "No one here."

"All clear," Lake called from his end.

When we met in the middle, Lake said, "I don't think they got off anywhere, not if they rode in a boxcar. We'd've seen them."

"With the girls, it's the only rail car they'd be traveling in," I said huffing like a little-toot-that-could.

He nodded, not looking at me.

The train gained speed. For the first time, I noticed the strong odor of onion in the rail car and fought a gagging reflex. I went to the door to breathe in fresh air, and quickly ducked back. We were passing the station. A man sat inside the iron-barred window with his nose pressing the print of a book or newspaper on his desk.

"Where to now?" Lake shouted, coming to stand behind me. "What's the next place on the map?"

"There's a freight switching yard not far from here. The South Georgia Agricultural Exchange Yard."

The fields and barns rolled by under low storm clouds. The engineer air-horned his way past a guarded crossing. We got to a trestle running above a county road when a flashing blue light passed below, going in the opposite direction from us. "Squad car," Lake yelled. "Going the wrong way."

Lake braced himself against the side of the boxcar and took out his cell phone. "Eight squares," he shouted. "Maybe we'll get lucky this time."

He punched in APD's number. "Can you hear me!" He shook the cell. "Can you hear me!" He punched nine-one-one. He looked at me. "I think they answered, but they can't hear me."

"So we must rely on triangulation."

While he continued to punch numbers and cuss the cell, I scanned the land and black sky outside, sighting blinking lights flying south. The small plane disappeared into turbulent clouds. Onion City had an airport, and I remembered its position on the railway map. Our kidnappers would not be flying out of Onion City, but I recalled the list of functioning and defunct airstrips Web had e-mailed. A flying school had operated for a time from a runway very close to the agricultural switching yard and about ten miles from the Onion City regional airport.

Folding his cell phone, Lake grumbled, "I can't hear a thing. Maybe someone made out what I shouted."

"Let's hope. Not far from the train yard, which we should come to soon, is an airstrip, an old pilot school. Closed now."

Lake's features took on a ray of hope. "But the runway could still be there."

The rails followed the interstate for a bit, then swept through pine trees and paralleled a hard road. We lost speed. Another plane flew overhead heading for the Onion City airport.

"That pilot better lay it down before the storm hits," Lake said.

He swayed to the other side of the car. We kept watch out opposite doors. No one was going to jump off this train onto the gravel decline. I held my breath for the squeal of brakes. I had that destination feel, as my mama used to call it, when you get near the end of the line.

The ground beneath our wheels flowed by, and then I noticed

a rail spur going off at a seventy degree arc. It crossed the hard road and disappeared into a forest.

Sure enough, the brakes hisssssed and the train jerked. We deceled, and the force tugged my body, threatening to twist my legs like they were rubber.

Moments later, the yard's sodium lights shined inside the car. The train halted. The string of cars trembled at idle—but not for long. A fierce racket reverberated through the yard. The train reversed course—backing onto a side track.

Lake said, "They're taking the rear cars off. That's us."

"So this string of boxcars stays here. That means the Rooks are heading for that old runway."

"Looks like," Lake said. "*If* they're on this train."

If. One day Lake's going to pay.

Lake unfolded his cell again and pressed the pad. "No service," he grumped.

Careful not to let the yard crew see us, we kept watch on the line of boxcars. All the yard action was on the left side, leaving the right side of the train deserted. Anyone could jump off and have a short dash to a three-foot concrete barrier.

But no one jumped off. The yard crew, uncoupling cars, worked so close I heard them holler above the tooting horn talk and the clashing rail cars. A passenger train shot past on the main track heading west.

Lake went to the action side of our boxcar and called out, "Dru." He pointed up the line. It looked like the gondolas and tankers in our string lost their locomotives. The two engines rolled ahead, switched onto the main track and then passed, going west—following the passenger.

That puzzled me. "The engineer said he was going to Savannah."

"He's probably going to a spur for a nap before he sets off again," Lake said. "Those guys are worse than truckers for catching catnaps whenever and wherever they can."

"I don't feel right about him," I said.

"I don't feel right about anything."

That shut me up.

Lake punched the pad on his cell. He waited. "Hmmm." He folded the screen. "I got a connection at State Patrol. Then a disconnect. Maybe they'll respond."

A small locomotive budged our line of cars further down the side track and halted by a line of warehouses that were separated from the track by overgrown weeds—a perfect place for men carrying two kids to run the hundred or so yards to the buildings.

But no sign of them. With every minute that passed, my nerves stretched. Not long, and something bad was going to happen. It was past time for the Rooks to make a move, unless they knew we were on this train. That old bugaboo intuition told me they did.

Lake asked suddenly, "Where'd you learn how to jump a train?"

His unexpected question—accusation?—recalled scenes from childhood. "A train used to go by Grandma's. She lived near the tracks in Roswell. Me and Portia used to hop on the ladders, and then let go when the train started speeding. Got cussed at by the crew, but it added to the fun."

Fret wrinkles scrunched his eyes. "You having fun now?"

"Not fun. Excited, juiced up, I guess."

He reached for a lock of my hair and rubbed it in his fingers. "Me, too. But I don't want you hurt."

"Me, neither." In case he wanted to go into the *if* again, I moved away to look up the line of cars. I wished I could keep the faith, but my brain betrayed me and I wondered if I hadn't jumped (not the gun but the train) by mistake, thus allowing the Rooks to get away—and the girls lost forever.

Lost forever—such horror can't be fathomed unless you look into the soulless eyes of children whose innocence is stolen. "Where in God's name are the Rooks?" I said, scratching my arms.

Lake touched my shoulder. "They can wait for a while to move out. Nobody's going to bother with these cars for a few days."

"They don't have a few days. They have tonight, period."

"No planes are taking off in this weather." I looked squarely at him, knowing what was coming. He asked, "What convinced you this was the train the Rooks were on?"

"You do doubt me."

"I wouldn't dare. It's never paid."

"It had to be this train. Besides something was wrong with the engineer."

"You said. What?"

"His voice maybe. He wasn't very good on the air horn when he took off—although he got better."

"Oh, I see," he said, like he was looking into a mud hole.

"No kidding. I learned a lot from Bassett."

"Maybe Bassett was teasing you—see if you'd get into his game."

I'd thought about that. But before I could speculate, the howl

252

of emergency sirens filled the air. "Here comes our backup," Lake said, and jumped from the boxcar. I followed, on the run.

The flaring blue lights flashed up the track. Two squad cars—sheriff's—threw gravel when they braked hard. As we dashed toward them, three men flipped the snaps on their holsters.

Lake held up his hands. In one was his police ID. My ID hung on a stout ribbon under the Rain Shadow. I raised the piece of plastic.

A round, burly man, wearing a campaign hat, kept his car between him and us. "Who are y'all?" he called out.

"Atlanta Police. Detective Lieutenant Richard Lake."

"Sheriff of Mortimer County. Throw those IDs on the hood."

I did as told, mindful of the two deputies who stood behind the sheriff, holding their guns on us. The sheriff looked over our IDs.

I looked back at the line of boxcars.

"What's Child Trace?" the sheriff asked, handing me the ID.

"I track and rescue missing children," I said. "That's what we're doing here."

"You answering my nine-one-one?" Lake asked.

"What nine-one-one?"

"We're after kidnappers, looking for two girls. You hear of the Rose girls yet?"

"Yet? We ain't Atlanta, but we ain't still on the Pony Express, neither."

"Sorry, didn't mean that." Lake had a way of looking apologetic that soothed even the highly insulted.

The sheriff said, "Ever one in the state has heard of them kidnapped sisters. Every county sheriff's got men on the roads, especially the innerstates."

"You won't find them on the interstates."

The sheriff looked at the boxcar from which we'd jumped. "You sayin' they came here on this here train?"

"We believe so."

The sheriff waved his deputies toward the train. "Check 'em out." But he looked unconvinced, and I had that ol' hollow feeling that makes you want to hang your head and cry. "If."

"There'll be at least two armed men with them," Lake called. "Watch for knives."

As the deputies searched the boxcars, Lake tried to rationally explain why we'd been on the train.

"But," the sheriff said, his doubts creasing his face, "y'all don't know for sure, do you?"

Lake and I exchanged glances. The sheriff walked away, toward the boxcars. A light rain began to fall. The deputies emerged from the dark side of the train, both shaking their heads.

Humiliation filled my eyes—don't you dare cry—as the sheriff and his deputies walked back to where we stood. The sheriff ordered a deputy to go fetch the yardmaster.

I was wrong. I'd led us on a wild-goose chase. A gentle hand clasped my damp shoulder. Lake was doing what he could, but it couldn't drag my spirit back into my body.

Lake turned to the sheriff. "Mind if I ask what brought you here?"

"Kinda funny, I guess. It's about the engineer that came out on the same train as y'all from Atlanta."

I perked. *The engineer?*

"What about him?" Lake said. "I don't know what the speed limit is for trains, or if there is one, but I'll testify he was going too fast for conditions."

The sheriff's mouth distorted—his version of a wry smile. "Won't matter to him now. He's been murdered."

The engineer's round face popped into my head. The man who'd led us on a roller-coaster ride was dead?

Lake grimaced. "When . . . where?"

"Up yonder, in Onion City, at the depot. That there train he was driving wadn't supposed to stop there. But it did, and somebody killed the engineer and the stationmaster, then the dang thing came on here. Lucky the passenger was late, or we'd have a crash on our hands instead of two murders."

Who brought the train from the Onion City depot to this yard? I looked across the yard. I didn't see any yellow engines.

Lake asked, "How were they murdered?"

"Throats slit."

The man behind the bars at the station pressing his face into a book. I'd assumed he was nearly blind. He was dead.

"Where was the engineer found?" Lake asked.

"On the side of the track," the sheriff said. "No blood there, though, not like the stationmaster, whose neck was about took off."

The sheriff went to his squad car and reached inside the back seat. His hand held a plastic bag. He took out a police radio. "This here portable look familiar?"

"It's mine," Lake said. "It's dead. I got through to GSP on my cell before you showed up. That's why I thought you were backup."

The sheriff reached in his car again and brought out a black leather backpack. "This here yours?" he asked Lake.

"It's mine," I said. "I dropped it when I jumped back on the train."

The sheriff took a wide stance and planted his thumbs in his waistband. "Something don't seem right. Murders are going on, yet you don't hear or see nothing."

"We couldn't see the locomotives," Lake said. "The train was curved away from us. Besides, our attention was on the boxcars."

I kept seeing the engineer as he looked down on us in Underground. A mental tick fell into place, like a key in the cylinder. "What did the dead engineer look like?" I asked.

"Young fella. Not more'n—"

"The locomotives!" I shouted. "They're in the yellow locomotives!"

The sheriff stared, astonished. "What!"

"They stole the locomotives! The girls are in them."

"Who stole the locomotives?"

I thought for a second. No sense talking about Rooks or Senor Shiv. Or the Knight—the false engineer. I said, "The man who brought the train in is a kidnapper. Two men are with him."

From his expression, the sheriff clearly thought I'd lost my mind.

Lake said, "The locomotives were uncoupled from the train cars. The fake engineer headed back west. Older fellow, heavyset. Wore glasses."

"We came on the highway," the sheriff said. "Wouldn't see no lone locomotives on the track."

"There's an unused airstrip near here, isn't there?" I asked.

He leaned his head to one side. "Airstrip?"

"A flight school runway near here."

He looked toward the south. "Ain't used no more. Used to be a place to go jump out of planes, too. Had an accident two years ago. Moved the school to Scarborough."

"Was there a spur near the property?"

"Used to be when there was warehouses there. Tore down the warehouses when the property sold for the pilot school. You saying they're heading there?"

"Yeah."

His bold eyes searched mine. I have no idea what he looked for, but whatever he saw—certainty, fear, the need to hurry—he nodded and took out his radio. As he spoke, the deputies brought the yardmaster.

The railroad man buzzed like a hornet when he said to Lake, "You seen them units you came in on?"

"They went west," Lake answered. "We're going to look for them."

"I'm in charge of this trick," he said, swiping the rain from his safety glasses. "Got a message from Dispatch. Nobody answered at the depot in Onion City. Now I hear tell Mr. Cartwright, the depot master's, dead. And so's the Atlanta engineer, a man named Smith. Who brought them units in?"

"A murderer and kidnapper."

The yardmaster's eyelids blinked behind his safety glasses.

"We passed a spur up the main track," I said. "Can a locomotive switch onto it and get to the defunct airport runway?"

He took off the safety glasses and rubbed them on his wet shirt. "Ain't been done since I been here, but don't know why the switches won't line for the crossover unless there's a break somewhere."

The sheriff looked at us and shook his head. "I'm going to find them engines. Y'all riding with me?"

"Guess so, sir," Lake said. "Don't have no other ride."

THIRTY

The sheriff raced west on the hard road, the deputies behind us, so near their headlights flooded light into the back seat where we sat.

"Train cars don't go down that spur no more," the sheriff said, turning his head so a cheek faced me. He talked out of the side of his mouth. "Don't know if it can, but it's a track to nowhere since they tore out the warehouses and built the concrete block shed they call a airport terminal. The spur crosses through the forest at Beaver Creek and Beaver Creek ain't dry now."

"The spur goes through a creek?" Lake asked.

"Used to be, Beaver Creek was a hunnert yards from where it is now. Time changed its course. Time and wet springs like the one we're having this year."

"How deep is Beaver Creek?"

"Maybe three foot now. It runs off quick and dries up in summer."

"Is there still a railroad right-of-way through the woods?" Lake asked.

"It was let go to the state Department of Transportation ten years ago. It's not kept up, but hunters and hikers use the trail so it's not so overgrown."

We rounded a generous curve. The sheriff screeched to a stop, two wheels spinning on the shoulder. We got out. The deputies pulled in behind us, but stayed in their cruiser. Thunder rumbled from the west and the rain beat the ground. I pulled out the roll-up hood of my rain jacket. My hair was soaked, but I needed warmth on my ears.

The sheriff shone his flashlight on train tracks embedded in the asphalt surface. The rails cut up the shoulder of the road and disappeared into the woods. The sheriff flashed his light up a break in the pines. "There's where the spur went, back in the days trains picked up cotton from the warehouses."

"How far through the woods to the airstrip?" I asked.

"Quarter mile maybe."

"Could a locomotive cut through a running creek three feet deep?" I asked.

The sheriff spit on the ground. "Don't know why not. Ain't no little body of water gonna wash a couple of locomotives off the rails. Trouble is, the rails may be washed out. I ain't been back there in a couple years."

"Wouldn't it be too steep for a locomotive to dip down into a creek?"

"Beaver Creek's wide. Grade's not steep. Got a lot of sand and gravel on the bottom, though. That'd mess with the wheels."

The sheriff ran his flashlight along the rails again. Soil and gravel stuck in the rust. I brushed the wet from my face. The sheriff asked, "Look to you like engines passed along these rails?"

I bit my lip. Lake shook his head.

"Let's look on down the main line," the sheriff said.

We got inside his car. "What's the quickest way to the runway, besides through the woods?" Lake asked.

"The way we're going. Toward town. The track runs over Main Street. You go on Main a little ways till you come to a road called Terminal. Used to be marked, not now. It's all growed up since the runway's closed."

The sheriff's police radio crackled. He reached forward and pushed the button. I couldn't make out Dispatch's words, nor understand the numericals. He listened for five more seconds, then yelled, "Kee-rap, on my way!"

Lake leaned forward. "What?"

The sheriff's mouth clamped as he spun the squad car. With lights flashing and wipers swiping rain off the windshield, he crossed the main track at an unguarded crossing. Going west, he met an intersection and whipped the car left. I think the tires on my side left the ground. A quarter mile up, he approached a guarded railroad crossing. The striped arm was down. Red lights mounted on it flashed. Bells clanged.

Two coupled yellow locomotives sat smack in the middle of the crossing on an elevated track.

"What in thunder!" the sheriff shouted, flinging his door. Lake and I jumped out. The rain had lessened, but I heard a distant rumble. I hoped it was thunder and not a train approaching. Across the tracks, I heard someone laying on a car horn. A dozen people stood on the track, gazing at the engines. The sheriff grabbed his portable and strode off, barking into it. I stood next to Lake and the deputies, looking up at the two hulks of silent, rain-slicked, yellow-coated steel as if they held magical powers.

"Is it stalled or what?" a deputy wondered. He was a giant of a man with a boyish, rosy face.

"Where's the crew?" the other deputy asked.

"We got to get those units off the main," the giant said. "This here's a busy track."

"When's the next train through here?" I asked.

He looked at his watch. "'Bout now."

Lake and I backed away. The sheriff said into his walkie-talkie, "Get that red board up."

I said to Lake, "Did the Rooks get away on foot, or did they have a vehicle waiting for them?"

"I'd bet the latter."

"We've got to get around the locomotives and get to the air-strip."

"Not with the berm. It'd take something on tracks like a tank to get over it."

Mounds of earth and gravel lined the track. Main Street was a strip over the railroad berm. "How 'bout we confiscate a car on the other side."

"You think the sheriff will go along with that?"

He was right; it was the sheriff's jurisdiction.

While I told myself not to panic, Lake ran toward the crossing and ducked beneath the arm. He reached for his gun. I drew mine from its holster.

The sheriff called, "Lieutenant, don't!"

But Lake was already on the ladder leading into the cab. He called back, "You call the yard?"

"Yeah," the sheriff shouted, heaving his bulk under the guard arm. I followed him. He motioned for his deputies to board the second engine and drew his gun. "We might have us a hostage situation," he said.

"I don't think so," Lake said, "but we have to check it out."

I believed Lake was right; we'd know by now if the kidnappers were turning this into hostage negotiations.

Inside, the cab was dark and cramped. I threw off the rain jacket hood and didn't hear or feel any sign of life other than our own. The sheriff unsnapped an LED light from his belt. "Don't know nothin' about these here engines," he said. "Do you?" Lake answered no. "Best we not go touchin' stuff that might be lights, but might not be lights."

"Anybody aboard?" Lake called out. His voice rang hollowly. "Police! Speak up. Show yourself."

"Sheriff, heah!"

Lake led, his gun held straight out, chest high, while the sheriff's flashlight shone on the controls, indicators, computer displays—all looking surreal in the arcing light. We walked single file alongside the turbocharger and the generator and the shiny diesel into the equipment-packed rear of the engine. "Oh," the sheriff muttered and shone the light on the floor. "My foot got something soft." His light shone on a body lying alongside the air compressor. I stood in its sticky blood.

"An unfortunate Rook," Lake said, holstering his gun.

The sheriff said, "Rook?"

"One of the kidnappers."

The unfortunate Rook's throat had been cut. The blood was fresh and bright red in the light, its iron odor mixing with the diesel smell. I wondered what those two little girls had seen or heard.

We about-faced, with the sheriff leading us to the front of the cab. I said, "We need to get to the runway."

He turned a cheek to me. "I got a murder investigation to see to, and I got to work with the railroad to get these engines back to where they belong."

I climbed down from the locomotive and spotted two men standing by a small concrete block building. The sign on the building said THE NO-NAME SALOON. I began to run. Lake was beside me.

"Police," he said to the men. "You see what happened here?"

"All's I know," a man said, "was them engines stopped. Two men climbed down each one dragging a kid and went 'round to the other side by where the Texaco station is. They took off in the Jeep parked there."

"How long had it been there?" I asked.

The man answered, "Couple days ago, a stranger asks the manager if he can put a Jeep at the corner of the lot with a FOR SALE sign on it. He hands the manager a hundred dollar bill and said he'd check back in a couple of days. Manager called me up a few minutes ago and said some people got off the train and stole the Jeep."

"What kind of Jeep?"

"Uh, real Army. Green, looked okay to me. I told the manager to tell the stranger I might be interested if the price was right."

"What were they wearing . . . the men?"

"One looked like an engineer. Heavy boy. The other was a Mexican boy."

"And the kids?"

"Two girls. Damndest thing I seen in my life. I owned this place for fifteen years and never had two engines stop on the track. Trains go slow 'cause the yard's ahead. Sometimes hoboes jump off, but I ain't ever seen two engines shut down and people run off."

We hurried to where the sheriff was speaking into his portable, reporting the latest events. Lake interrupted, "We need a deputy."

The sheriff 10-4'd and shook his head. "You really think they're taking those kids somewhere in a light plane in this weather?"

"That's the reason they came to your county. What's the quickest way to the strip?"

"Six miles up the road's another crossin' but that's takin' you away from the strip. You got to backtrack over country roads."

"Any flat places along this track a car can cross?" Lake asked.

"The banks have been built up to keep folks from doin' just that. In some places there's fences."

"We'll go back to where the spur is," Lake said. "If your man can't drive through the creek, we'll wade across."

The sheriff motioned the giant deputy, who was climbing down the ladder of the second locomotive. The giant deputy told the sheriff a brakeman had been knocked out, but was alive.

"Jimmy Ray, what I want you to do, you take the lieutenant here, and this lady, to the spur."

Jimmy Ray looked euphoric.

We hurried to the cruiser. "You been in those woods lately?" Lake asked.

"Just last month," Jimmy Ray answered. "Turkey huntin'."

We got in the back and I looked out the rear window. A dot blinked low in the night sky. "A plane coming from the south."

Lake stared at it. The dot winked intermittently and veered east, the way the deputy flung the cruiser around the corner. "They're nuts in this weather," he said.

"They've got nothing to lose. We have everything."

THIRTY-ONE

Ah, to be enthusiastic and brainless. Jimmy Ray hit the siren and almost a telephone pole. His big hands got the car righted, then he floored the gas. The speedometer hit a hundred, and we almost missed the turn at the spur. He must have been going sixty when we breached the first trees in the pine forest. "Hold tight," he said. "We'll be running with the track and through brush and stuff."

I held the hand strap as the car jostled over the old railroad ties, the headlights glowing off wet leaves and glistening darkness. The trail widened as it gently flowed downward. Suddenly the car swung sideways. *Don't let us be near a drop-off.* Jimmy Ray got the cruiser under control and straddling the track again.

He told us, "This here's turned into a swamp. Didn't used to be back when the railroad came through to get the cotton in the warehouses. Now the farmers take their stuff by truck to the warehouses up the way, and the swamp's takin' over." The car suddenly skidded. "Hold on. Traction's bad. Real muddy along here."

My side of the car scraped along some pines. The crunching, banging, and cracking sounded eerie in the rain. Finally, the car ground to a stop. "Watch your step," Jimmy Ray said, throwing the gear shift. "It gets real squishy here." He'd left the car lights on, and we trotted, three abreast, toward the creek.

He swung the bright lamp across the defunct railroad line. Sawgrass grew up in the middle and alongside the rails. Although there were places where it was beaten down by animal or human passage, it still came to my knees.

Jimmy Ray continued to swing his lantern in a wide arc to lead us to the water's edge. Pelted by rain, the water glimmered black. Lily pads floated and there was a sandbar near the middle of the creek.

Suddenly something moved on my right. "Lake," I said softly. "Something's there."

I lifted my ankle, freed the automatic from its holster, left the rail path, and stepped into the reeds and sedges. One of my feet sucked into the mud. I yanked it out without losing my shoe. I raised my head to see two fiery little eyes about twenty feet away.

Alligator. They feed at night. Springtime. Mating season. Mean . . . hungry . . . guarding-the-nest alligators.

My blood turned to ice water. "Alligator," I whispered to Lake, who'd followed me off the path.

His breath caught audibly. "Don't move."

Despite wanting to jerk the gun up and shoot, I stayed frozen.

Shortly, Jimmy Ray called from the trail, "What's over there? Y'all get stuck, or something?"

We didn't answer. My mouth was too dry, my heart beating too fast.

How big is the thing? It was as motionless as we were, eyes fixed and glinting.

Jimmy Ray stomped through the mud.

"Alligator," Lake hissed.

"Nothing to fear," Jimmy Ray said with a cackle. "It's a little ol' thing. Not more'n a two-footer. No big ones around here. Not enough big stuff to eat."

He shoved ahead of us. I couldn't see past his bulk, and I couldn't hear if the alligator slipped away. I listened for a splash or crackling through the brush. All of a sudden, Jimmy Ray about-faced and ran, almost banging into me. "Get out! Get out!" he shouted, reaching the trail and fleeing toward the cruiser.

I caught sight of the gator in Jimmy Ray's retreating lantern, his armor plates moving like black rolling sea waves, his wide-spaced claw feet pounding the ground. I jumped away and felt something hit my right foot as the reptile thundered toward the deputy.

Lake grabbed my gun, took aim, hesitated, and then lowered it.

I could read his mind. Gun sounds carry. Warning the Knight.

A car door slammed. Jimmy Ray had evidently made it to his car. But where was the gator? And what about others in this creek bottom?

Lake shoved my gun in my hand. "Storm's fifteen minutes away, I'd guess," he said.

"Doppler radar wears a suit," I said.

The squad car's engine roared to life. As it crept toward us, no creatures appeared in the headlights. Jimmy Ray got out of the car and brushed his hands together. "He's gone now."

"What about others?" Lake asked.

"Cain't understand that big fella being here."

"What if there are other big fellows being here?"

"Might be a big ol' female," Jimmy Ray said. "We'll watch out." For having just run for his life, he sounded indifferent. He unfastened his holster and took the gun from it, fingering the trigger. That frightened me more than the gator. He said, "Now, let's see if this here creek's too deep for the cruiser." He waded in. I couldn't see his shoes.

"Too deep," I said, and saw two bright dots floating toward us. The same fixed glinting eyes.

"Come back," I called to Jimmy Ray. "Gator!"

He splashed to the bank. "We're jes fine. Car can get right through."

"Don't get us stuck," Lake said.

"No, sir."

Jimmy Ray changed gears and the cruiser glided through the creek like it had an outboard on the back. The cruiser climbed the shallow bank. Jimmy Ray switched gears, and the car picked up speed. "Gators," he said with a smile in his voice. "That one, and its mate, ain't gonna be around here long. Make some nice shoes, anyone catches it. Good eatin', too."

The car straddled the rail line, and we listened to the thunder moving closer.

"Up ahead's a fence," Jimmy Ray said. "Gotta gate, but the lock's nothing can't be handled. We'll go up yonder 'bout a hundred yards, and we'll come out at it."

All of a sudden the rattle of automatic fire mixed with the undulating thunder. The deputy swerved away from the ammo bursts and ducked to his right. When Lake and I went down on the back seat, my head collided with his. He pulled me beneath him, against the rounds bombarding my side.

"Assault rifles," Lake said. "Two of them."

Jimmy Ray called, "Coming from the other side of the chain link."

The back end of the cruiser fishtailed and hit something.

The shooting stopped. So had we. A bolt of lightning struck a tree. Lake opened his door. "Stuck!" he shouted. The interior lights had the shooters firing again. Slamming the door, he called, "Deputy, you okay?"

"Sure am." Jimmy Ray raised a shotgun.

"No," Lake shouted. "Useless. Get us out of here."

Jimmy Ray's head appeared above the headrest. Lake shouted. "Get down!"

Jimmy Ray slid down. "I can follow the tree line." He pressed the gas and the car lurched forward. The lightning apparently helped him differentiate the trees from the sky overhead.

Automatic rounds pelted the car. It stalled. Lake smashed the inside light with the butt of his gun and swung his door open. Clutching the window frame, he stood on the running board. He shouted to the deputy, "Turn right, you're up against a fence." Jimmy Ray jerked the wheel to the right and bounced the car away from it. "Now, left," Lake called. Then: "Straighten! Straighten!" Jimmy Ray fought the wheel while we rocked forward.

The gunfire became sporadic, the rattle of guns further away and behind us now. Lake pulled himself back inside the car. Jimmy Ray heaved his body upright and tromped the gas. The engine roared and the back wheels broke loose, spinning a back fender into a pine tree.

"Fuck," Lake cried.

Jimmy Ray threw the gears into reverse, slew the car sideways, and rammed the back bumper into thick bramble. It thrust the back wheels up, and when the deputy shoved the shifter into drive, the cruiser shot from the brush and nearly crashed into the fence. The car rolled forward, making bizarre noises.

At the end of the fence, we turned for a gate. A chain locked it.

"Shoot it out," Lake ordered.

Jimmy Ray grabbed the riot gun. His elbow shot back with each pull and boom. The steel lock flung apart. The gate hurled backward. The car roared through and Jimmy Ray braked in front of the plate glass window of a small, white block building.

Through it all, my gun stayed in my hand, my heart in my throat.

Jimmy Ray jumped out, shotgun to shoulder, flashlight in hand, and ran through an open door into the terminal. Lake was on his heels and I was on Lake's.

The building was a simple structure. No electricity. Jimmy Ray snapped on his light. A quick sweep of our guns—no one in the small office. In the hangar, no one. No automobiles, no planes, no Jeep. We went outside and Lake told the deputy to keep watch in front. He grasped Jimmy Ray's light, and we circled to the back of the building.

Spent shells littered the tall, wet weeds. Topping them lay the body of a Hispanic man with a long knife attached to a belt at his waist and another with its hilt buried in his chest. "Senor Shiv, I presume," Lake said, nudging the wet body with his foot. He bent and felt for a pulse. "Not many minutes dead."

"Stupid shithead," I said.

"Let's see what our fearless sidekick is up to," Lake said. "And go find our Knight."

"He knew, didn't he?" I said.

"He had to believe we got on that train. He had to believe we got on to him, and he had to know we'd come after him. He had to think ahead of us."

As we rounded the corner of the building, we heard Jimmy Ray's whispered shout. "Lieutenant! Lieutenant!"

"Here!" Lake called.

The big man pointed toward something white near the woods. "Plane!" he yelled. "Gas tanks used to be kept back there. Must be still are."

Lake said, "He had gas stored there for the plane to refuel. It's come a long way."

Lightning flashed from the west, illuminating the plane as it cleared the woods' line, maybe two hundred yards away. It was white with blue stripes. I'd ridden in similar planes. The craft turned away and bounced across the uneven ground toward a clearing in the distance.

"Beech Bo," Lake said.

"Headed for the runway," the deputy said as we sprinted to the cruiser. Jimmy Ray got the car rolling, no small surprise. "She's got a lot left in her," he boasted.

Ahead, the plane's wing lights came on. It gathered speed and turned west.

"It's got to the runway," Jimmy Ray called. He crushed the gas pedal. The car shuddered for a second or two, then rocketed forward, smelling oily, ghastly.

We reached the grassy runway and gained on the plane, but in seconds it would soar away.

"Cut it off," Lake shouted. "Watch out for fuel tanks."

"Going to," Jimmy Ray said.

The car bounced on the uneven surface but caught up to the plane. Jimmy Ray hit the siren. Irrationally, I giggled. Imagine pulling over a plane. But then, imagine trying to outrun one, which was exactly what Jimmy Ray was trying. The cruiser drew even with its right wingtip, now on the level with my nose. I looked at the porthole window above the wing. A lightning bolt flashed, illuminating the face staring from the window. The smug face of evil glared at me. The Knight—the devil who'd taken us all in.

Jimmy Ray jerked the wheel to the left. My God, he was going to sideswipe the cruiser against the wingtip. Pure suicide. I opened my mouth to scream. He wrenched the wheel right, fishtailing and spinning away. He muscled the wheel into a fast one-eighty. The cruiser snarled toward the plane's tail. If the plane shot upward, we'd miss her tail by a whisker.

Jimmy Ray yelled, "Now! Get down!"

A loud crack came from under the car's hood. A rod—or the entire engine blew. But the cruiser jumped under the tail piece.

I'm going to die.

The car hung up under the tail for a second before the plane broke free, taking the car's roof. Pieces of the Beech's tail flew overhead. The plane swung left. The car's sideways momentum pulled my neck. An abrupt halt or roll would break it.

Jimmy Ray fought to keep the car on four wheels. It teetered, whined, and snaked, but didn't roll. And finally, it stopped.

Jimmy Ray looked back at us. "Y'all all right?"

I couldn't find my voice. I shook my head no and flung back to let the rain slide down my face, to let the adrenaline drain down my brain stem.

Lake put a hand on my shoulder. "You okay?"

"No," I whispered, shivering. My thoughts flew to the Rose girls, and I reached for the door. It wouldn't budge. I stood up. A single headlight beamed from the cruiser's front end. I made out the white plane at the end of the runway. In the eerie wet night, it stood out against the heavy thicket into which it had plunged. Its nose and starboard wing were held up by brambles and scrub pines.

"Quick, the flashlight, Jimmy Ray," Lake said.

Jimmy Ray bent to the passenger side floor and brought it up. Lake pulled his gun. "Let's go."

I got my automatic and scrambled out, willing my boneless legs to hold me up.

Lake asked, "You got an extinguisher, Deputy?"

"Yep, if I can get the trunk open."

The trunk lid was the sole body part that hadn't been wrecked.

Jimmy Ray ran with us—the extinguisher under an arm, a flashlight in one hand, his gun in the other.

No movement came from the plane. My imagination saw dead children inside.

As we approached, Lake asked, "You smell gasoline?"

Jimmy Ray and I answered, "No."

"I don't either, but that doesn't mean some's not leaking. Dru, you and Jimmy Ray go to the port side."

Except for the missing tail piece, and what looked like bent propellers, the plane appeared in one piece. From what I could see, debris hadn't penetrated the fuselage. I circled and wondered why no one stirred inside.

All of a sudden, the pilot's door thrust outward. Something white flew out—a paper towel. Another flew out. "*Me entiego*," a voice called.

Lake ran from the starboard side and took an armed-cop stance. "Hands in the air."

A small Hispanic man in a muscle shirt and jeans stepped carefully onto the black strips of the wing, his hands held out. The wing wobbled and the man jumped to the ground. He had no weapons.

"Hands behind your head."

When the man didn't comply, Jimmy Ray stomped toward him and jerked his hands above his head.

Lake ordered, "March him to the other side."

On the other side, Lake pointed to the cabin door. "Open it!"

I couldn't tell if the man didn't speak English or was simply uncooperative. College Spanish flashed into my head. *"Abierto!"*

I held my breath as the man reached for the handle and pulled the door.

"Now back away," Lake ordered.

The man was too slow. Jimmy Ray grabbed him by his shirt, tossed him to the ground, and, in seconds, had him in plastic cuffs.

I rushed to the door, gun ready, and lifted my foot onto the iron leg-up. But Lake called, "Back up, Dru. Let's take it slow."

I stepped backward, to where he stood. I stretched out my arms, my fingers wrapped around the gun butt. Lake called out, "Come out now. Hands in the air."

No answer.

"Come out! Now!"

No answer.

Lake turned to the pilot on the ground. "Are they dead in there?"

Jimmy Ray shone the flashlight in the pilot's face. His large black eyes blinked in three-second intervals. If he spoke English, he didn't give it away.

Summoning up more college Spanish, I hoped I could make him understand. *"Son muertos en alli?"*

His face registered understanding. *"Sí,"* he said, nodding his head yes. *"Muerto. Sí."*

Muerto. Dead. The end. I'll never survive this.

THIRTY-TWO

Lake walked cautiously to the step-up, gun thrust forward, and pushed his head in the door opening. Suddenly his legs flew upward and his torso collapsed inside the cabin. I dashed forward, my arms outstretched, both hands clutching the gun, finger ready to fire.

A voice called out from the cabin. "Stay put, Miss Dru. Lieutenant Lake is a dead man, you come any closer."

I froze. I heard the pilot on the ground spit, turned my head, and saw Jimmy Ray kick him in the face. In the fuselage, I heard a flesh-on-flesh whap and looked to see a foot kicking Lake out the door, his body bouncing off the wing and sprawling in the mud.

The Knight called, "You, Miss Dru, throw the gun on the ground where I can see it. Deputy, you, too." I threw my gun between Lake's spread-eagled legs and waited for the deputy. He didn't move; he didn't toss his gun. By the look on his face in the light of his lantern, Jimmy Ray wasn't giving up his weapon.

"You have to do what he says," I said.

"No, ma'am," he said, rain dripping from his hat. He meant it.

"Deputy!" the Knight yelled. "You ready to die! Throw the gun!"

"Send out the Rose girls!" I called.

The Knight's voice was oily. "You'll have to come and get them, Miss Dru."

"Are you serious?"

"Come look inside."

Holding my breath, I walked toward the listing plane and climbed on the metal step. I angled to get a glimpse inside and came face-to-face with the Knight. The hole in the barrel of the Smith & Wesson .45 looked as evil as he did, and I lurched backward. My foot slipped off the wet metal step, and I fell on Lake's legs, near where I'd dropped my weapon. I pawed in the mud after it.

The Knight jumped from the cabin and yanked me to my knees by the collar of the borrowed rain jacket. He said, "You want to die, keep up the tricks."

"No tricks, Captain Turquin," I said, getting to my feet. "I slipped. It's raining, in case you didn't notice."

He looked so different than he did this morning with his fireman's steel hat hiding most of his face and all of his silver hair. In the drizzle and fog, by the light of the cruiser's one headlamp and the deputy's flashlight, he looked like a tired old Roman senator in an expensive British raincoat.

I started to say something when I heard Jimmy Ray say, "Drop the gun, mister!"

Oh no, not heroics!

Turquin grabbed my hair—coiling it in his hand until I faced

Jimmy Ray—and took dead aim. The gun roared in my ear. Blood spurted from the deputy's shoulder. His flashlight fell, but the giant wouldn't go down. His face burned with rage. He charged, raising his hand to fire his pistol. Turquin flinched enough to let me break free. I went down on top of Lake to give Jimmy Ray a clear shot. My fingers found my gun and closed around it.

Jimmy Ray's shot missed, nicking the door of the plane. He staggered and sagged to the ground, clutching his bloody torso.

I became aware of screaming sirens piercing through heavy wet air.

"You're over, Captain," I said, getting to my feet. I hadn't been able to get my hand in firing position, so I'd slid the gun into a pocket.

"Maybe not," he said. "I'll tell you what. I'll let these girls stay here with your boyfriend, and you can come with me. Fair trade?"

"Where to?"

"Does it matter?"

No, I guess it doesn't.

"Back up," he ordered. I stood away from Lake and Turquin kicked him in the thigh. His eyes fired into mine. "If I didn't like Richard Lake so much, I'd enjoy putting a bullet in his head. That goes for you, too. Now let's move."

I dug in my heels. "Let me see the girls, or you'll have to kill me here."

He considered the sirens closing in and waved a hand toward the fuselage. "Be quick."

I looked at Lake. I thought he moved. God, don't let him be dead. I climbed into the opening and picked up the flashlight on the floor. The beam of light caught the girls as they sat fastened in their seats, their heads plastered against the leather backs, their eyes frozen like blue marbles. But they were alive. "You're safe now," I whispered to the children whose fright I'll never forget.

Turquin called. "Let's go!"

When I climbed out, my ankle touched Lake. He flinched. I ran ahead before Turquin realized Lake was waking. The next knock on the head would be fatal.

I let Turquin grab my hand. For a man of his bulk, he was fast. He pulled me to the edge of the trees, and before we plunged into the dark wet forest, I looked back. The sirens had reached the runway. I said a prayer for Lake and for the little girls who had witnessed so much violence in their short lives.

The confusion the authorities would confront at the plane was enough to let us get a good head start—the hog-tied pilot, an unconscious cop, and a bleeding, maybe dying, deputy.

Dying deputy? Jimmy Ray couldn't die.

Turquin pulled me along a dark path by the arm that, had it been free, would have gotten the gun in my pocket. A Jeep hulked on the path. He held the .45 close to my head and shoved me inside. I crawled past the driver's seat to the passenger side. He got in and laid the gun on his lap with the muzzle pointed at my thighs.

He stepped on the gas and the Jeep heaved ahead. He didn't flick on the headlights. Once my eyes got used to the dark, I could see the forest road. We climbed upward until the Jeep's transmission changed pitch. We topped a grade and descended. With a splash and a mechanical whine, the Jeep's wheels hit water. The going was easy, then the Jeep climbed again. I didn't know South Georgia had this many hills. When Turquin got to the hard road, he flipped the lights, brightening the slick asphalt.

"Where are you taking me?"

"Where do you want to go?" He sounded as if we were discussing which movie to see.

"I'm not in the mood for games, Captain Turquin."

The windshield wipers filled the silence for a brief time. "I like games. I like to win against a worthy opponent."

"So do I, but I think worthiness means something different to you than it does to me."

His meaty lips pressed together. "You're a smart aleck, aren't you?"

"Call me anything you like."

"I am a worthy opponent, Miss Dru, but I didn't want you or Ricky against me. Ricky was supposed to be off this weekend."

"How did you . . . ?" No need to ask. This man knew his way through the information highway.

"Easy enough to get Ricky's shifts. And you were supposed to be in San Francisco."

He didn't have to crack into a Web site to learn that. It was in the news that I was trying to find a girl in California. I would be there if the girl hadn't turned up DOA. I said, "Ricky would have been off if you hadn't burned down the Barnes house."

"When things didn't go right from the start last night—goddamn storm—I was bent. Then you and Ricky showed up. You can't imagine my shock. But at least I could make a game of it."

"All those lives gone and you call it a game."

He made a guttural noise. "You need to change your attitude if we're going to get along."

"We're not going to get along."

"Why not? We're in this together, aren't we?"

"In what together?"

"The denouement. The End Game."

"The girls are safe. That's The End Game for me."

He cackled. "Doesn't mean you're safe."

"Nor are you."

"No one ever is," he said, glancing at me. "This has been one unlucky operation."

"Where were you taking the girls?"

"I, myself, wasn't planning on taking them anywhere until you spooked their transportation and I had to step in."

"Where were the Rooks taking them?"

"The islands."

He turned onto a state road. "How?"

"Beechcraft to Miami. Boat to the islands. Hand over to the King. The last leg was the King's problem. He only paid to get them to the islands." He came to a stop sign and turned right. "You beat me out of a million bucks, Moriah Dru."

"It wasn't yours to begin with."

"I made the sale."

"You sold something not yours to sell."

"Whose was it?"

"Human beings aren't for sale."

"Every man, woman, and child gets bought and sold every day."

"What life experience got you to that conclusion?"

"Personal life experience," he said. "Now hush for a while."

"Was I the only one talking?"

His eyes shifted from the road to his rearview mirror. He was careful to drive the speed limit. It began misting again. We went through a tiny town, then rolled by small houses separated by pastures and outbuildings. After twenty minutes or so, Turquin braked and ran upon the shoulder of the road. He turned into a dirt road running through loblolly pines. The Jeep's wheels spun in the mud.

After he'd settled the Jeep into a slippery waddle, he said, "Mama was the first to sell me out."

Confession time—one of his reasons for bringing me along. A couple of other reasons were too horrible to contemplate.

When I was a cop, I honed my ability to keep egomaniacs talking. Whether a jumpy street thug or a patient mastermind like Turquin, they *needed* to be *understood*. "How did she sell you out? Why?"

"Mama loved money. Too bad we never had any."

The apple hadn't fallen far from the tree. "What about your daddy?"

"He died, working on the railroad. Then Mama went totally crazy."

"He have anything to do with her going crazy?"

The muscles in his neck strained. He fingered the gun on his lap. "He was an honorable man. Not like the hick she took up with a month after he died."

He made another turn and ran along a farm road where you couldn't see the red soil for the moonless sky. He continued, "Mama's cousin was insane. The strain in the family ran down and deep."

It took restraint to keep from blurting what came to mind, but what I said instead was, "Lots of kids don't get along with their stepfather."

"Don't even use that word. He wasn't any kind of father. The hick didn't want me anywhere near him. When I was ten they made me move my stuff to the barn. I could never have friends in. You say to a friend, 'Hey, Johnny, come to my house and play.' And Johnny comes and says, 'Your room's in the barn? Wait till the kids hear about this!' "

I looked at his profile. "People of strength and intelligence don't worry about what others think."

He glared sideways. His hand tightened on the gun. Then he laughed. "You'd tempt the devil, wouldn't you?"

I faced away and watched the woods go by.

"You're right about strength. Two years later, he hit me . . . broke my nose. I hit back . . . broke his jaw. Then I moved into my old room. On my sixteenth birthday Mama called the sheriff and had me evicted. I moved to Savannah to live with an uncle. He had one condition on taking me in—I get my education. I did, too. I liked learning. I liked reading. I do a little writing— poetry when I'm in the mood."

"What's the C stand for in your name?"

"Want to guess?"

"Claus?"

"I was born on Christmas Day."

"Your mother ever kill anyone?"

"Not unless you consider my soul."

"Ever think of killing her?"

"Over and over, and she wanted me to. I used to come back and visit a cousin, lived down from Mama. I never went to see her to sit down and visit, but I used to drive by when she was out-side. She stood there, looking at me. She burned herself up in her house. I still own the place. You'll see."

Where was this monster taking me? I didn't care about his life's story. Who wants to understand someone who kills a helpless old lady by smothering the life out of her? It would take insanity itself to understand. But I'd listen and look for a chance to get my hand in my pocket when his guard was down. Monsters get cocky and careless when they get a chance to unload a lifetime's mental baggage on their hostages.

He came to a fork in the road, went left, and drove along a lake lane. We were in duck country. I could make out a few blinds in the marshes. Rain fell again, making splashes in the black water.

Turquin eased off the gas and turned the car into a weed patch. The crunch of gravel under the tires spoke of a lane of sorts. The headlights fastened on a single brick chimney stalk stretching skyward.

"Welcome to Mama's," he said. "Shall we visit a spell?" He leveled the gun at my head. "Get out and put your hands on the hood."

He kept the Jeep's lights on and stayed in the driver's seat. I could see his eyes as I lay my palms flat on the hood. Slipping from the Jeep, he held the gun easily in his hand. The head-lights in the foggy drizzle made his face look like Satan's. His fist squeezed my arm, and I angled myself away so he wouldn't feel the gun in my pocket. We slogged through shin-soaking weeds to three concrete steps leading nowhere. He waved the gun casu-ally. "Come into the parlor, my dear."

The ground beneath my shoes was slimy, and I made myself slip, but I was too close to him. He caught me before I went down, one hand above the pocket with the gun. "When did this house burn down?" I asked, pulling my arm from his fist.

"Twenty-three years, six days ago."

"It looks like the fire just happened."

"Couple times a year I come and burn off the weeds. Keeps

the memorial fresh." He led me to the other side of the burned area. "What does it feel like here, Miss Dru?"

I knew what he wanted me to say. "Like standing on someone's grave."

"You're standing on the very spot where Mama burned up."

I willed myself not to jump away. "Your mother's spirit isn't restless."

"You believe in ghosts?"

"Yes, and monsters."

"Monster, from Latin to Old French meaning a divine omen." Taking my arm, he led me back to the Jeep. "Come, let's go to the barn. I can take my friends to my room now."

I pulled my arm. His hold was loose, so it came free. "What for?"

He grabbed my arm again and tightened his grip. "Don't forget who holds the gun, Miss Dru."

"What's the point?"

"What do you think the point is?"

"Getting even?"

He snickered. "Something like that."

THIRTY-THREE

He fetched a lantern from the back seat of the Jeep. I saw the assault rifles next to it. He switched on the light and held it out. I took it, and he leaned over the Jeep's steering wheel and turned off the headlights. "Walk on," he said.

Approaching the barn, the rain fell harder and we hurried. No use, since we were already soaked. I was glad for the borrowed raincoat. I'd keep it forever as a reminder of the evilest day in my life. The barn was picturesquely painted rust-red with white trim. He unlocked a large Dutch door, ushered me through, and flicked a switch. Track lights gave the vast, one-room interior a golden glow. I saw it for what it was—a place where a psychotic came to deepen his hatred for his dead mother and to nurture the evil growing within himself. One end of the room was a stable. Three mahogany stalls were ready for the horses or cows or sheep that would never stand in them. On the other end stood a giant, shiny John Deere tractor that would never plow a field—not for this owner. Behind the tractor, an island bar separated it from the kitchen, which was stainless steel sleek. I'd seen plenty of kitchens like his in home-and-garden magazines.

In the center of the barn was the great room. Against the back wall stood an enormous and expensive peninsula fireplace; its smokestack rose and cut into the fourteen-foot raftered ceiling. In the outsized firebox, logs lay ready for a match. Leather sofas, loveseats, chairs, and tables were placed haphazardly, yet with a decorator's eye. Two walls were floor-to-ceiling bookshelves, filled with leather-bound volumes.

"I'm impressed," I said. "I wondered where and how the flesh peddler spent his money. How much did you get for the Yates and Patterson girls?"

"Not nearly as much as you've gypped me out of."

"So you sank it in here, in this shrine to your mad mother and your unhappy youth."

He pointed the gun at my temple. "Watch your mouth."

"Do your neighbors know about this place?"

"I'm my own neighbor. I've bought all the land near here and was looking to buy more. You see, this is the one place I could spend money without arousing suspicion. Where would a simple fireman get the money to live in Atlanta's posh neighborhoods? Let me move onto West Paces Ferry and see the eyebrows go up. Some busybody would call the newspaper to investigate the Atlanta fireman that moved in."

"If you wanted wealth, why'd you choose a low-income profession?"

"I didn't choose it, Miss Dru. It chose me. Let's get something to drink and I'll light the fire. It's chilly in here, don't you think? And please, don't make a run for it. I'm very fast."

I walked beside him to the kitchen area, my right forearm feeling the metal in my pocket.

"I can't offer you an alcoholic drink, because I don't keep the stuff in my home. Will Coke do?"

"Coke's fine."

We returned to the great room, and he lit the logs.

I sat on the sofa. He sat in a leather chair opposite me, his back to the fireplace. I felt unnaturally calm. I knew I should be feeling my nerves sticking out from my skin. Instead, something satisfyingly tight built in my chest and I felt my life had come down to this. He contemplated me while he drank, curiously composed, since we both knew that soon it was going to be him or me. I needed to keep him talking—bragging. "I see by your books you're a scholar."

He gave an unpleasant laugh. "Scholar. My uncle didn't have the money for college. My paycheck was needed for my aunt's necessities like her hairdresser and her nail lady. And, oh, don't forget the gin. However, I've educated myself and I'm proud of it."

"As you should be." I about gagged at flattering him. "Where'd you learn to drive a train?"

"Like my daddy and uncle, I started as yard crew and went on to become a brakeman. Railroading changed and I got laid off. So then I went to work for the Savannah Fire Department. Before I was there a year, I was blamed for letting a fire get out of control and got fired."

"Is that what you meant when you said your career chose you? You are an arsonist, aren't you?"

At first he didn't answer. He stood and went to the fireplace and picked up a poker. He shoved it at the burning logs. He faced me, poker in one hand, gun in the other. "Ever hear a real fire-

and-brimstone preacher?" I nodded. "I grew up hearing them. The Fires of Hell." He stoked the logs, flaring sparks.

"What happened after you got fired?"

He came back to his seat, planted the poker next to him, and placed the gun on a knee. "I went to Atlanta—the big time. I didn't tell them about Savannah, and got hired."

I laid a hand in my lap, casually palm up. "You did all right. You got promoted."

The muscles in his jaws bulged. "You can't eat on promotions. I got shorted on raises my whole thirty years with the department. Police get raises. We get promises. Then there was the fire at the cotton mill."

"The Cabbagetown mill fire?" One of the cotton mill buildings caught fire when it was being turned into apartments. A crane operator was removing part of the old tar roof when fire broke through from the floor below. The man had no way down.

"I volunteered to go up and get the crane operator," Turquin said, his eyes narrowing. "I had heavy rescue training but they tagged the younger man. He's still basking in the glory."

A man like Turquin could turn a slight into a soul-festering boil. To deflect his ire, I changed the subject. "Did you marry? Are you married now?"

"I married bad. Didn't know she was bad when I married her. She took up with a cop."

Lake was a cop. Turquin stared at me like I was his bad wife. "What happened to your wife?"

"Cancer got her and the cop gave her body back to me." He rose, knocking the poker to the floor. While he picked it up, I got my hand to my pocket. Suddenly he raised his head, gave me a hard stare, then took the poker to the hearth.

"Why didn't you divorce her?"

"I wouldn't give her the satisfaction." He grabbed a large log. My hand eased back to my pocket. "Ever think of killing her?"

"I did." He tossed the log in the fire and got another, but I knew he was watching me from the corner of an eye. I folded my hands in my lap. "But she did me a favor and died on her own."

"How did you meet Miss Goddard?"

"She was a friend of my wife's. Millicent made her shroud."

"Was it then when you and Miss Goddard developed a relationship?"

"Relationship?" he snickered. "Not by what the word means today. Millicent was . . . ah . . . Millicent." He watched the fire, his hand clutching the gun like he was ready to whirl and fire. "She could sure kick a man when she took a mind to."

"She spurned you."

He rotated his torso so the gun barrel stared at my forehead. "She had no right over a dog. I loved my dog, but he was old. I slit its throat. Why is that worse than taking it to a vet and crying crocodile tears as if life was endless? Life is death. The best death, like the best life, is quick and painless."

"Miss Goddard was aware when you went to the kids' schools to give fire awareness lectures, you often made use of your name Claus."

"Ho. Ho. Ho. The kids ate it up." His face had reddened and now glistened with perspiration.

"How could you sell the very children you entertained?"

Instead of answering, he strode to a small desk planted in front of a bookcase. Opening a drawer, he took out a tube. It looked like a mailer.

"Miss Goddard confronted you in the street, didn't she?"

"You're guessing."

"We have film from a chopper."

"I told her I'd be in to see her shortly and we would talk. But you didn't see me go in her house. The helicopter was out of range."

"Clever of you. She opened her back door for you, didn't she?"

"She wanted to be discreet, too."

"She and Wanda knew—or believed—you were responsible for those other kidnappings."

"Millicent had a knack—like you—for figuring things out." He'd put the tube underneath an arm. The gun drooped in his hand.

"But she never turned you in, never went to the authorities."

"She cared for me once." His eyes appeared to tear. But maybe it was sweat.

"And yet you killed her."

He turned the gun a couple of times in his hand as if deciding what to do with it. He said, "She told me not to hurt those girls, and I told her I wasn't going to. She lay back against her chair and looked up. It was time, she was telling me. It's my time. She didn't resist when I put my thumb and finger over her nose and mouth. It was done in no time. Like life . . . done in no time."

"My, a scholar *and* a philosopher."

"You know, Miss Dru, we live to die. What difference does it make the manner of our death? Or when?"

"You tried to kill Lake and me—twice."

He took the mailer from under his arm. "I didn't succeed, did I?"

"Why did you kill the Barneses?"

"Wanda called the firehouse. She told me she'd seen me in the neighborhood a couple times—that I was there for no good reason. Shit. Firemen check things like hydrants all the time."

"Wanda and Miss Goddard weren't going to let you abduct anyone else."

"I'd already put things in motion—couldn't back out." His eyes clouded into another dimension. "Girls. Like kittens . . . cute when they're little, but they get big . . . and mean. Wanda was mean. Millicent was mean." He stared at me. "You're beautiful, but inside, you're mean, too."

"When I have to be."

"I read about you. Your family life wasn't so hot. Neither was holier-than-thou Ricky Lake's."

"So, does that mean we should've been sold to pedophiles?"

"I've offended you?"

"Murderers, rapists, slavers offend me."

He shrugged. "Look at it the way I do. Little girls who come from low-life, become low-life. I was giving them a jump on the kind of life they were born to. When they grow up, people like you go after them for abusing their own children."

"You're making excuses. You did it for the money and because you have no heart."

He hit himself lightly on the head with the tube. "And here I thought I was performing a service."

"What happened last night? Were the girls asleep in their beds?"

"They sat up when I came in. I told Jessie I was there to take them to their uncle in the mountains."

"She bought that?"

"Yes, because I'd planned to make a game of it. I told her my friends would take them to see the Lion of the Confederacy first. She believed her kin were buried under the stone. Her daddy filled her head with nonsense, and she had no judgment." He paused and shook his head. "I mean, for Christ's sake, it was the middle of the night."

"She's nine."

He stared at me and tapped the tube against his leg. *The tube is an incendiary device.* Keep speaking. "You had access to Oakland. Firehouses have access to public places in case something happens when the place is deserted. You also have access to rail yards." I was reaching the apex of a dam, ready to crest it. "You're good at deflecting attention. The authorities zeroed in on Cyrus Bassett for the Yates kidnapping. Do you always carry a Santa hat in case you come upon a kid you want to kidnap?"

"I plan, I don't let things just happen. Too bad Bassett was in church or he might be in jail now."

"When you encountered the Rose girls on the street Friday, Dottie remembered you from her speech school. I bet Wanda went wild when she learned you had disregarded her warning to stay away from her girls. She called you, didn't she, and threatened to go to the authorities?"

"Yes," he said, smiling with no mirth.

"Why did you bring me here?"

When he spoke, his voice came straight from the crypt. "I brought you here to make up my mind. Do I want to kill you, or don't I?"

If he meant to ramp up any fear I might have, he failed. He made me mad. "And the answer is?"

"I'm still making up my mind."

"Don't let me rush you, Captain Turquin."

"You don't have to call me Captain any longer. I've retired."

"I stopped by the firehouse. I saw your retirement party setting up."

"Did seeing my farewell banner give you a hint of any kind?"

"I didn't see the banner, just balloons. I didn't know it was for you."

"When did you suspect me?"

"The media tape, the overview of your scenes. I saw you talking to Lorette, the speech teacher. Hugle was right there, too. He brought her to talk to me. What's she to you?"

"I've had dinner with her a couple of times. I asked her out for tonight. Didn't know then I wouldn't be able to keep the date."

"Where are you going?"

His left eye winked, but he evaded answering. "I thought Hugle was going to be the best suspect."

"He didn't have the imagination, nor the contacts, to plan the abductions. He's a closet case."

He grinned. "In that regard, I've done you a favor."

"I can't wait to hear."

"Look in Hugle's closet. He's hanging out there."

I felt limp, like my bones were melting. Besides hearing this madman gloat, the room was terribly hot. "You're not joking, are you?"

"I thought you'd be glad to—ah—get him out of your hair."

"Your murdering him doesn't do me any good."

"You should have spoken up sooner. He let Dwight go to prison for something he didn't do."

"I suspected; so did everyone, but you knew it for a fact."

"Susie confided in Santa Claus like he was her therapist."

"Why didn't you snatch Susie for the slave trade?"

He stretched his arm straight out, the gun barrel pointing at my nose. Would I see the flash before the bullet went into my brain? He said, "Time wasn't right. No buyers—and then she wasn't right." He lowered his arm, and the gun went slack in his hand. His eyes half closed. "South America's nice this time of year."

"You got your ticket yet?"

He went to the hearth, picked up the poker, poked the logs, and threw two more on the fire. He held the tube underneath his arm. He faced me and said, "I'm a rich man. I can go anywhere I want to. I've traveled to places most people can't afford, but I've never been able to talk about what I did on my summer vacation."

"I've listened to your reasons for making your choices. You're no different than millions of others. Nobody has a perfect life. So, what's next for you—for me?"

"What do you want to come next?"

"I've achieved my goal, which was to save two little girls from a man who can still weep for a woman he killed. Who can murder two people and snatch two children for slavers. I can't understand you, Captain Turquin."

"And I can't understand you, Miss Dru. If life is so sweet, why do you think yours is less important than two little girls? You and Richard Lake took a chance that everyone in the plane, and in your car, would be killed, including the two little girls you meant to save."

What was there to say? I would be thinking about that for a long time to come.

He sat on the sofa. "Cat got your tongue?"

"I've nothing more to say."

The gun wavered in his hand. "Think of something."

I let my words pour forth in no particular order and not knowing if they made sense. "I love life, yes. I love my life. I wish everybody loved their life as much as I do—even you." I rose from the sofa and moved to the side. "But there are those who don't get the chance because of things that happen beyond their control. That's especially true of children . . . the little victims. They come from families ranging from the well-intentioned but cruel to the downright depraved. I can't save all the child victims, but if I can save a few, I'm happy. Yes, ex-Captain Turquin, it makes me gloriously happy to rescue kids. I was thrilled beyond anything you can conceive to look into the plane and see those two girls alive. I hate evil and death. I can't conquer it, but I like to spit in their eyes whenever I get a chance. Maybe that's why I stand here and listen to a monster like you threaten to kill me."

He let the gun rest on his knee and clapped. "Very nice." He pushed the gun off his knee onto the sofa, got to his feet and took the tube from under his armpit. "Do you want to kill me?"

"No."

"But you could?"

"Yes."

"Would it make you gloriously happy, too?"

"No."

"Have you killed before?" he asked, going to the fireplace.

"Yes."

"Why?"

I had to be careful not to fall in his trap. "It was necessary."

"A necessary evil?"

"Yes."

He raised the tube. "So, to wipe out evil, you must kill it—cause death, something you despise."

I stepped back, putting my hands in my pockets. My right hand clamped the gun butt, my finger found the trigger. "I'm not going down your screwball road."

"Oh yes you are." Then he laughed and raised the tube. "You will be my salvation. You will cleanse me. You will bring mercy to my soul." He bent to the firebox and threw the tube. The flames threw a white flash back at him. He spun around, his shirt on fire. He propelled forward. "Have mercy," he cried. "Gun from your pocket . . . kill me."

The smoke was thick. I held my breath. The flames licked at the back of him.

"Have mercy! Kill me!" His hair caught fire.

I aimed my automatic at the human torch. Then lowered it. Let the son-of-a-bitch burn. I dashed for the door . . . twisted the crystal knob. Locked. My hands shook. I reached for the dead bolt and looked back. The inferno came at me.

"Shoot me!" He dragged his burning body forward. His fiery arm reached out, nearly touching my shoulder. The lock snapped and I yanked the door inward. He grabbed for me just as I cleared the threshold into the soaking rain.

Glancing back, I stared at his sinking, burning body before it crumpled facedown in his hell of a sanctum.

The lightning god threw a bolt into the firestorm. The ground shook. My foot slipped. The side of my head hit the mud. Oblivion washed in.

THIRTY-FOUR

"Dru! Dru!"

The voice echoed from behind consciousness.

Too, too wet . . .

"Dru! Can you hear me!"

Someone moved me as I lay drowning. My eyes flashed open.
Drowning?

"You're awake!"

Lake.

"Good girl. Let's sit."

"No."

Lake was on one side of me and someone else on the other.
They pulled me to sitting. When their hands relaxed, I folded,
pressing my face to my knees. My chest hurt. I coughed smoke.

Lake said, "Good, now darling we need to get you out of the
rain."

I was already soaked, so what was the hurry? "I can't . . ." I
coughed.

"Darling, don't speak now. Here, let's get you standing."

What's with the *let's*?

Standing wasn't easy. Someone shoved me into Lake, and, as we were about to topple, Lake hardened the muscles in his legs and grabbed my arms. I staggered, but stayed on my feet. Lake drew me into him. I looked past his shoulder. Smoke poured into the night sky from the building. The fire was losing to the rain.

Turquin. The dreadful reality snapped back—the tube, the fire, the burning man.

"The barn," I said, pulling back from Lake's embrace. "He's in . . ."

"It's almost out now," Lake said, pulling me closer, trying to cradle my head against his neck.

I leaned away. "He's in there."

"Yes."

"I watched him burn up."

"We were coming down the road when you ran out the door. We saw him fall."

"I couldn't . . . shoot him." The greasy smell of cooked flesh clogged my nose. My olfactory memory picked a bad time to kick in. I turned away and swallowed hard. "I'm sick."

"Let it go."

I didn't throw up. I resist even when it's supposed to make you feel better. As I was about to suffocate, I put my hand across my mouth and sucked in air. I stared into Lake's dark face. "Retribution."

"For what?"

"I should have put him out of his misery, instead I played God."

"No, darling, you didn't play God. C.T. played the devil."

"He begged for mercy."

"You know what I think?" He put his arms around me.

I buried my nose in the sweet smell of his cheek. "I always want to know what you think."

He rubbed the back of my head. "First of all, he knew you wouldn't shoot him. He wanted to make you feel guilty."

I pulled away for an instant. "Like I feel now."

"Secondly, if it had to be his End Game, he played it the way he wanted to. He's first and last an arsonist."

I believed Lake. His wisdom filled a portion of the void in my soul. I stood straight and breathed in the smoky air. The awful odor had disappeared.

The sheriff emerged from the shadows of the dying fire. He wore the expression of a doctor about to deliver bad news. He laid a gentle hand on my shoulder. "The ambulance is on the way."

"No, thanks. I'm all right. Where are the Rose girls?"

"At the hospital."

"Then, I'm going there." Remembering Lake had been knocked out, I scanned his face in the light of the sheriff's lamp. The skin above his left temple was dark red. "You come, too."

" 'Fraid not," he said. "Too much to do here."

The sheriff said, "It's not your case now, Lieutenant. It's not the county's neither. It's the FBI's and the GBI's. They're coming in the gate now."

"Like the cavalry charging in after Wild Bill shoots the last Indian," I said, feeling much too giddy for the situation.

I wish we could have gotten away before we had to make statements to the federal and state agents. For ten minutes they badgered us with whys and how-comes. I finally said, "Now I'm going to get in the ambulance."

The FBI agent snickered, "First time I've heard of suicide by PI."

I grabbed Lake's hands so he wouldn't make fists.

At the hospital, I learned the sheriff had either lied to get me to the hospital, or didn't know what he was talking about. The girls weren't there. They had been examined and whisked back to Atlanta by the Highway Patrol. As long as I was in the emergency room, I let a boyish doctor put a tongue depressor in my mouth and a light up my nose. He took my pulse and temperature and listened to my heart. He pronounced me fit medically, but said, "You look beat. We have beds available, go on, take advantage."

I didn't feel beat. I was ready to get back to Atlanta. After an X-ray showed Lake didn't have a skull fracture, we walked to the exit. An unattended squad car sat next to an ambulance.

I looked at Lake. "How're we getting back to Atlanta?"

"The GBI promised a ride back in one of its planes."

"When's it leave?"

"Who knows?"

"Why don't we hop a fast freight?"

Lake hardly ever giggles, but his laughter now had a high pitch to it. "It's something I've always wanted to do."

The emergency room door opened behind us. "Lieutenant!"

I recognized that voice. Delighted, I faced it. "You're all right."

Jimmy Ray grinned. I hadn't noticed he was gap-toothed. "Little ol' bullet, cain't hurt much."

He'd been bandaged and given a green hospital shirt that covered the arm in a sling.

"No need for this," he said, flapping the arm. "Humor the doc."

"Can you drive?" I asked.

"Sure can."

"What time's the next train going to Atlanta?"

"Amtrak?"

"No," Lake said, "the next high-baller."

He looked at his watch. "Let's see, she should be in the station now. Leaving 'bout half an hour, if she's on time."

"Let's go."

"Is it 'cause you're superstitious?" Jimmy Ray asked.

"What do you mean?"

"Mama always said you need to go home the same way you came."

Despite getting shot, the man hadn't slowed down. We raced to the train yard where the string was taking on a couple of piggyback semis hauling logs.

"How'd you like to ride under them?" Lake asked.

"Having my druthers, I'd rather be crushed by a truckload of Mercedes."

The yardmaster introduced us to the engineer. Lake began his pitch, when the engineer said, "Glad to have you aboard, Lieutenant. We heard what happened to Smitty, and we know about the man who killed him. Glad the bastard's dead."

We climbed the ladder to the second locomotive. I had the honor of the engineer's seat, and Lake took the conductor's. The narrow seats were mounted on high springs. Mine had armrests, Lake's didn't. The second engine faced east and the train traveled west, but going backward didn't bother my nightmares—which were vivid short takes about how the devil couldn't make me do it. Funny thing, though, the devil was sometimes me.

THIRTY-FIVE

It was eight-thirty in the morning when the engineer stopped the train at Underground's parking lot. Lucky for us, the squad car was still parked between two concrete pillars. The glass was intact, the fenders hadn't been mashed, and it hadn't been booted. "Maybe they don't boot on the Sabbath," Lake said.

"Maybe because it has a blue light on the dash and the tag says it's an APD car."

"Maybe because I put a five-dollar bill in the pay slot."

"Maybe because it's warm enough for the homeless to sleep al fresco."

"Where did you learn to speak Spanish?"

"That's Italian."

"Spain, Italy—they're right next to each other. Aren't they?"

"Take me there and see for yourself."

"Can we get there by rail?"

For the rest of the drive to my place, we didn't speak. The city's mood was like ours—that of a quiet Sunday morning after storms had washed the mean streets to a freshness Atlanta seldom sees. Even a wino's bottle gleamed from the gutter.

In my driveway, with my hand on the door handle, I hesitated, waiting for Lake to say something. One beat, two beats, three beats . . . I sighed and looked at him. "It's been quite a time."

"Yes, it has," he said. He plucked at strands of my hair like they were harp strings. "Like never before."

I tried to grin, but the forlorn feeling in my soul didn't allow it. I was flat let down. The thrill had ended; it was back to everyday life. "Like never again."

"We hope."

"Yes."

"Dru . . ."

Uh-oh. I recognized that tone.

He swallowed. "We need to resolve this thing . . ."

"What thing?"

"The other night."

"I shouldn't have pried."

"Of course you had to. You got calls."

"You believe me, then?"

"You might lie to a bad guy, but never to me."

"Not even when it's about you."

"It isn't about me."

"Who's it about?"

"That crazy reporter."

"I don't understand."

"I guess not."

"Help me then."

"She wanted to do a piece about the Hat Squad."

"The Hat Squad? It's been done . . . many times." The Hat

Squad was the Atlanta Homicide unit's unofficial name. It began with legendary Danny Agan and his fedoras. His disciples, of which Lake was one, emulated him with the trademark chapeau.

"She's new to the city," he said. "She saw me at a homicide scene and asked about the hat. I told her about Danny. She said she wanted to do a TV magazine piece about it."

"Okay."

"That's it."

"How many interviews have you given her?"

"Dru . . ."

"Sorry—not my business."

He put his hand in mine. We walked up the path and up the steps, to my front door. I unlocked it. In the foyer, he cupped a hand around each of my shoulders. "I don't like it when you don't trust me."

Trust, blind unthinking trust. It had been the crux of the matter. Trust—and the fact Lake doesn't like to explain himself. I took a step back and his hands fell to his sides. I said, "And I don't like husky-voiced women calling me in the middle of the night saying—"

"Women? More than one?"

I sort of laughed. "Especially red-haired ones."

"You could tell she had red hair through the phone?"

"I ran her down."

I could have smacked the satisfaction off his face. He reached out and caressed my cheek. "Dru, my Dru. Look in the pocket of the spare suit I keep in your closet. You'll see an envelope. Inside is a date with the words, 'Dru will have discovered her identity by this date, or before, or I'll have to start dropping obvious clues.' "

Although my spirit soared with relief, I crossed my arms like I was pissed. "You jerk."

"I hope in time you'll come to find out the truth of what I'm telling you. It'll mean more than my word."

"No it won't. Give me your word."

"On what?"

"Your relationship with her."

"I told you I have none."

"She said you call her all the time."

"She lies. She calls me."

"But you talk—"

"It's business, my duty. She'll get tired of it."

"Tell her to get lost."

"You tell her for me."

"I will." But I didn't think I'd have to.

He kissed the tip of my nose. "Now why don't I get in the shower and you lay out my spare suit, then get naked and come wash my back? We promised Susanna brunch, don't forget."

In those moments, my spirit's kaleidoscope clicked into one helluva spectacular pattern.

THIRTY-SIX

I like Lake's ex. I'd met Linda Lake before I knew her husband was a cop. She was the Fire Department's spokeswoman before she gave birth to Susanna. She's the opposite of me: tiny and blond, pert and gabby . . . more gabby . . . and engaged to a real estate tycoon.

She answered the door wearing a tennis outfit from Saks. Whenever I get the chance to play, my game is golf and I play it in plain ol' khaki shorts and ten-year-old golf shirts. Lake plays both tennis and golf, but I can't remember the last time he enjoyed either. I looked at him and thought, The man really needs some serious time off. But I probably didn't look fresh either.

Susanna ran from behind her mother. "Daddy!"

When a five-year-old says "Daddy!" like that, it makes your heart zing.

I looked at Linda. Worry lines framed her pink lipstick and blue eye shadow. She motioned me aside. "He's a good man to have when danger comes. I wouldn't want anyone else."

"Nor I."

"I can't believe Claus was behind those kidnappings. He was the kindest man. I'm shocked. How can people change and become something horrible. He was such a gentleman. Ricky told me once Claus would be chief one day. Golly, you don't know about people, do you?"

"No, you don't."

Her mouth turned down. "He died like he lived, the television reporter said. Were you there when . . . when . . . ?"

"He died like he lived."

"Where are the little girls now?"

"In protective custody."

"Oh, good. I heard on the news." She fidgeted with the hem of her short skirt. "I didn't think y'all'd make it back in time to get Susanna."

"Had to."

"I told Mama that. I said, Ricky might get tangled up and can't make it. After all—isn't that why we split? That's in the past, but I told Mama, Moriah would see to it Susanna isn't disappointed. You ever think of having children, Mo?"

"I'd have to think about . . . a few other things first."

"You and Ricky ought to get married. He's a good man, really. He needs someone like you. You two share the same things. You know, goals and all. You want the same thing out of life."

I thought she would never shut up. At that moment, Lake's instinct intervened. "Lin, we're skipping Ray's on the River today."

Linda looked as if we were going to strand her at home in her tennis outfit. "Oh?" But then she recovered. "It's okay. I guess y'all are tired. After all y'all've been through . . ."

"Lin," Lake said. He always looked at Linda kindly, as if she were a favorite cousin. "We're going someplace else."

Her eyes rolled from him to me and back to him. "Where?"

"It's a surprise for Suze."

"Oh?"

"We're going on a picnic."

Her mouth turned down. "Where?"

"A special place."

"You're not going to tell me? Ricky, you know I have to know where she is at all times in case, God forbid, something—I need to get in touch with her fast."

"We won't be long."

"I'll be back from tennis by three."

Holding his five-year-old in the fold of his arm, Lake said, "Susanna will be back then." As we walked out, he called back, "If you can't ace 'em, then beat 'em up with your best punch volley."

We left Linda at the door smiling uncertainly.

Lake hadn't let me in on his secret, but there was just one place in Atlanta that was perfect for our picnic.

We drove through Oakland's imposing gates. "Oh Daddy," Susanna cried. "Look at the iron man sitting on the chair."

Lake told her he'd been one of Atlanta's founding fathers, but she had already moved on to other statues. She paused at the fountain where concrete children stood under an umbrella with the sun dancing on the water. Then she skipped the paths, ooohing and ahhhhing at the winged angels and the marble doves and the bronze lambs. I wondered what it would be like to look at gravestones without thinking of what lay beneath them. Only a five-year-old could. Six, they tell me, is the age when death becomes a concept. Oh, to be forever five at heart.

Lake picked up Susanna, and we headed to our favorite monument. We were almost there when I spotted a car parked on the lane. Portia. My heart skipped and I looked at Lake. The man's grin split his face. It infected Susanna because she began to giggle. "Daddy and me have a surprise just for you."

I kissed his cheek, then leaned down to kiss hers.

Susanna walked between us, her small hands in ours, as we followed the path into the Confederate section. Portia kept her gaze fixed ahead while she held her seven-year-old son's hand. I stopped next to her and entwined my fingers in her free hand. She gently pressed them.

Dottie and Jessie were dressed in pink linen and each held a white wicker basket. They were picking daisies and roses from the baskets and laying them at the base of the Lion of the Confederacy. Tears wet my cheeks. I looked at Lake. His wondrous eyes told me what I should have known all along. He loved me and only me.

I breathed in the sweet spring air and wondered what Susanna thought, standing between us, looking like a perfect alabaster angel while she watched the Rose girls at their solemn task.